SECRETS, SECRETS ARE NO FUN

PENELOPE ROSE PALMER

For information, contact:

Penelope Rose Palmer

peneloperosepalmer@gmail.com

979-8-9933148-0-8 (paperback)

979-8-9933148-1-5 (hardcover)

979-8-9933148-2-2 (ebook)

CHAPTER ONE

Mark opened the back door to his office for me as I was ready to leave, its creaking sound just enough to break the silence of the moment. Without a second thought, I turned around and rushed back to the chair in his office, my footsteps echoing on the hardwood floor. I grabbed my purse from where I'd left it. The familiar weight felt grounding as I quickly slung it over my shoulder, not daring to take too long. Turning back to Mark, I leaned in and planted a soft kiss on his cheek, the brief contact sparking a familiar warmth that lingered even as I pulled away.

"I'll see you in a few days," I said, my voice light but laced with barely restrained anticipation. I didn't linger for a moment longer than necessary, quickly turning and walking out the door.

As soon as the door clicked shut behind me, I felt a sudden rush of longing. The urge to turn back, to cross the room, and feel his warmth against me once more was almost overwhelming. I wanted to run my hands gently across the back of his neck, to feel the way his hair would fall through my fingers, and to give him a kiss that could erase the distance already growing between us. But the clock was ticking, and I knew if I didn't leave now, I'd be late.

Mark's office was one of many in the sprawling building, but while the main entrance was reserved for his receptionist's sitting area, the back door led to far more serene settings. A secluded courtyard, a hidden oasis that the executives used for lunch breaks and impromptu meetings, stretched out behind the building; it also had a separate entrance to the executives' offices. The area was a green paradise, with vibrant flowers and ivy creeping up trellises. High-top tables were tucked among the foliage, offering a peaceful place to step away from the rush of work. Brick pathways crisscrossed the garden like veins, guiding pedestrians and passers-by to different back door entrances to the executives' offices. There was even a side exit from the courtyard that led to the back parking lot, where I had parked my car earlier that day, away from the eyes of the other employees.

Stepping lightly onto the smooth bricks, I made my way through the garden, letting the beauty of the space soothe me even though I was rushing. Double French doors loomed just ahead, leading me out of the lush garden and into the parking lot. I snuck by the few cars in the area as quietly as possible, hoping no one would spot me. Since I was at the back of the building, it was unlikely anyone would see me, but I still couldn't shake the need to slip away unnoticed.

Once I reached my black SUV, I quickly jumped in.

Having sat under the midday sun for a while, it felt like an oven on the inside. It was the middle of June, and the heat was starting to set in. I rolled down the windows slightly, hoping for a breeze, and took off toward my next destination. I had only driven a few minutes when my phone rang through my car. It was Mark.

"Rachel," his voice came through the car Bluetooth, warm and full of longing, "I can't wait to see you again." The words sent a wave of heat through me, and I felt my cheeks flush, knowing just how much he was looking forward to seeing me again. Mark stood at an impressive 6'2", naturally commanding without even trying. His skin already carried the golden glow of summer, likely from time spent on the golf course whenever he could steal a few hours away. The sun had deepened his tan just enough to complement the sharp, dark brown of his hair, which he kept neatly trimmed in a professional style. He was fit—strong and well-built, but not in an overwhelming, obsessed way.

There was something about him, an effortless confidence that drew people in. When he spoke about business, he had a way of making every word sound important. When Mark got serious, when his professionalism took center stage, it only made him that much more magnetic.

The sun was pouring through the windshield, and already I could feel a light sweat forming from both the heat of the car and the flurry of emotions Mark always stirred in me. I smiled to myself, trying to stay focused on the road as we chatted for a few minutes, finalizing plans for our next time together.

I was driving across town to meet Ellie for drinks, as the

sun hung in the sky, casting long shadows over the streets. It had been a day full of appointments and then Mark ... Though I was physically heading somewhere else, part of me was still with Mark.

CHAPTER TWO

"Ellie, Ellie!" I called out softly, waving from my seat to get her attention.

"I'm over here!" I added, a little louder as she scanned the bar, looking for me. Blue's was the heart of the local country club here in Glen Springs, a growing town. It was an upscale establishment, and most of our neighbors were members, spending weekends at the golf course, at the pool, or at exclusive events. Glen Springs Country Club was an integral part of life here, especially since a golf cart path connected our neighborhood directly to the course, making it easy for residents to visit. The bar itself had a luxurious feel, with rich dark wood accents along the walls that gave it an air of timeless elegance. Yet, it also had a modern flair —sleek brass lighting fixtures overhead and a pristine white quartz bar top that contrasted beautifully with the deep tones of the wood. The back wall of the bar was adorned with elegant light grey tiles that gave way to a stunning mosaic pattern.

"Good to see you, sweet friend! You look absolutely lovely!" Ellie exclaimed as she gave me a side hug before sitting down. As her arms wrapped around me, I felt a wave of affection for her—Ellie always knew how to make me feel at ease.

I smiled, though I could feel the faintest flush creeping across my face. I'd just come from Mark's office, my heart still fluttering from our time together. Before walking into Blue's, I'd taken a few moments to adjust my outfit and check my appearance. I wanted to make sure everything looked just right.

I was wearing a black, sleeveless dress that stopped just past my knees. It fit perfectly—slightly snug, but with just enough room to feel comfortable. A row of buttons ran from top to bottom in the front, and I couldn't help but smile as I thought about how easy it would be for Mark to undo them, to slide his hands over my skin—which is why I'd chosen this dress this morning. Paired with strappy black heels, it gave me a sleek, confident look. The dress, my heels, and the tan from a few sunny days outside had all come together perfectly for the afternoon I'd spent with him.

We settled into our lunch, munching on fresh salads and hearty sandwiches while making small talk. The kind of conversation that flowed easily between close friends— casual, comfortable, and full of the day-to-day thoughts that kept our lives moving forward.

"Hey, what do you think about getting together this weekend? Maybe we could even come back here tomorrow and lounge by the pool? The weather is supposed to be beautiful," I suggested, already imagining the golden rays of the sun and the cool, refreshing water of the club's pool.

June in Glen Springs meant long, hot, and sunny days—ideal for outdoor activities. Nestled in northern New York, Glen Springs had become known for its pristine golf courses, some public and some private, and it was only a short drive from New York City. Every summer, wealthy city-dwellers—their golf clubs in tow—flocked to the area to escape the heat of the city and spent their weekends in luxury. The town had grown exponentially in the past few years, and with the influx of out-of-town guests, places like Blue's were often crowded. But the ambiance, the familiarity, and the luxury of the place made it all worth it.

"I've got a new bathing suit I can't wait to wear! Let's do it—let's plan for tomorrow," Ellie replied with a sparkle in her eye.

Ellie didn't have a job, which made her schedule far more flexible than mine. While I was constantly juggling work deadlines and obligations, she seemed to move through life at her own pace. I remember her casually mentioning once that she had studied business at the University of Alabama, but she never spoke about a career —past, present, or future. It was as if work had never been part of her plan. I often wondered if she had always intended to transition straight from college into family life, bypassing work life. But I never found the courage to ask.

After we finished eating, the waitress came by to clear our plates, and I used my club account to cover the bill for both of us. We continued chatting, savoring the moments of relaxation before we had to face the world again. Eventually, we decided it was time to head out.

As we walked toward the door, we were stopped by Jeremy, the restaurant manager, who always greeted us like old friends.

"My favorite ladies!" Jeremy boomed, grinning widely as he stepped between Ellie and me; he wrapped his arms around us in a quick, friendly hug. Jeremy was a social butterfly, so he probably said that to everyone who came through the door. But it didn't matter. His energy was contagious, and his enthusiasm made it impossible not to feel special. He was always ready with a smile and quick to help if anyone had a special request. On countless occasions, I'd watched him go out of his way to make sure every guest was satisfied, and I'd never once seen him without that big, welcoming smile.

As we pulled away from the embrace, Ellie and I giggled, shaking our heads at how effortlessly Jeremy could brighten anyone's day.

Once outside, we stood between our cars and kept talking, the afternoon sun casting a soft golden light over everything. Just as I was about to say something, I heard a voice from behind me.

"Looking good, little lady," said the familiar drawl of an older man. I turned and saw Jim Beck, one of the club's more flirtatious members, coming toward us. Jim was probably in his late 80s, but he had the charisma of a man half his age. Always offering compliments, always with a twinkle in his eye.

Before I could reply, Jim waved a hand and turned to address Ellie with another compliment. I couldn't help laughing as Ellie and I exchanged amused glances. Jim continued on his way, chuckling to himself as he walked past, and we shook our heads in good-natured amusement.

After a quick goodbye hug, Ellie and I parted ways, heading toward our respective cars. I pulled my phone from my purse, checking for any missed calls or texts. I was careful not to keep my phone out in front of anyone. No one knew about Mark and me, not a single person. It was our secret, and I planned to keep it that way.

CHAPTER THREE

I made the turn into our gated neighborhood, the heavy gates swinging open to reveal the rows of grand, million-dollar homes lining the streets. Each one stood out in its own unique way: some were sprawling estates of brick with majestic front entrances, while others had intricate stonework or elegant wood accents, but all of them were equally opulent. The homes were massive, each one spanning at least five thousand square feet of living space, and the landscaping was nothing short of perfect. Though the homes were vast and imposing, the land they stood on was far from expansive. The properties were compact, with each mansion nestled tightly against its neighbor. Every lawn was meticulously manicured, each flowerbed strategically placed to complement the architectural beauty of the house. Past the large, circular drive in front of my own home, I pulled into the garage with a quiet sense of contentment. I was never the type to boast about the wealth or luxury surrounding me, but I couldn't deny that there was something special about where I lived.

I stepped out of the car and made my way inside. The house felt like a sanctuary, a place where I could unwind after a long day. Jax, my energetic dog, greeted me at the door with his big brown eyes fixed on me. I quickly let him out and back in, and then I headed upstairs to my bathroom. The soft sound of water filling the tub welcomed me as I unbuttoned my dress, letting the fabric slip to the floor like a whisper. The familiar scent of Mark's cologne lingered on my skin. I took a slow breath, savoring the moment, as the scent clung to me for just a few seconds longer. It must have been from when he had leaned in, his body brushing against mine. I closed my eyes for a brief moment, enjoying the connection, even though it was fleeting. It was still early in the afternoon, but the idea of a warm bath was irresistible. I sank into the water, the heat enveloping me as I stared out the window, lost in thought. I thought about the way Mark's hands had roamed over me, the memory lingering like a slow burn. But soon, reality crept in. I had more work to do, and as much as I wanted to stay in that moment, I knew I had to push forward.

After a long soak, I reluctantly pulled myself out of the bath and dressed in a simple but professional outfit. I needed to get some work done, so I made my way downstairs to my office. As a realtor specializing in high-end homes in our area, my days were often filled with calls, emails, and appointments. There was always something to stay on top of. I enjoyed the flexibility of my job, but I was always mindful of looking the part—whether I was meeting clients in person, closing on a house, or even working at home, I made sure to stay presentable. Just as I was about to call it a day around six p.m., Jax appeared at my side, his tail wagging furiously, a silent plea for a walk. I couldn't help but smile as I went to change into my workout clothes and tennis shoes, slipping the leash onto him before heading out the door.

On the way, I passed by Ellie's house, which was just across the street and one house over. Something in her front window caught my eye—a rapid movement, almost too quick to make sense of. It looked like someone running back and forth inside her house, but I knew there were no children in her household, so that didn't add up. I stole another glance, trying not to appear too obvious. The motion persisted—someone was definitely moving around quickly. It felt strange, out of place. I shook my head, trying to push the thought aside, but curiosity gnawed at me as I continued my walk.

Jax and I strolled for about forty minutes, but as I made my way back to my house, my eyes were drawn once again to Ellie's home. There it was again—the strange, rapid movement in the window. It bothered me, but I didn't want to dwell on it. Just as I reached the halfway point of my driveway, I heard someone calling my name.

"Rachel, wait! Rachel!" Ellie's voice rang out.

I turned around to see her jogging across the street toward me, her face flushed with the effort.

"We're still going to the pool tomorrow, right?" she asked, catching her breath.

"Yeah, I'm still planning on it," I answered, trying to keep things light.

Jax, ever the attention-seeker, immediately started jumping up on her, barking excitedly. He began sniffing her leg, which was unusual for him since she had no animals. I quickly tugged him back, feeling a slight wave of awkwardness wash over me.

"Sorry, he always does that," I said, though I knew that wasn't exactly true. It just felt like the right thing to say at the moment.

It was odd that Ellie had come out to ask about a plan we had already discussed. Why didn't she just text me? It seemed like more than a simple check-in. I couldn't shake the feeling that maybe she was trying to distract me, perhaps even subtly deflect attention from whatever was going on inside her house.

"Okay, I was just making sure," she replied, her tone just a bit too casual.

"Do you want to walk up to my house with me? Or I can walk you back to yours," I offered, trying to keep the conversation moving.

"No, no ... let's walk up to your house," she said, her tone insistent as she turned toward my driveway. She started walking ahead, clearly trying to steer the conversation away from her home.

I glanced back one more time at her house, my curiosity piqued, but I followed Ellie up my driveway. Once inside the garage, I grabbed a couple of water bottles from the garage fridge and offered one to her.

"So were you just out for a walk?" she asked, fiddling with her water bottle and clearly trying to keep the conversation flowing.

"Yes. Jax kept jumping around in the house and seemed to have a lot of energy, so I thought I would take him for a walk," I said, offering a smile. I wasn't sure if she was just making small talk or if there was something more going on.

I had only been working as a realtor for about two years, but it had come naturally to me. I enjoyed meeting new people and finding them their perfect homes. As we stood in the garage, I noticed how Ellie's fingers fidgeted with the bottle, a subtle sign that she was still on edge. It made me wonder if she knew I had seen something inside her house earlier.

As Ellie started to leave, my phone buzzed in my pocket. I discreetly pulled it out after she was several steps away, glancing at the message on the screen. It was from Mark.

> Baby, I've been thinking about you. Let's not wait until next week to get together. Can I see you soon?

I didn't react. I made sure my face remained neutral just in case she looked back. I couldn't help but think about the effect he had on me, even as I hid my emotions behind a mask.

CHAPTER FOUR

The next day, I arrived at the pool to the sight of Ellie
lounging on a chair in the distance, looking perfectly
relaxed under the sun. She had already claimed a spot for
me, a bag placed neatly on the lounge chair next to hers. I
walked past several families who were enjoying the warm
day, their laughter and chatter filling the air, until I reached
Ellie.

"Wow, it's a hot one today," I commented as I gently
placed my bag on the ground between us, shielding it from
the blazing sun.

Ellie smiled up at me from her chair. "Definitely feels
like summer today," she said, adjusting her sun hat to cover
her face a little more.

"Cute suit! Is this the one you were raving about?" I
asked, eyeing the vibrant red polka dots on her swimsuit. It
was bold, fun, and effortlessly suited her personality—like
it had been made just for her.

"It is," she confirmed, glancing down at it.

I stretched out on the lounge chair beside her, laying

out my blanket and feeling the scorching heat of the sun almost instantly. My skin was beginning to tingle with the first touches of sunburn, and I quickly began applying sunscreen to my arms and shoulders.

I leaned back, letting my thoughts drift, reflecting on just how much my life had changed. My new life in New York now was a far cry from my roots in California. My father, the president of a major car company based there, and my mother, an ambitious restaurateur, spent their days expanding her five-star dining empire. Recently, her restaurant had opened its fourth location in Southern California. Despite the distance, I still spoke with my parents weekly. I had grown up in what I always felt was a loving home, alongside my younger brother, who was now studying business at the University of Southern California.

That was where my path had first crossed with Steven. I was twenty, studying business at USC, when we met in a study group. Steven always had a polished way about him —always turned out in crisp, well-chosen clothes that looked intentional, not flashy. He stood just about eye-level with me, and his hair—lighter in color and almost too perfectly styled—seemed to fall into place like it had rehearsed the part. At first, he carried himself with a kind of quiet uncertainty. But as our study group sessions unfolded, I realized there was a sharp mind tucked behind that hesitant demeanor.

One thing led to another—friendship turned into something deeper, and before long, we graduated from college, became engaged, and then married. When he was offered a job in Glen Springs, New York, the opportunity was too good to pass up. So, we packed up our lives and made the leap. And now, here I was, thousands of miles from where I started, marveling at how different everything had become.

"Here's some water," Ellie said, handing me a chilled bottle.

I opened it immediately, splashing a little on my skin to cool down before taking a long sip. "Thanks," I said, feeling the relief spread over me as the cool water hit my throat.

"We might need one of those umbrellas today," I said, squinting up at the sun. "You really have to be careful in this heat, so you don't burn."

Ellie nodded in agreement, pulling her sun hat down over her eyes and settling in for some shade. She didn't seem in the mood for a lot of conversation, so I grabbed the magazine I had brought and started flipping through the pages. Ellie and I were good friends, so we didn't feel the pressure to fill the silence with small talk all the time. The comfortable quiet between us was just as nice. Unlike me, Ellie was a New York native. Yet, she rarely spoke of her family—just the occasional mention of a sister she visited now and then, as if the rest of her past was a story left untold.

Steven and I had moved into the neighborhood about three years ago. This was our second move within the area, a step toward something more permanent. Our first home had been a modest little place—just a temporary refuge to help us settle in—but somehow, it became more than we'd anticipated. I was in my twenties, well into my career as a realtor, while Steven was already established in his work, which kept him busy. We had bought our home in this upscale community to escape the hustle of the city and to be closer to Steven's job, which required frequent travel. Steven was the president of investor relations for a national tech company. The move had been a bit of a challenge at first—new neighborhood, new faces. But Ellie had reached out to me after a few casual encounters around the neighborhood, and we'd hit it off immediately.

The country club was like something out of a dream. The pool area was lined with expensive, cushioned lounge chairs perfectly arranged in rows, with large umbrellas providing shade at regular intervals. The area was spacious, stretching all around the pool. On the opposite end, there was a stunning stone hot tub and a splash pad for the kids. To the side of the pool, there was even a large outdoor restaurant, whose staff would walk around taking orders from the members as they lounged by the pool. This restaurant was separate from the fine dining restaurant inside the golf club. The view of the golf course stretched out beyond the pool, with rolling green hills and mature trees dotting the landscape, creating a peaceful, serene backdrop. It was the kind of place where the men played golf while the wives and kids soaked up the sun and relaxed.

"I'm going to get one of those umbrellas," Ellie said, sitting up suddenly. The sun was definitely taking its toll, and I could see her squinting uncomfortably.

She began dragging a large umbrella over to our lounge chairs, and one of the staff members quickly came over to help.

"Thank you, sir," Ellie said with a wink, smiling at him as he assisted with setting it up.

I chuckled to myself, knowing Ellie could be quite charming when she wanted to be. Once the umbrella was in place, we both sank back into our chairs, grateful for the shade.

I handed her one of the magazines I had brought, and

we both started to flip through them. As I turned a page, I noticed my nails were starting to grow out, and I frowned, knowing it was time for another manicure.

"We should go get manicures tomorrow," I said, glancing over at Ellie. "Mine are starting to look a little out of control."

"Yeah, same here," Ellie agreed, inspecting her own nails. "Mine look gross."

I couldn't help but laugh. "Eww, what did you do to yours?" I asked, raising an eyebrow as I looked at the state of her nails.

"It's just from gardening," she replied, grimacing at her nails. They were jagged and scratched up.

"Intense gardening, huh?" I said, half-laughing as I gave her a playful nudge.

Ellie laughed too. "You have no idea," she said, shaking her head.

"Well, let me check my schedule, and we can definitely meet up to get them done tomorrow," I said, reaching for my phone.

Ellie nodded in agreement, her focus returning to the magazine.

"Are you ladies good? Or can I get you anything?" A voice interrupted us, and I looked up to see that it was the outdoor staff member who had helped Ellie with the umbrella.

"Well, since you helped me move the umbrella, do you happen to have any of those cute little slushy drinks?" Ellie asked, flashing him a flirtatious smile. Something gave me the impression they already knew each other, even before he had helped her with the umbrella.

I bit back a laugh at their playful banter. Ellie definitely knew how to flirt when the mood struck.

"I'll see what I can do," he said, smiling back at her. They locked eyes for a few seconds before he turned and walked off toward the restaurant.

A few minutes later, he returned with two drinks that looked like pina coladas, complete with the tiny umbrellas. I looked at his name tag—it read "Gabe"—and couldn't help but notice how polished and put-together he seemed. He looked to be in his mid-twenties, his dark hair neatly combed, and his crisp work shirt suggesting he took his job —or at least appearance—seriously. He was definitely a few years younger than us.

He handed us the drinks, his gaze lingering a little longer on Ellie, and I couldn't tell if it was just friendly interest or something more.

"Are these pina coladas?" I asked, taking a sip to confirm. "They are delicious," I continued with a smile, savoring the tropical taste.

"Uh, yes, they are," Gabe replied, his voice a little more awkward now. He looked away from Ellie for a moment, his gaze shifting uncomfortably.

Ellie and I were both twenty-nine; however, our appearances were different. I was a blonde, standing about 5'7" on the thinner side. I did my best to stay toned by working out. Ellie's complexion was much fairer, and her jet-black hair was always impeccably cut to ear length, her whole look often topped with a bold red lipstick. Ellie exuded a quiet confidence, and she always managed to look effortlessly chic. She stood at about 5'10" and was thin as well.

I had a feeling the situation was getting a little

awkward. There was a lot of staring between Ellie and Gabe, and the conversation had stalled. To break the tension, I decided to leave for a moment.

"I'm going to get a salad," I said, standing up from my lounge chair. Sensing the uncomfortable vibe between them, I wanted to give them a little space. It was almost as though they were waiting for me to depart anyway.

As I waited for the salad, I occasionally glanced back at Ellie and Gabe. Ellie was sitting up on the lounge chair, looking animated and engaged, while Gabe had now moved to the foot of her lounge chair and was sitting down. They were both laughing over something, clearly enjoying each other's company. It looked like their little flirtation was heating up.

When I returned with my food, I saw Gabe standing up quickly as the outdoor manager called out from behind him. "Gabe, you're needed at the restaurant."

I could tell that Gabe had been caught in a compromising position. He looked startled, almost embarrassed, and hurriedly excused himself.

As Gabe rushed off, the outdoor manager, a man named Max, turned toward Ellie. "So, is Mr. Duncan out golfing today?" Max asked, his voice carrying a hint of disapproval as he looked over at Ellie. I couldn't help but notice the subtle reminder in his question.

"Yes, he is," Ellie answered coolly, nodding toward the golf course.

Max walked off, and I watched Ellie closely. There was a subtle glow to her, an almost triumphant look in her eyes.

In all the years I'd known Ellie, I'd never seen her behave like this—so flirtatious and playful with another man. It made me wonder if she was looking for something more.

"So, what was that all about?" I asked, trying to keep my tone light but curious.

Ellie turned to me with a mischievous grin. "He's hot. Don't you think so?" she said, a glint of excitement in her eyes.

CHAPTER FIVE

The sun was blazing, the heat was almost unbearable, and we spent most of our time tucked beneath the shade of the umbrella. The moment we stepped out from its cool shelter, the warmth hit us like a wave, making the air feel thick and heavy. So, we would retreat back to the poolside, to the water glistening invitingly under the sun. I could barely resist the pull of the pool, and every now and then, I would slip into the cool, refreshing water. It felt like a slice of heaven against the oppressive heat. I could almost feel the stress of the day evaporating with each dip.

After spending nearly three hours lounging by the pool, I began to wonder if it was time to wrap things up and head home. My mind started to drift, and I realized that I had already flipped through every magazine I had brought with me.

"I think I'm going to head out," I said, sitting up and starting to gather my things. "I'm getting tired."

I noticed Gabe was still wandering about the pool area.

I couldn't help but wonder if Ellie was just waiting for me to leave so she could continue flirting with him.

"Can we reschedule our manicure for Monday instead of tomorrow?" Ellie asked. "My sister is planning to stop by quickly to drop something off, and I'm not sure when exactly."

"Sure, no problem. Monday works for me. I'll text you later to figure out the details. Have fun," I replied with a wink, a playful smirk crossing my face. I was sure she knew exactly what I meant.

The club's pool area was enclosed by a large wooden gate at the front, offering a sense of privacy, which I appreciated. I gave Ellie one last glance before stepping through the gate. Sure enough, as I looked back, I saw Gabe standing over her. He wasted no time.

Once I was in my car, I barely started the engine when a message popped up on my phone. It was from Mark.

It's a hot one out there today.

It is. Just leaving the pool now.

Can't wait to see you again. Been thinking about you.

Looking forward to it.

My office again on Monday? Come through the courtyard. Everyone will be gone for the afternoon. How about 12:30?

12:30 works. See you then.

I let out a long breath, smiling to myself. My mind

drifted to Monday, to the quiet anticipation of seeing Mark. Tossing my phone on the passenger seat, I remembered I had promised Ellie I'd get that manicure with her. I'll sort the timing with her later.

I made my way out of the country club, driving back through the scenic route that led to our neighborhood. As soon as I walked through my front door, I sent Ellie a quick message as the timing for the manicure was obviously weighing on my mind more than I had thought.

> Is 11 a.m. good for the manicure on Monday?

I took my phone with me to the bathroom as I washed off the day's sunscreen, savoring the cool water. Afterward, I settled onto the couch in my living room with my laptop, trying to catch up on work emails. I kept glancing at my phone, waiting for Ellie's response.

Nearly twenty minutes passed without a reply. Usually, Ellie was much quicker to respond, and I wondered what might be keeping her. Another half hour slipped by, and just as I was starting to wonder if something had come up, I noticed her black Mercedes driving by my window, heading to her house. A minute later, my phone buzzed with a new message—from Ellie:

> Yes, 11 a.m. works.

I knew we always drove separately to the nail salon, so I didn't feel the need to offer her a ride. We lived right across the street from each other, but with my unpredictable work schedule, it was always easier for us to meet there. That way, we didn't risk either of us running late if something came up.

Looking at the time, I realized we needed to finish our manicures by 12:00 or ten minutes past twelve at the latest. I had a much more pressing engagement at 12:30 with Mark, and I couldn't afford to be late.

I couldn't help but wonder if Ellie had been distracted because she had been chatting with Gabe all this time, which would explain her delayed response. I was sure I'd find out more when we got our manicures.

CHAPTER SIX

Today had all the weight of a Monday—endless tasks piling up and my mind running in a dozen different directions. I walked into the nail salon just a few minutes before eleven, and the subtle scent of polish and spa aromas immediately relaxing me. I waved a casual greeting to the ladies working behind the counter, who smiled back warmly. Ellie and I were regulars here, and over time, we had built a rapport with the staff. They always appreciated our business, but it was our generous tips that really made us stand out. They had always told us that we didn't need an appointment— just walk in, and they would fit us in. Today, though, as I looked around, I realized I hadn't seen Ellie's car in the parking lot before I walked in, which meant she wasn't here yet.

I made my way over to the row of nail polish bottles, the vibrant colors arranged in neat lines. I paused for a moment, eyeing the current shade on my nails—white, simple, and clean. I wanted something soft this time, so I reached for a light pink hue that would complement my toes. The creamy rose shade felt right, like a fresh beginning, and I liked how it seemed to mirror my mood.

Settling into the plush leather chair, I sighed deeply, feeling the comfortable cushion support my back. The salon was small but charming, tucked in the heart of a quaint shopping district—one of those places that offered everything a family might need, though all with a slightly upscale twist. A gourmet grocery store, a sushi restaurant with a chic atmosphere, a cozy pizza spot, and even a dog grooming salon dotted the strip. There were many more unique and charming stores as well. It was a little world unto itself, and the type of place where you could find almost anything without ever having to leave the area.

As I sank into the chair, I glanced around the room, my thoughts wandering. A few minutes later, I heard the bell above the door chime, and in walked Ellie, a little late. She looked a bit frazzled, her face flushed and hair slightly out of place. Despite her hurried arrival, she didn't offer any explanation for her tardiness, though it was clear something was bothering her.

"Don't you look cute," she said, out of breath from rushing, her voice tinged with exhaustion. She glanced at me, the compliment seemingly more out of politeness than anything else.

I brushed it off, not really in the mood to explain my outfit. She likely assumed I was dressed up for a house showing or closing. I was wearing a white, sleeveless blouse that was light and airy, the buttons open just enough to reveal a hint of my tan. It draped loosely over me, giving off an effortlessly chic vibe. My light brown silk pleated skirt swished slightly as I shifted in my seat, the fabric catching the light. My feet were adorned with brown strappy sandals. Light makeup highlighted my features, and a sheer pink gloss made my lips shimmer just enough. My blonde hair flowed loosely down my back. The undone buttons of my blouse were a subtle invitation, a deliberate move meant for someone specific.

"Are you okay?" I asked, concerned as I took in her rushed demeanor. "You seem a little flustered."

"Yeah, just a crazy morning," she replied with a sigh, her frustration still evident in her voice.

"So, what's the deal with you and that Gabe guy?" I asked playfully, raising a curious brow.

Ellie flashed me a coy smile. "Oh, you know ... just friends," she teased. But something in her eyes told me there was more to the story.

I opened the flap of my purse and reached inside, my fingers grazing my phone as I subtly checked the time. I still had a little over an hour to get my nails done before I needed to leave. Luckily, we were called back just a couple of minutes later, and the rhythmic process of having my nails done gave me a moment to relax. By the time the last coats of polish were applied and dried, I was out of the salon with plenty of time to make it to Mark.

When I arrived at the back of Mark's office, just as I had promised, most of the cars were gone. I took a quick look at myself in the car mirror, making sure my makeup was still fresh. Reaching into the console, I pulled out my small bottle of perfume and spritzed a bit onto my wrists and neck. The scent lingered, light and intoxicating.

I left everything in the car except my phone and keys. I turned the volume down on my phone as I walked toward the courtyard, wanting to avoid any distractions. As I approached the path leading to Mark's office, I could already picture him inside, waiting for me. He always kept the door unlocked, knowing I would arrive soon. I took a steadying breath as I walked through the familiar entrance and into the quiet of his office. He was seated at his desk, talking on the phone. The other door, the one leading to his receptionist's office, was closed and locked, offering us privacy. Mark was the president of a national plastics company that manufactured everyday essentials like food containers, storage bins, and coffee cup lids. I recall him once mentioning that the former CEO had a knack for scaling the business in ways that were nothing short of impressive.

I chose to sit on the large leather couch in the middle of the room, remaining quiet and still as I waited. I had no intention of interrupting him while he finished his call. The seconds stretched out as I watched him from across the room.

As soon as he hung up the phone, he turned toward me, his eyes dark with focus. He didn't walk over to kiss me right away. No, he moved with purpose, his arms open, ready to pull me into him. I stood up, meeting him halfway.

"Come here, baby," he murmured, his voice low and commanding. His arms wrapped around me, pulling me close as if nothing else in the world mattered. And in that moment, nothing else did.

There was something different about the way he had been holding me lately, something more intense. It was clear this moment was more than just about the physical connection—it was about something deeper, something unspoken.

CHAPTER SEVEN

Mark's lips were warm as they pressed gently against the curve of my neck. A shiver ran down my spine, and I tilted my head back, surrendering to his embrace. His strong arms held me securely, his breath hot against my skin. His lips traveled slowly, teasingly, from just beneath my ear, tracing a path downward along the sensitive curve of my neck. Each kiss seemed to linger, igniting a fire that spread through me.

Mark paused briefly, stepping back to loosen his tie. His fingers deftly worked the knot, tugging it loose with a practiced ease. I couldn't help myself—I reached out, pulling his shirt free from his pants. He tossed the tie onto the couch with little care, and I eagerly began unbuttoning his shirt, my fingers brushing against his chest with each movement.

His hands slipped beneath the back of my blouse, the warmth of his palms sending goosebumps across my skin. He captured my lips in a deep, passionate kiss that left me breathless. I tugged his shirt free from his shoulders and tossed it carelessly over the arm of the couch, already moving to lift his plain white T-shirt.

Just as I started to pull it over his head, Mark stopped me, his hands closing gently over mine. His hesitation caught me off guard.

"What's wrong?" I asked.

"Nothing," he replied, his tone tinged with embarrassment. "I just have an allergic reaction to something on my back. It looks awful, and I'd rather keep the shirt on."

I smiled softly, letting my hands fall back to his chest. "It's okay," I said reassuringly, dismissing the matter with a casual wave of my hand. His imperfections didn't bother me.

His lips found mine again as his fingers moved with deliberate precision, unbuttoning my blouse. He opened it slowly, revealing the delicate lace of my bra. His belt was already undone, and my hands worked quickly to unfasten the button and zipper of his pants.

With a sly grin, he guided me backward until the edge of the couch pressed against the backs of my legs. "Lie down, baby," he whispered in my ear.

I sank into the plush corner of his dark brown leather couch, leaning back as he climbed over me. His weight was comforting, his presence magnetic. Mark kissed me again, deeply, passionately, before pulling back to look at me. My legs were wrapped around him, his hands resting firmly on my thighs.

His touch was electric. He hooked his fingers into the delicate band of my black lace thong and slid it down my legs with agonizing slowness. My heart raced, my body responding eagerly to every move he made.

The moment our bodies aligned, a gasp escaped my

lips. "Ohhh," I moaned instinctively, unable to contain myself.

Mark chuckled softly, his laughter a warm rumble in my ear. "Shhh," he teased, his tone playful. "There still might be a few people here. I don't know who left for lunch, but just in case."

I stifled a laugh and nodded, biting my lip. "Okay, sorry," I whispered back, trying to muffle the sound of my own pleasure. But the humor faded quickly as we lost ourselves in the intensity of the moment. His hand caressed my upper leg, and we moved together as if perfectly in sync, the rest of the world fading into oblivion.

Afterward, as we lay tangled together on the couch, Mark's arm draped protectively over me, he pressed a kiss to the side of my head.

"I wish I didn't have meetings today," he added wistfully. "I'd give anything to stay here with you all day."

"Me too," I whispered, brushing my lips against his neck.

We stayed there, cocooned in the aftermath of lovemaking, his strong arms wrapped tightly around me as we lay side by side on the couch. I gazed around the spacious office, taking in the rich decor—his mahogany desk in the corner, the fireplace, a well-stocked bar, and an impressive flat-screen TV. The room was impeccably designed, every detail polished to perfection. It was clear a professional decorator had worked their magic on it.

It was hard to believe that just forty minutes earlier, Mark had been seated at his desk in his work attire, focused and professional. And in another forty minutes, I would be working on my next client case for a showing.

The memory of how we first met surfaced in my mind

—a chance encounter at the country club's spring meet-and-greet two years ago. Steven and I had already been members for a year, and we thought it would be nice to mingle with new members. Mark had been wandering around admiring the new golf items as I was. We struck up a conversation, which led to him mentioning that he and his wife were house hunting. As a realtor, I naturally offered my help, giving him my number.

Looking back, I remembered my initial impression of his wife—a woman I found interesting. But business was business, and I worked tirelessly to find them the perfect home. Mark appreciated my dedication and referred me to several of his friends.

A few months ago, one of Mark's colleagues was looking to upgrade to a larger home in the area. After referring him to me, Mark called to share how pleased his friend was with my help in finding the perfect place. I told him I owed him lunch, and soon after, we found ourselves at a cozy sushi spot near his office. The chemistry was instant, and the conversation flowed effortlessly between us. When we parted, he brushed a soft kiss on my cheek and told me he had a great time.

The next day, I got a text from him asking if he could call me in the afternoon. When we spoke, the conversation was light and easy, but I could sense he was holding something back. Toward the end, he told me he wanted to see me again. I was undeniably drawn to him, so I agreed. The very next night, we met at a charming bistro about twenty minutes outside of town, near my last showing of the day. The flirtation continued, and that's when the story of us began.

Mark's voice pulled me back to the present. "I'll miss

you," he said, his tone serious as he sat buttoning his shirt. His eyes lingered on mine, filled with an emotion that made my heart ache.

"Will you come closer to me?" he asked, patting the cushion beside him.

I moved to sit next to him, and his hand found its way to my leg. He rubbed it gently, his thumb tracing soothing patterns. He seemed pensive, as though something important was weighing on his mind.

"I was supposed to have a work dinner tomorrow night," he said after a moment. "But it got canceled. Can you meet me here? I have an idea." His smile turned mischievous, his eyes sparkling with anticipation.

"Yeah, I'd love to," I replied, matching his grin.

"Good. Meet me here at nine-thirty," he said, his voice dropping to a conspiratorial whisper. "It was supposed to be a late work night, so it'll be dark by then."

"I can't wait to see what you have planned," I said, my curiosity piqued.

He kissed me one last time before walking me to the door. As I stepped out into the warm air, my heart raced with excitement, already anticipating what tomorrow night would bring.

CHAPTER EIGHT

I pulled into the familiar back parking lot at Mark's office, the low hum of my car the only sound breaking the stillness of the evening. The sun had just dipped below the horizon, leaving behind a soft blue-gray haze that signaled the arrival of dusk. The lot was mostly empty except for a couple of cars parked far down at the other end of the building—likely belonging to the nighttime cleaning crew. Mark's car was parked snugly in the small covered garage near his office.

Excitement and curiosity fluttered in my chest as I parked and stepped out of my car, the cool evening air brushing against my skin. I glanced around, taking in the shadowy expanse of the courtyard I needed to cross. The lush greenery, so vibrant and inviting in daylight, now felt dense and imposing in the growing darkness. There were dim landscape lights along the pathway leading to his back office door, and the quiet amplified the faint rustle of the trees. It wasn't the fear of being seen that quickened my steps—Mark had been careful about getting the timing just right—but rather the uneasy solitude of the courtyard at night.

I was dressed for the evening in a light, flowing dress, unsure of what Mark had planned but knowing how much he appreciated the elegance of it. There was something intoxicating about wearing a dress for him, knowing that at some point, his hands would find the buttons or zipper, sliding the fabric from my body with deliberate precision.

I tapped lightly on the cool surface of the door before pushing it open. The office was dimly lit, a faint glow from a small desk lamp casting long shadows across the room. Mark wasn't at his desk, hunched over paperwork or a phone call as usual. Instead, he stood near the corner of the room, a bottle of wine, his phone, and keys in hand. He looked up as I entered, his lips curling into a smile that made my heart skip.

"Are you ready?" he asked, his voice warm and teasing.

I raised an eyebrow, mirroring his smile. "I guess so, though I don't know what I'm ready for," I replied, the skepticism in my voice edged with amusement.

I stepped toward him, and he pulled me into an embrace, his hands firm against my back. His body felt solid, grounding, as he leaned in to kiss me. His lips lingered on mine before traveling to my ear, his breath hot and uneven. The rest of the world melted away, leaving just the two of us locked in that intimate moment.

"Let's go. Oh, I ran out at lunch and picked us up a very nice bottle of wine," he murmured, pulling back just enough to look into my eyes. The mischievous glint in his gaze sent a thrill through me.

"Where? Where are we going?" I softly asked.

Mark guided me toward the door. He locked it carefully

behind us with his keys, the metallic click of the lock echoing softly in the quiet night. Without hesitation, he walked around to the passenger side of my car and slid in.

"We're going to your house," he said, taking my hand and pressing a kiss to the back of it, his lips lingering just long enough to make me blush.

I blinked at him, surprised. "Are you serious?" I asked, my voice laced with equal parts excitement and hesitation.

"Yes. But are you okay with this? Especially since ... he's passed?" Mark asked gently, his tone thoughtful.

I hesitated for only a moment, then nodded. "Yes, I am. Are *you* okay with this?" I asked, studying his face.

"How've you been holding up since Steven ... left?" Mark asked gently, genuine concern in his voice. "I imagine there are still some tough days."

I nodded, my gaze drifting for a moment. "There are," I admitted softly. "But they're not as constant anymore. The weight's still there ... just not as heavy all the time."

I glanced back at him and offered a faint, grateful smile. "Thank you for asking."

He exhaled softly, his hand still holding mine. "It's dark now. So we don't have to worry about anyone seeing us," he said with a small smile. "I just want to be with you in bed. Not on a couch, not on a chair—*in bed.*"

The sincerity in his voice made my chest tighten. "I know," I said softly. "Me too."

We pulled out of the lot and onto the quiet streets, the city fading behind us as we approached my neighborhood. The entrance to the gated community loomed ahead, the keypad glowing faintly in the darkness. I slowed the car to a crawl and carefully entered the code. My pulse quickened as I glanced around, hoping no one was driving out or walking nearby. The gates creaked open, and I breathed a sigh of relief as we slipped through unnoticed.

The streets of Checkerberry Lane were still, the neatly manicured lawns and perfectly trimmed hedges bathed in the faint glow of streetlights. I scanned the sidewalks and driveways, relieved to find no sign of neighbors taking an evening stroll. The tension eased slightly as we turned onto my driveway, the path winding back toward the garage. The house stood shrouded in shadows, its familiar outline comforting in the darkness.

I parked the car, waiting until the garage door had fully closed behind us before stepping out. The house was silent. Mark followed closely, his presence a steady reassurance.

For the first time, the reality of bringing him here—a place that held so many memories—hit me. But as his hand found mine, squeezing gently, all those doubts faded. Tonight wasn't about the past; it was about us, the pull between us too strong to deny any longer.

CHAPTER NINE

As we stepped into the kitchen, Mark quietly set his things on the counter, and I followed suit, placing my purse down beside them. The air between us was thick with anticipation, unspoken words crackling like static electricity. Without a word, Mark turned to me, his lips finding mine in a kiss that was soft but filled with meaning.

In a matter of seconds, Jax was at our sides, bounding around with excitement. He wasted no time, giving Mark a few investigative sniffs. With a quick, satisfied huff, he granted his approval, as if he were the official gatekeeper of our little world.

"Where are your wine glasses?" Mark asked, his voice low and smooth.

"I'll grab them," I replied, glancing at the bottle of wine he had brought.

Once the glasses were on the counter, I turned and made my way to the front of the house. The blinds in the living room and my office were still open, leaving the spaces exposed to the world outside. One by one, I drew them closed, a sense of privacy settling over the room like a comforting blanket.

The fireplace in the living room, though unused during the warm summer months, beckoned to me. I knelt down and lit it, the soft glow of the flames casting a golden hue across the room. The flickering light played on the walls, adding an intimate warmth to the space. Behind me, I heard the faint click of the kitchen light dimming. Mark entered the living room moments later, carrying two glasses of wine. He handed one to me with a quiet smile before pulling a blanket from a wicker basket near the wall.

He spread the blanket out in front of the fireplace, its soft folds creating an inviting space on the floor. He settled down, leaning back against the couch, and looked up at me with an expression that seemed to say, *Join me.*

"How's work been going?" he asked casually, his tone light but genuinely interested.

I sank down onto the blanket beside him, taking a sip of the rich, velvety wine before answering. "Good," I said, smiling. "I really like what I do."

Mark leaned in slightly, his gaze flickering between me and the table before settling on me again. There was a sincerity in his voice that caught me off guard.

"How's everything else going? I mean, I feel like we don't really talk about ourselves—about *us*—very much. I want to know more about you," he said, his fingers idly tracing the rim of his glass.

I studied him for a moment, unsure of how deep he truly wanted to go. "Everything's good with me," I answered, though I knew that wasn't what he was really asking. "I get what you mean. Our relationship has mostly been … physical. Are you sure you want to go down the road of *us*—the personal stuff?" My voice held a serious edge, my heart bracing for his response.

Mark didn't hesitate. "I do," he said firmly, meeting my eyes with an intensity that sent a small shiver through me. "I want to know more about you."

His words settled over me, warm and unexpected. I hadn't realized how much I'd assumed I was just an indulgence to him. But this—his wanting to *know* me—felt like more.

A soft smile tugged at my lips as I nodded. "Okay," I said gently. "Then we'll keep getting to know each other ... more and more."

For the first time, it felt like we were stepping into something real, something deeper than just physical desire.

As I spoke, my gaze drifted, and over Mark's shoulder, I noticed a vase perched on the sofa table. It was a gift from Steven, and its presence caught me off guard. A sudden wave of emotion surged through me, not painful but poignant—a reminder of how far I'd come and how much my feelings for Mark had grown.

Mark's voice pulled me back to the present. He was talking about the real estate market, enthusiasm lighting up his face. I tried to focus on his words, nodding as he shared his insights. When he paused, the room fell into a comfortable silence, the kind that feels more like a connection than an absence.

Without a word, Mark shifted closer to me, his hand gently cradling my face as he leaned in for another kiss. The firelight danced across our skin as our lips met, the warmth of the moment rivaling the heat of the flames.

"Do you like the wine?" he asked softly after the kiss, his voice a tender murmur.

"I do," I replied, my voice equally quiet.

Mark stood up and extended his hand to me, guiding me to my feet. We walked upstairs together, each of us carrying our glasses of wine. The quiet of the house seemed to deepen as we entered the bedroom. I took one last sip of wine before setting my glass on the nightstand. Mark's eyes met mine, his gaze intense yet tender.

"You look so beautiful," he said in a hushed, reverential voice.

I felt a flush rise to my cheeks as his words consumed me. Just as I began to lose myself in the moment, a practical thought jolted me back. "Hang on," I said with a soft laugh. "I need to close the blinds."

"Good idea," he replied with a smile.

The master bedroom faced the street, and the large front window left little to the imagination. I walked over, pulling the blinds down and glancing outside. The neighboring houses were quiet, though a few porch lights glowed in the distance. Satisfied that we were shielded from prying eyes, I returned to Mark, who was watching me with a look that sent a shiver down my spine.

I paused again to step into the bathroom and retrieve a candle I sometimes used for baths, its scent of rose filling the air as I lit it and placed it on the nightstand. The flickering flame added to the intimacy of the room. Mark and I began to undress each other, the motions deliberate and unhurried, savoring every second.

"I don't want tonight to feel rushed," he continued. "I wish I could stay all night."

I smiled shyly, overwhelmed by the intensity of the moment. We kissed deeply, the world outside disappearing as we explored each other with a mix of urgency and tenderness. Time seemed to slip away as we alternated between passionate embraces and languid caresses. The candlelight played over our bodies, the soft crackle of the flames becoming a soundtrack to our intimacy.

Hours later, we lay side by side, our faces close enough to feel each other's breath. Mark broke the silence. "I should go soon," he said in a voice tinged with reluctance.

"I'll take you back," I replied, brushing a strand of hair from his face. "I'm really glad we came here."

"So am I," he said, sitting up and beginning to dress. His expression grew serious for a moment as he pulled on his shirt, and I noticed faint scratches on his back. They were too numerous and deliberate to be random. They were the scratches from yesterday that he didn't want me to see. He said it was an allergic reaction, not scratches, so that had me puzzled.

Still, I said nothing, filing away the thought for later. As we left the house, the stillness of the street reassured me. Just half an hour after midnight, the neighborhood felt like a world apart, quiet and undisturbed. Mark and I slipped away into the night, leaving behind the secrets of the evening.

CHAPTER TEN

I woke up to the gentle chime of my phone, blinking sleepily at the screen. It was a message from Mark.

Last night was really special. I will never forget it.

A smile spread across my face before I even finished reading it. The memory of the night before washed over me, warm and vivid. Without hesitation, I typed back, *It was truly special.*

I lay there for a moment longer, clutching my phone as if it were a tangible connection to him. The world outside could wait—last night had been one of those moments that linger in one's soul.

Reluctantly, I pulled myself from the comfort of my bed, moving more slowly than usual thanks to the late night. After a long, warm shower, I moved downstairs, where the cool morning air greeted me. Jax wagged his tail impatiently by the door. "All right, all right," I laughed, letting him out into the yard.

While waiting for the coffee to brew, I flipped open my calendar. My first meeting wasn't until eleven—a rare luxury—followed by two house showings, a closing, and another showing in the late afternoon. As the smell of fresh coffee filled the kitchen, I poured myself a cup and transferred it into my trusty travel mug. Jax barked to be let back in, and with him trailing behind, I grabbed my work bag and headed out the door.

The drive to the office was a quick one—just fifteen minutes along quiet, tree-lined streets. Our real estate office was nestled in one of the many charming shopping districts, surrounded by upscale boutiques and cafes. It was one of the things I loved about this town: Everything I needed was close by, except for Mark's office, which was a short distance away. That distance felt like a small blessing, a safe buffer.

As I pulled into the parking lot, my phone buzzed. It was Ellie. She and I had an unspoken agreement to check in with each other at least once a day and catch up.

"Hey!" she chirped as I answered.

"Hey, yourself. Just got to work. What's up?" I asked, balancing my phone between my ear and shoulder while gathering my things.

"Do you want to grab a drink tonight?" she asked.

After I painted her a picture of my jam-packed day, we swiftly agreed to meet at Blue's at six sharp—the very first block of free time I'd have all day. With that plan set, I stepped into the office, determined to tackle my day.

But no matter how hard I tried, my thoughts kept drifting back to last night. It hadn't been rushed like other times, and the setting—a bed, not his office—made it feel more intimate, more real. The thought of him leaving at the end of the night still stung.

Midway through my last house showing, my phone

buzzed again. A message from Mark lit up the screen as I discreetly slid it out of my dress pocket.

I miss you. I'll call you later.

A soft smile played on my lips. I didn't respond immediately, not wanting to break the flow of the showing. The couple was exploring every nook of the house, opening drawers and testing faucets. Their attention to detail was promising.

When they asked for a moment to talk privately, I seized the chance to reply.

I miss you too, I typed. *We'll talk soon.*

Sure enough, they returned with grins that couldn't be contained. "We love it," the wife exclaimed. "We want to make an offer."

Back at the office, I navigated them through the process on my iPad, seamlessly guiding them through each step as they signed electronically. With a reassuring smile, I promised to print copies of everything for them before they left. Yet, as they scrolled and signed, my mind wavered between the structured flow of real estate paperwork and the restless anticipation of Mark's call, a quiet thrill humming beneath my professionalism. As we wrapped up, I glanced at my watch. I was cutting it close, but still had a chance to make it to Blue's on time.

Ellie was already waiting when I arrived, her face lighting up as I walked in. The familiar hum of the bar wrapped around us, and I remembered Mark's earlier message. I had forgotten to let him know I'd be out tonight. As Ellie waved me over, I made a mental note that I needed to find a moment to text him and let him know I was out.

For now, I let myself settle into the moment, ready to savor good company and a much-needed drink.

CHAPTER ELEVEN

"Guess what?" I exclaimed as I slid onto the barstool beside Ellie, barely able to contain my excitement. My purse tumbled onto the counter as I leaned toward her, my voice bubbling with energy. "I sold a house just before I got here! That always makes for a good day."

Ellie arched an impressed eyebrow, her grin spreading wide. "No way! Congrats! I was starting to wonder if you'd make it—thought for sure you'd be late since you said you had a really busy day."

"I thought so too," I admitted, still catching my breath. "But I managed to pull it off."

"Well, that's cause for celebration," she declared, already grabbing the drinks menu from the counter. "What are we having? First round's on me." She waved down Tom, our go-to bartender, who approached us with a knowing smile.

"What can I get for you ladies tonight?" Tom asked, drumming his fingers lightly on the counter.

Ellie leaned in conspiratorially. "We need something festive. Rachel just sold a house!"

"Hmm," Tom mused, tapping his chin for dramatic effect. "How about our chocolate raspberry martini? It's new."

"We'll take two!" Ellie said decisively.

As Tom went to work crafting our drinks, Ellie turned back to me. "So, spill—how much was it?"

I flipped open my purse absentmindedly, double-checking for my phone inside. "One point seven million," I said, trying to sound casual but unable to suppress my excitement.

"Well, look at you! Drinks are just the start; you should be treating yourself to a weekend spa day after closing a deal like that."

Tom returned with our martinis moments later, the glasses glistening under the warm bar lights. Ellie raised hers in a toast. "To you, Rachel—the ultimate realtor!"

We clinked glasses, and I took a sip. The flavors danced on my tongue—rich chocolate with just a hint of tart raspberry. It was indulgent, decadent, and exactly what I needed.

Ellie picked up the food menu, scanning it with interest. I, however, was distracted. My thoughts kept drifting to my phone resting in my purse. I needed to find a way to text Mark, let him know not to call while I was with Ellie. She had a knack for peering over my shoulder, curious about who I was texting.

"Chips and queso? Maybe the sliders, too?" Ellie asked, glancing at me for approval.

"Sounds perfect," I said, though I was barely listening.

My nerves were buzzing. "I'm going to run to the bathroom real quick."

"Well, I will order the food then," Ellie added.

Grabbing my purse, I walked across the now-busy restaurant. The mid-summer crowd had filled Blue's, and I weaved through the clusters of diners and laughing groups. The moment I stepped into the restroom, I was greeted by a familiar voice.

"Oh, hi, dear!" Mrs. Stewart, an older member of the country club, stood at the sink, her silver hair impeccably styled. She was a spirited woman in her late seventies, always full of life. Her and her husband's frequent appearances at the golf course had made them minor legends among the members.

"Hi, Mrs. Stewart," I said, mustering a smile even as my mind screamed at me to text Mark.

She launched into an enthusiastic account of her recent golf achievements and the impending visit of her grandchildren. I nodded and murmured the obligatory "Oh, that's nice" and "Wow," all the while glancing at my phone tucked into my purse. I decided to pull it out slowly and hold it, so I would be ready to text Mark as soon as she left.

After what felt like an eternity, Ellie walked in. "So this is where you've been! Hi, Mrs. Stewart."

Mrs. Stewart turned to her with a warm laugh. "Oh, I've been talking her ear off. I'll let you girls get back to your evening."

As she left, I sighed in relief. "I still have to use the bathroom," I muttered. Ellie grabbed my phone and purse from me abruptly. "I'll hold this for you. Use the bathroom quickly."

Panic surged through me. My phone was in her hand.

My hands were shaking as I hurried out of the stall a minute later. Ellie raised an eyebrow. "That was fast. Wow."

Back at the bar, our food was delivered in a few minutes. Just as Tom set the food down, I heard a familiar voice behind me.

"Dear, look who's here!" It was Mrs. Stewart again, this time with her husband in tow.

After a few minutes of polite conversation with them, my phone rang. It was lying next to my purse, opposite where Ellie was sitting. *Why did I leave it on top of my purse?* I thought. My heart leapt into my throat as I saw the name flash across the screen: Mark. Tom noticed, too, sliding the phone discreetly under my purse while wiping down the bar around our plates as Ellie was still preoccupied talking to the Stewarts. A minute later, they left, and Ellie glanced at me, as if asking who was calling me. "Probably the couple I just sold the house to," I said.

We moved on to talking about going shopping or meeting for lunch within the next few days, but my mind kept circling back to Tom seeing my phone.

As we left the restaurant, my phone buzzed again. Ellie noticed the sound of it again. "Answer it, if you need to."

I dug into my purse and looked down at the screen discreetly on my phone. "It's just my mom," I said, silencing the call. "She's probably worried about some skin spots she had removed." It was Mark, not my mom. I hid it well.

In the car, I finally called Mark. His voice was eager as he said, "Can you come to my office? I have a quick evening meeting over the phone with people out west, but it'll only take about ten minutes." Twenty minutes later, I was in his office.

He paced the room with the effortless confidence that had always drawn me to him, his voice calm and assertive as he navigated the end of his phone call. I couldn't help but admire the way he carried himself, so sure, so composed, even in moments like these. While he spoke, I wandered around his office, taking in the small details I'd overlooked before—the neat stacks of papers on his desk, the size of his desk, his oversized leather chair.

Eventually, I found myself in his private bathroom. It was pristine, the kind of space that attested to his meticulous nature. But what caught my eye was the small collection of items on the counter: a tube of antibiotic cream and several large bandages. My brow furrowed as a flicker of concern sparked in my mind. *Why would he need something like this? What happened?* The question lingered, heavy and unanswered, as I drifted back into the main office, trying to push it to the back of my mind.

Finally, he ended the call. Without a word, he dimmed the lights further, and the room took on a soft, intimate glow. He crossed the space between us in a few long strides and pulled me into a kiss. His lips were warm, firm, and intimate, igniting that familiar rush in my chest. "I'm glad you're here," he murmured in a low voice, his hands circling my waist.

The scent of his cologne wrapped around me, intoxicating and heady, mingling with the heat of his touch. His hands moved slowly, deliberately, sliding along my sides until his thumbs rested just below my ribs, the gentle pressure sending a shiver through me. He continued upward, stopping just beneath my breasts, his movements deliberate and intentional. Then his hands slid behind me, finding the buttons of my blouse, and with a practiced ease, he unfastened them.

Our breaths mingled as we lingered lip to lip, heavy and shallow but not yet kissing. He tugged the blouse up over my head, letting it fall to the floor in a soft heap. Then he reached for the zipper of my skirt, easing it down. The fabric pooled at my feet as I fumbled with the buttons of his shirt, my fingers trembling slightly from the rush of it all. One by one, the buttons gave way until his shirt hung open, exposing the firm planes of his chest.

"Let me take your T-shirt off," I whispered, reaching for its hem.

But he stopped me, his hands covering mine gently. "Not right now," he said, his voice quieter, almost hesitant. He glanced away for a second, a flicker of embarrassment crossing his face. "My back ... It's still messed up. I'll explain later."

I froze, the words hanging in the air between us. So many questions swirled in my mind, but his kiss brought me back, his lips seeking mine as if to distract me from whatever was troubling him.

Still, the thought lingered. What was he hiding? And why did it feel like he was carrying more than just physical pain?

CHAPTER TWELVE

When we were done, Mark didn't pull away. Instead, he lingered close, trailing slow, hungry kisses along my neck and back to my lips, as if trying to stretch the moment into something more permanent. He always wanted more afterward—more closeness, more time, more of me. And the truth was, I wanted it too. I was trying to be careful, trying to protect myself from getting pulled too deep, too fast.

Just as I was slipping on my clothes, my phone buzzed. I grabbed it quickly—it was Ellie calling. At the same moment, Mark glanced down and caught sight of her name glowing on the screen.

"You can take it," he said, his voice soft but neutral.

"Okay, I'll be quick," I replied, stepping a few feet away, already pressing the phone to my ear.

"Hey! Tonight was fun," Ellie chirped, her voice bright and full of leftover laughter. I could feel Mark moving behind me, the quiet rustle of him getting dressed.

"Yeah, it was," I said, forcing lightness into my voice.

"Wanna grab lunch tomorrow at Blue's?" she asked.

"Sure. Let's meet at 1:30," I said without thinking too hard.

"Perfect," she said, and then we hung up with the usual easy finality that close friends have.

As I set my phone down, Mark let out a quiet giggle—the kind that made me smile without meaning to. He walked over, shirt still clinging to his chest, and kissed me—long, slow, and full of an unexpected tenderness. Then, I grabbed my bag and headed out the door.

On the drive back home, my thoughts started to unravel. I kept circling back to the small things I hadn't paid enough attention to at the moment. Like the way Mark had hesitated when I tried to pull his shirt off earlier. Or the medication bottles I'd seen on the bathroom counter. What was all of that supposed to mean?

CHAPTER THIRTEEN

When I arrived home, Jax greeted me, his tail wagging furiously as he barked and spun in circles. His boundless energy always brought a smile to my face. I leaned down to ruffle his soft ears before heading upstairs to change. My body still buzzed from the emotional high of being with Mark, a mix of exhilaration and restlessness.

Jax followed me eagerly to the bedroom, bouncing around and occasionally pawing at my legs as I slipped out of my clothes. I pulled on a pair of leggings, a hoodie, and my sneakers, grabbing his leash and a flashlight. It was dark now, but the cooler night air and the steady rhythm of a walk seemed like exactly what I needed to clear my mind. *The antibiotic cream? Mark not wanting to take his T-shirt off? Why?*

We left through the garage, the faint hum of cicadas filling the quiet neighborhood. I decided to turn away from Ellie's house, heading in the opposite direction. After a few moments of walking, I picked up the pace, breaking into a light jog. Jax trotted happily beside me, his ears flopping in time with his steps, as we made our way down to the gated entrance of the community. I looped around the gates before heading back toward my house.

Making my way back toward the other end of the street, I approached Ellie's house. It was then that I heard it—a sharp, unmistakable yell cutting through the stillness of the night. I slowed down instinctively, my heart giving a slight jolt as I strained to make sense of the sound. The noise grew louder as I neared her property, and soon I recognized Ellie's voice, unmistakably angry.

I hesitated, caught between curiosity and a hesitation to intrude on her privacy. Her garage door was open, a soft light spilling onto the driveway. My mind flicked back to earlier visits, recalling the screen door that separated her garage from the main house. If the inner door was open, the screen would do little to muffle the sound. I stepped closer, pretending to adjust Jax's leash as I peered toward the house.

Through the faint glow of light, I saw a shadow—Ellie's silhouette, moving frantically back and forth inside. The sound of something crashing followed her raised voice, and I caught a glimpse of her figure, erratic and wild, as she gestured sharply. This wasn't a cry for help but the kind of raw, unfiltered anger that made me uneasy. My instincts told me to keep moving.

I turned back to the sidewalk, pulling Jax gently along, but my mind was working overtime with questions. What was happening in there? Was she alone and needed help? No, she wasn't alone; her husband's car was in the garage too. The tension in her voice and the chaos I'd glimpsed unsettled me. I was confused. I felt guilty for not helping, but noticing her silhouette as the agitated one, I decided to stay away.

I wandered aimlessly for a while, letting the quiet streets stretch ahead of me as I tried to think. The night was warm and calming, but my thoughts were anything but. Part of me wanted to circle back, to check on her, while another part hesitated, unsure about whether I wanted to get involved in something where *she* was the violent one.

Eventually, I looped onto another street, the soft glow of porch lights and the occasional rustle of leaves offering a sense of normalcy. I even passed another walker—a reassuring sign that the neighborhood was still safe, even though it was getting dark.

Soon, I was back on my street and only a couple of houses away from mine, on Ellie's side of the street. The yelling continued, though not as loud as before, and I could see her moving quickly from room to room. Her gestures, though less erratic, were still animated. I tried not to make it obvious that I was looking, keeping my head turned only slightly while my eyes darted toward her window. Whatever had caused the outburst wasn't over yet.

Feeling uneasy, I crossed the street toward my house, the leash taut as Jax tugged me forward. I quickened my pace, heading up my driveway and into the garage. Once inside, I closed the door behind me with a sense of relief, the chaos of Ellie's house lingering in my thoughts. Something about her felt off now, and I couldn't shake the feeling that this wasn't just a passing argument.

CHAPTER FOURTEEN

I woke up at half-past two in the morning, unable to push the gnawing thoughts of the disturbance at Ellie's house from my mind. The unsettling images and sounds of the previous evening replayed on a loop, leaving me restless and unable to sleep. Sliding out of bed, I walked to the window and parted the blinds, just enough to peer outside. Her garage door was still open, a hollow gap in the otherwise quiet, orderly street. That struck me as strange—nobody in the neighborhood ever left their garage doors open overnight, especially given the high value of the houses in this area. The vehicles inside were visible, parked neatly in their usual spots, but there was no other sign of life.

I went on scanning the surroundings for movement or light from within, but there was nothing. With a sigh, I let the blinds fall back into place, retreating to my bed. I reached down to scratch behind Jax's ears. "What do you think, buddy?" I whispered, knowing full well he couldn't answer. His only response was a sleepy yawn before he settled back down.

When morning came, my head was foggy, and my limbs felt heavy as I made my way to the kitchen. The aroma of freshly brewed coffee helped shake off the lingering haze, and I sipped from my mug while getting ready for work. The morning routine felt mechanical, a series of motions without much thought, as my mind stayed fixed on Ellie.

At work, I sent Ellie a quick text:

> Are you up for lunch later today? How about noon? I know we just met last night, but I thought it could be fun.

I didn't even know why I texted her. I was tired from the night before. I think I was looking for an explanation for the many odd things that had been happening at her house lately. I wanted to give her the chance to explain.

Her response came quickly:

> Yes, Blue's, I assume? I have a few errands to run near there.

> Yes. See you soon.

As I stared at the screen, a realization crept in: I couldn't even remember the last time I'd been inside Ellie's house. It had been quite a while. She came over to my place often, but lately she was always quick to avoid me setting foot in hers, even when I had a reason to visit. That thought nagged at me as I sat at my desk, absently staring out the window.

About an hour later, as I was typing away, my phone rang; it was Mark.

"Hi, baby. I miss you," he said as I got up to close my office doors. There were a few other co-workers down the hall, and I didn't want to risk anyone hearing anything. They would just assume I was having a private conversation with a client, another realtor, or a bank.

"I keep thinking about the last few times we were together. I really miss you too," I said, smiling. "Can I see you again tonight? I know it's been a lot recently, I just miss you."

"I would love to," Mark replied. "I miss you just as much. Come to my office tonight. Around 6:30? I'm going to get a bottle of wine and some sushi for dinner. I will put something together special for you. I have some other things I wanted to talk to you about, also, if we have time tonight."

Mark's office had become our unquestioned sanctuary, the one place we could always count on when we needed a quick, reliable hideaway. It had started as a convenient choice, but over time, it had become almost second nature to head there without a second thought. The ease of it was comforting, though perhaps a little *too* comforting.

"Wow, all that sounds really nice. I can't wait," I said.

"Another thing I wanted to tell you—I have a work meeting out of town next week. It's overnight. Do you want to come with me? It's only an hour away in Syracuse. I can get a hotel room away from everyone else at the meeting," he added.

I smiled. "Yes, I would love to. It would be so nice to spend a whole night together."

"That's what I thought," Mark said.

"What was the other thing you wanted to talk to me about?" I asked.

"It will be better in person," he said.

I took a moment to evaluate what I had on for tonight before we hung up. Somehow, I always wanted the outfit—including the lingerie—to be perfect for him.

I left a while later to meet Ellie for lunch. When I pulled into the parking lot at Blue's, I looked around and didn't see her car. The hot sun was hitting my shoulders as I walked from my car to the entrance of the restaurant. I thought about walking faster because I didn't want to feel sweaty when I met Mark later. I walked through the bar area where we normally sit and made my way out to the deck. The back deck sat up higher and overlooked the long fairway to one of the holes of the course.

I sat down at a covered table in the shade. A few minutes later, a waitress showed up to greet me and poured me some much-needed water. I quickly drank it down as I had so many things going through my mind.

"Hey, you," Ellie said, sliding into the chair beside me with her usual easy smile.

"How's your day been?" I asked.

"Just laundry and getting things ready for my sister's big milestone birthday in a couple of months," she said casually.

In all the years I'd known Ellie, I never really had much contact with any of her family. They existed only in fragments—brief mentions in passing, never enough to form a complete picture. She spoke of them sparingly. Her sister, though, was the exception. Ellie visited her often, and since she was originally from the area, it made sense that her sister still lived nearby.

Her father, however, was a different story. I asked about him once—just once—and the shift in her was immediate, like a storm rolling in without warning. Rage flickered across her face before she forced it back down, swallowing whatever words had nearly escaped. That look alone was enough to tell me all I needed to know. I never brought him up again.

As we talked, I noticed her nails—rough, chipped, and jagged again.

"Your nails ... what happened again?" I asked, unable to hide my surprise.

She glanced at them briefly. "Oh, just gardening again this morning. I was out there digging forever, and carrying some heavy rocks without gardening gloves," she said with a dismissive laugh.

Something about her answer felt off. She hadn't mentioned gardening until just recently, and the state of her nails didn't seem consistent with a morning spent in the dirt.

"Look over here," Ellie said suddenly, standing up and motioning for me to follow.

She led me to the edge of the deck, pointing out a newly installed waterfall feature in the landscaping. The sound of trickling water was soothing, but I couldn't shake the feeling that she was trying to distract me.

"See those flowers over there by the waterfall? Those are called coneflowers. It's like a blanket of purple. The other colorful ones are dahlias. All the phlox around the bottom is so pretty too," Ellie said.

Whoa, I thought. She had caught me off guard. I had no idea that she did indeed have a green thumb.

"The dahlias and phlox I just put in our backyard. All over the last few weeks," Ellie continued. Turns out, all the damage to her nails may have really been from gardening.

"You will have to show me what you have been doing in your backyard," I said in an awestruck voice. "I had no idea."

"It will be ready soon. I'm still working on it. Just adding more things before I'm ready to show it off. I'm really picky, and I don't let anyone back there until it's done. It's come a long way already, and it looks so pretty," said Ellie, looking proud.

We walked back toward our seats. Just as we turned around, I noticed Ellie's gaze was fixed on someone off in the distance near the pool. I followed her line of sight and saw Gabe, the pool guy.

He gave her a small wave, which she returned with a smile that lingered just a bit too long. She continued to look his way more often than she should have.

We ordered some drinks, and I couldn't take my eyes off her nails. She was wearing a sleeveless shirt, so I naturally looked up and down her arms and didn't see anything that looked like it shouldn't be there—no obvious marks or scratches. Everything looked normal on her arms.

CHAPTER FIFTEEN

Ellie and I had agreed on sharing a slice of dessert. As I glanced around the table, I thought, *Why not?* I was planning on getting up early the next morning to do a workout, which I hadn't managed to fit in that morning. Steven had done something amazing when we bought the house—he had added a state-of-the-art gym to our property.

I had quickly made it a habit to use it several times a week. There was something incredibly satisfying about having a gym right at my fingertips; it made it so much easier to stay consistent with my fitness routine.

Curious, I turned to Ellie. "So, what are you doing for the rest of the day?" I asked, genuinely interested in hearing her plans. But she seemed distracted, her eyes scanning the room in search of someone. I couldn't help but notice the way she glanced around as if looking for someone in particular, but I didn't have to wonder for long—soon enough, Gabe appeared at our table. He must have been lingering nearby, waiting for the right moment. He approached our table and then wasted no time jumping into the conversation, effortlessly slipping into flirtation mode with Ellie.

From the moment I met him, something had felt ... off. I couldn't quite put my finger on it; maybe it was the way he carried himself—too polished, too controlled. Or perhaps it was his kindness, which felt just a little too practiced.

I was feeling a bit out of place, not really knowing how to join in on their banter. I didn't want to pull out my phone and start scrolling through social media, which is what I normally did when I felt disconnected or bored in such situations. Instead, I picked up the drinks menu and pretended to look it over, even though we were almost ready to leave. I found myself glancing up at them from time to time, offering the occasional smile and a simple "Aww, nice" or "That's great," just to acknowledge their conversation. They mostly chatted about how the lunch had gone, whether it was busy at the pool, and other small talk that seemed to come effortlessly to them.

Then, out of nowhere, Gabe asked, "Is Mr. Duncan here today?" I frowned a little at the formality of his question. For some reason, hearing him say "Mr. Duncan" rubbed me the wrong way. There was just something about the way he said it, as though he was talking about some old, dignified gentleman. I always got the sense that Gabe was trying to measure the room, gauging if "Mr. Duncan" was around so he could make his move on Ellie without any interference.

"No, he's working today. Not golfing," Ellie replied, quickly putting that question to rest.

The conversation continued, light and flirtatious, with Gabe throwing in more of his usual charm. It didn't take long for him to broach the inevitable question. "I'll be working tomorrow—will you ladies be here?" he asked, in the same formal, almost absurdly polite manner he always used. I almost wanted to laugh at how over-the-top it sounded.

Ellie turned to me, giving me the look—the look that meant I was supposed to back her up. "I'm not doing anything, are you, Rachel?" she asked, her eyes silently pleading with me to say that yes, I could make it work. I could tell she was counting on me to be her wingwoman.

"I can make it," I said with a nod. It didn't take much to agree, though I was still a little unsure about how often we were hanging out at Blue's lately. I'd definitely extended a few invites myself, but lately it felt like we were there more often than I would have liked.

"Oh, good. We'll be here then," Ellie said with a smile, and Gabe grinned widely at her, flashing his signature charming smile before walking off to rejoin his friends.

I returned to work after lunch, trying to focus on my tasks. My mind kept circling around what Mark had to share with me tonight. What could it be? I had a showing scheduled later that afternoon, and as I checked my calendar, I realized I wanted to try to head home afterward to freshen up before meeting Mark at his office. It would be a tight window, but I could manage it. Sitting outside made me feel a little too sweaty, even though we had been in the shade.

After the showing, which went well enough despite the couple's rather picky nature, I drove home. As I pulled into my driveway, I found myself glancing at Ellie's house across from mine, wondering if something had changed, if anything looked out of place. It dawned on me that she had said nothing at lunch about the events at her house last night. For now, the house seemed as quiet as usual, but there was a peculiar feeling about it. All the strange movements and behaviors seemed to happen in the evening hours.

Once inside, Jax greeted me with his usual excitement. I let him into the backyard and waited a few minutes for him to return. Then I headed upstairs to change. As I passed my bedroom window, I caught another glimpse of Ellie's house. Her garage door was open, and I could see her car parked inside. Nothing seemed out of the ordinary, but I still felt that nagging curiosity. Instead of pulling the blinds shut, I opted to pull the curtains together, stripping off my work clothes and tossing them onto the bed. I quickly gathered my long blonde hair and clipped it up, planning to shower before heading out.

The warm water mixed with the coconut-scented body wash helped wash off the sweat from a long, hot day. Once I was done, I stood in front of the mirror, contemplating what to wear with Mark. I decided to go for something different—a pair of jeans, though I planned to dress them up. I rummaged through my drawer and found a black lace and velvet teddy I had bought a couple of weeks ago on a shopping trip. I had Mark in mind when I bought it, wondering how he would like it. I slipped it on, adding a pair of jeans over it, and topped it off with a silk blouse.

I finished the look with a pair of brown heels, letting my hair fall free and touching up my makeup. I imagined running my hands over his chest, feeling the warmth of his skin under his work shirt, and everything felt so charged with an electric energy.

After what felt like a perfectly timed transformation, I grabbed my purse and headed out the door, giving myself just enough time to make it to Mark's office. As I walked down the path through the courtyard, I couldn't help but notice that all of his blinds were shut tight. Normally, he kept them slightly open, even with the lush green trees surrounding the courtyard. Something about it felt off, though I pushed the thought aside and focused on getting to the door.

I reached out to grasp the cold, metallic handle of the door, only to find that it was locked. A sigh escaped my lips. I gently tapped on the door, a rhythmic pattern that felt almost like a secret invitation. The silence that followed seemed to stretch on for a heartbeat before I heard the faintest sound—the soft click of a lock being disengaged.

As the door inched open, a sense of anticipation built in my chest. The room beyond was mostly enveloped in shadows. For a moment, I couldn't make out much—just a play of shadows and light, the kind that creates a romantic setting.

Then, through the darkness, a voice broke the silence. "I missed you," Mark said, his tone playful yet warm. His confident voice immediately drew me in, and when I looked up, I saw his flirtatious smile, his eyes gleaming with mischief and affection. He extended his hand toward me, and without a second thought, I placed mine in his, feeling a rush of warmth spread through me.

As I stepped inside, I noticed the fire crackling softly in the fireplace. Around the room, numerous candles flickered, their flames casting a soft light that gave the space a cozy, intimate feeling. The contrast between the warmth of the fire and the cool darkness of the office made everything feel just a little bit magical.

I took a deep breath. "Wow, this is beautiful," I said, my

voice barely above a whisper as I continued to look around, still in awe.

Mark chuckled softly, walking over to me with a glass of red wine in his hand. "I know it's still my office," he said, his voice tinged with a lightheartedness that only made the moment feel more special. "But I wanted to do something different for you. Something that feels ... well, more like us." He paused for a moment, his smile turning a bit more earnest. "Next week will be even better, I promise."

I raised an eyebrow, curiosity piqued. "When? How? How did you do all this?" The questions tumbled out before I could stop them.

He winked at me, a playful glint in his eyes. "I ran out quickly after work and grabbed a few things. You know, nothing too fancy." He shrugged nonchalantly, but I could tell he was proud of the surprise he'd orchestrated. "Let's eat," he added, his tone shifting toward a more casual, inviting note.

I followed him as he led me to a small, low table, placed on the blankets set out in front of the fire. The table was set with what appeared to be two expensive plates, each filled with a variety of sushi rolls. But these weren't just any plates—they were proper, ceramic ones. I recalled one late night when we were the only ones here and he'd given me a tour of the kitchenette down the hall, a surprisingly lavish space. I can only assume he had borrowed the elegant plates from there.

"Tell me about your day," Mark asked, his voice warm and attentive as he sat down beside me. "Any house showings?"

I took a small bite of sushi, savoring the delicate flavors before answering. "Just one," I said, my tone lighthearted.

"A new couple, and I can already tell they'll be super picky. But they've got a high budget, so it's worth the effort." I giggled, amused at the thought of their meticulous demands.

Mark smiled at my words, but there was something wistful in his gaze, something that shifted in the air between us. "I like this," he said, his voice quiet. "I like just talking about us, our everyday lives." His smile faltered, and a shadow seemed to pass over him, his mood shifting unexpectedly.

Concern bloomed in my chest. "What's wrong? Are you okay?"

"I am," he said, forcing a small smile. "I'm okay because you're here with me."

His words hung in the air, and for a moment, we simply sat there, gazing at each other. The room around us felt almost too still, the only sound the crackling of the fire. We resumed eating, the silence between us comfortable, but I couldn't shake the feeling that something was weighing on him.

As I looked at Mark, I noticed how professional he looked in his crisp white button-down shirt, his dark grey tie neatly knotted at his collar. It was the same professional look he always wore to the office, but somehow, it had a power over me. There was something about the way he carried himself, the quiet authority in the way he moved, that made me feel both drawn to him and incredibly proud to be in his presence.

He took another sip of wine, his gaze never leaving mine. That familiar, intense look was in his eyes again—the one that always made my heart race. Slowly, deliberately, he set down his glass, and I felt the air between us shift as he moved closer.

Without saying a word, he leaned in and captured my gaze, his fingers brushing lightly against the buttons of my blouse. One by one, they were undone with gentle precision, the touch of his hands sending a wave of warmth through me.

"I love you," he whispered, his voice so soft it was almost lost to the crackling of the fire.

The words took me by surprise, though I'd felt them in every touch, every glance, in the way he had been caring for me more lately. This was the first time he had said it, and the sincerity in his voice made my heart swell.

I froze for a moment, uncertain of how to respond. But then, I realized that I had felt it, too—lately, more than ever before. Slowly, I whispered back, "I love you too."

Mark's face fell a little, as if his serious confession had caused him to lose some of his usual confidence. "I'm sorry," he said, his voice tinged with regret. "I know it's not the best of situations, but I do love you."

I reached out and touched his arm gently, my voice soft and reassuring. "Don't apologize," I whispered, my hand trailing up to cup his face. "We'll figure it out. We'll figure it all out at some point ."

He smiled at me, but there was something sad in his eyes, something unresolved. "I wanted tonight to be perfect," he said, his voice steady despite the underlying vulnerability. "With the fire, the wine ... I wanted to tell you how much I love you. I wanted it to feel special."

I smiled, my heart full. "Listen," I said, my voice soft but firm. "Tonight has been perfect. Just being here with you is all I need."

Mark didn't respond. Instead, he reached out and gently undressed me, his hands slow and reverent, as if each movement was an unspoken expression of his love. It felt different this time, more than being just physical. I could feel the heat of the fire on my skin as the layers of clothing fell away, and in that moment, I felt both vulnerable and cherished—wrapped in the warmth of the fire, the wine, and the love that flowed between us. I had known for a while that I loved him, but I guarded my heart, afraid of what it might cost me. Yet, lately, the way his eyes lingered on me, soft and searching, made me believe he might just feel the same.

"Wow, you look absolutely stunning," he said, his voice thick with admiration. I could feel his gaze sweeping over me, his eyes drinking in every inch of the teddy I wore and my exposed skin. My blouse and jeans had already been discarded on the floor. The intricate lace and velvet teddy traced patterns against my skin. I found myself on one of the plush blankets laid out in front of the fireplace. The heat of the flames mixed with the warmth of his gaze.

His shirt, now unbuttoned, hung loosely around his frame. His hands caressed my body as I lay in front of him, the fire and candles glistening all around us. He slowly rubbed my body up and down. I arched my body and moaned for him. I lifted my hands, gently sliding his shirt off. He hovered above me, his gaze locking with mine, a quiet intensity passing between us.

Nearly two hours later, I eased back into my teddy. The room felt warmer.

I stepped toward him. His arms reached out, pulling me into him with a warmth that felt inviting.

"You really look amazing in this," he murmured appreciatively, as his hands wandered over my body again.

Even in the midst of the moment, a thought lingered in the back of my mind. A question I'd been meaning to ask but hadn't found the right moment.

I pulled back just a couple of inches, giving us both space to breathe, and looked at him. "I didn't want to stop this, not at all, but I noticed something earlier. What happened to your lower back again? It looks like you still have a lot of cuts, or was this part of the allergic reaction to something?"

"No, no, it's not cuts or an allergic reaction," he said, shaking his head slightly, his gaze moving away for just a moment.

"Can I explain next time when we are together?" he said hesitantly. "There is something I've been wanting to talk to you about ... something important. But tonight has just been so perfect, and I don't want to spoil it." There was obviously something big he was keeping buried.

"I don't want to bring you down, and frankly ... I don't want to bring myself down either," he said, his voice trailing off as he slowly turned and began to finish dressing.

"Yeah, sure. I understand. I was just concerned about you," I said softly, my voice a whisper of reassurance. "I just want you to know I'm here, if you ever want to talk about it."

He paused, and I could feel the way his entire body seemed to release a breath he'd been holding in.

CHAPTER SIXTEEN

The next morning, I woke up feeling a strange need to work from home. I knew that if I were in the office, my mind would wander more than if I were at home. At home, I was able to focus more.

I texted Ellie early in the morning to reschedule our so-called lunch at Blue's for today. I just wasn't up for it, although I told her I had a lot of work to do. Plus, I just wasn't mentally ready for Gabe again. She agreed, and we set a time for tomorrow.

I kicked off my morning with the workout I had promised myself. My home gym was a place where I could lose myself, pushing my body through a grueling routine that left me exhausted but satisfied. I was surprised at how focused I stayed throughout the day as a result—there was an unexpected sense of clarity, like the sweat had washed away any lingering doubts.

Still, there were moments, brief but persistent, when my mind drifted back to Mark—his back, the tightness in his voice when he had brushed off questions about it. I could tell it unsettled him, but I also knew he'd open up in his own time. That thought, that sense of patience, gave me comfort, even though I couldn't help but wonder what had happened.

By mid-afternoon, I remembered that I still had a task to complete—returning some open house signs to the office for another realtor. It was a quick errand, but one that broke my routine. As I pulled out of the driveway, I couldn't help but glance over at Ellie's house. Once again, there was no sign of her doing the yard work she had claimed to be busy with lately. It was hard to ignore the feeling that something wasn't adding up, but I told myself that maybe she just wasn't working on it today. I decided to give her the benefit of the doubt—after all, she was my neighbor, and I wanted to believe the best about her.

The errand was quick, and before long, I was back home, settling into my usual rhythm. I had new clients to schedule showings for, and as I worked, time slipped away faster than I realized. Before I knew it, it was seven in the evening, and my stomach rumbled. I hadn't eaten much all day, too absorbed in work. I changed into something more comfortable—and headed to the kitchen to raid the fridge.

I wasn't in the mood to cook, and the idea of going out or ordering takeout seemed like too much effort. So I poured myself a glass of red wine and wandered into the living room, sipping it slowly as I considered my options. The soft glow of the TV beckoned, and as I clicked it on, I decided to order food after all. I was too comfortable now to even think about leaving the house, and besides, I had a show I'd been meaning to catch up on—one that a couple of women in the office had recommended.

About thirty minutes later, the doorbell rang. When I

opened it, I was greeted by a teenage delivery boy, but we were interrupted by a loud sound coming from across the street toward Ellie's house. We both turned our gaze toward her house. I saw one car parked in her garage and one in the driveway.

"Wow, what's going on over there?" he asked, his voice tinged with concern, his eyes never leaving Ellie's house.

I didn't hesitate. "Oh, it's okay. She told me she was cleaning out her garage today, so probably just moving stuff around over there," I said, offering a tight smile as I reached for my food.

I could feel his gaze lingering on the house. "I tipped online," I said quickly, trying to steer the conversation back to something normal. "I tipped pretty well. I know you guys are out all hours."

He blinked, clearly distracted. "Oh, yeah, yeah. You're all set," he mumbled, his eyes flickering back to me, although he seemed hesitant to tear his focus away from Ellie's house.

I offered him one last, lingering smile as he stepped past the threshold. I stood there for a moment, my heart ticking faster than I wanted to admit.

My thoughts spun like a carousel, each question more insistent than the last. *What exactly was happening over at Ellie's house?* There was something off—something that tugged at the edges of my intuition. I couldn't explain it, not fully. It was the kind of gut-deep suspicion that crept in silently and refused to be ignored.

Fear kept my questions locked inside. I couldn't bring myself to ask Ellie, not directly. Not yet. Maybe I was afraid of what her answer would be—or worse, that she'd lie. And as for calling the police... well, that was a whole other problem. We lived in a neighborhood where people hosted wine tastings on Thursdays and waved politely while pulling into their three-car garages. A picture-perfect, million-dollar facade where the idea of calling the cops feels more scandalous than whatever crime might be happening behind those manicured hedges.

And what if I *was* wrong? Then the whispers would start. The glances. People would talk—not to me, of course —but about me, behind gleaming windows, over charcuterie boards and glasses of imported Chardonnay.

So instead, I stood there in the silence, alone with my spiraling thoughts, staring at a closed door and wondering if it had just shut on something far bigger than I was ready to face.

I walked into the living room and settled in front of the TV, my food delivery forgotten for a moment as I kept an eye on Ellie's house. The anxiety that had crept up inside me made it impossible to focus on anything else.

On impulse, I grabbed my phone and texted Ellie. I didn't know what else to do. A part of me wanted to check on her, to make sure everything was okay, but I couldn't bring myself to ask directly. Instead, I tried something simpler.

> I'll see you tomorrow for lunch, 1:30, right?

Ellie's answer came a couple of minutes later.

> Yes, I can't wait.

I couldn't help but feel as though she was trying a little too hard to make everything appear perfectly fine.

I went to the kitchen to unpack my dinner, still in wonder and shock. The tension in my shoulders was hard to ignore as I tried to unwind. While eating, I went back to my show, finishing a few more episodes. Every now and then, I would glance at Ellie's house, wondering what had caused all the chaos.

The next morning came too quickly. My alarm went off at six. I had promised myself I would get in a workout before my showings. I pushed through the hour-long session, sweating out the knots of tension and frustration that had built up since last night.

As I stretched out afterward, I told myself, *Don't worry about it. It's not your issue.* But somehow, I wasn't convinced. The more I tried to push it from my mind, the more it lingered, like a shadow I couldn't shake.

The morning had gone smoothly, with the usual mix of excitement and minor hiccups that came with introducing fresh clients to new properties. But now, I was ready for a break, eager to catch up with Ellie and take a moment for myself. I glanced at the clock in my car and thought, *I should start heading to Blue's to meet Ellie.*

My car's dashboard read eighty-three degrees as I cruised down the road toward Blue's. I had already anticipated the heat of the day, so I slipped off my thin sweater and tossed it onto the passenger seat. The warm breeze felt good, and the sunshine made everything feel just a little more carefree. I was already mentally preparing myself for a hot outdoor lunch. The fresh air and the view of the golf course had a way of putting me at ease, even if it was hot.

As I walked through the front door, I spotted Gabe right away. He was lingering near the hostess stand, as if he were waiting for Ellie and me to arrive. It was no surprise—he always seemed to be around or had a way of showing up, whether as a waiter or as the pool patrol. Today, it seemed, he'd taken a shift in the restaurant.

"Hi, Rachel," Gabe greeted me with his signature grin, his eyes sparkling mischievously. "Follow me."

He led me to the deck, and sure enough, the table he pointed out was the one he was serving. I sent Ellie a quick text, letting her know where I was sitting, and made myself comfortable, knowing this would be our spot for the afternoon.

Gabe took a step back, glancing at me with that charming, almost too-perfect smile. "Would you like anything to drink?"

"Just two waters, please," I replied, giving him a polite but distant smile. I had learned not to engage too much in his overly enthusiastic chatter.

"Do you work in the restaurant part often?" I just had to ask so seriously.

"So, sometimes I wait on the members by the pool," Gabe chattered on, "and other times I work up here. There was an opening again today, so I figured I'd take it and get someone else to cover for me at the pool. That way, I can still keep an eye on you two lovely ladies." He added a wink for emphasis, which made me roll my eyes internally while keeping my face neutral.

A brief, awkward pause ensued. "I'll get those waters for you," he said and walked away.

I didn't bother responding, choosing instead to let his words hang in the air. I knew I wouldn't be escaping his attention anytime soon. I wouldn't have to worry about Ellie getting intercepted by him at the door—he would be our waiter the entire time we were here. And while part of me wished for a little more privacy, I had to admit that Gabe's charm did make him hard to completely dismiss.

A few minutes later, Ellie arrived. I decided not to spoil the surprise by mentioning Gabe's presence. I wanted to see her reaction when she realized that our waiter was none other than him. But to my surprise, when Gabe returned with the waters, Ellie didn't seem shocked at all. In fact, she looked entirely unfazed by it. That made me pause for a moment—had she known he would be here? The only way she would have known was if they had been talking or texting beforehand. The realization hit me like a small shockwave, and suddenly I wondered what was really going on between them ... and for how long?

But I let it go for now. It wasn't the time or the place. Gabe didn't hover around the table too much, which was a nice change. It seemed like he was giving us some space to talk.

When lunch arrived, we both decided to order a pear martini to go with our meal, and I couldn't help but notice how strong they were. Gabe had clearly made them himself, and they hit harder than usual. As the afternoon wore on, and we continued chatting, our next few drinks became stronger and had a noticeable effect. We started to relax more, the tension of the morning and the stress of work starting to melt away. We sat there, overlooking the golf course, laughing about everything and nothing. The conversation drifted from topic to topic, and for the first time in days, I wasn't thinking about the noise from Ellie's house the night before. The martinis had loosened me up enough that I could let go of any lingering thoughts about what was really happening over there.

At some point, I glanced down at my watch and saw

that it was already 4:50 pm. I hadn't realized how much time had passed.

"Wow, have we really been here that long?" I giggled.

"We have," Ellie replied with a laugh, her smile wide and carefree.

"I'm done at five, so I'll close you ladies out," Gabe chimed in.

"Do you want to move inside to the bar?" Ellie asked, her voice light and playful.

"Yeah, sure."

As I used the arm of my chair to stand up, I couldn't help but laugh. "Wow, I'm so glad I didn't have anything else on my schedule today. What was in those drinks? I feel tipsy."

"Me too," Ellie said, her voice tinged with the same lightheartedness.

And then, as if on cue, she added, "Gabe is so cute, isn't he?"

I smiled, my thoughts momentarily interrupted. "Yeah, he's definitely ... something," I replied, my mind swirling from the martinis.

When Ellie had a few drinks in her, she became a whole different person—an open book, no longer holding back her thoughts or emotions. She was like one of those people who'd share their entire life story with a stranger, no hesitation. I, on the other hand, was always the opposite. I prided myself on being a vault, locking away any personal details behind a carefully constructed wall. My lips rarely parted on anything too revealing.

We walked into the bar, and it was already buzzing with life. The atmosphere felt warm, inviting, but also a little bit crowded. Golfers and couples out on date night filled the space. There were a few familiar faces—regulars from the club—chit-chatting over drinks. Ellie and I stood for a few minutes, waiting for the crowds to shift, trying to find a place to settle in. It wasn't exactly uncomfortable, but it was a little awkward, standing behind the rows of chairs at the bar.

"Thank goodness we still have our martinis to keep us company," Ellie giggled, taking another small sip from her glass. Her eyes sparkled, and her laughter seemed a little more carefree than usual.

"I don't know if I can handle another one after this," I muttered, glancing at my half-empty glass, already feeling the familiar warmth in my chest from the alcohol.

Finally, a couple of stools were freed up. We slid onto them, with Ellie already making herself comfortable. The bartender, Tom, came over with a friendly smile.

"Can I get you ladies another round?" he asked, his eyes flicking between Ellie and me.

Before I could respond, Gabe, who had slipped into a newly open seat beside Ellie, spoke up. "Get them both one of my special martinis, Tom. And put it on my tab. Their martinis are almost gone."

I raised an eyebrow. The martini in my hand already felt a bit stronger than usual. I'd already made a silent pact with myself to steer clear of the new martini Gabe was so eager for us to try—no matter how charming his pitch or how pretty the glass.

I glanced over as Gabe sat next to Ellie, making it feel like the two of them were in their own world. I suddenly felt like the odd one out—like the third wheel in a situation I didn't really want to be in. A small part of me considered calling it a night, even without taking a sip of my new martini Gabe had insisted on. I contemplated heading out and calling for a ride home. I knew my limits, and after the couple of drinks I'd already had, I wasn't about to risk driving.

But I stayed a while longer, occasionally making small talk with Tom over sports. Ellie, meanwhile, was already showing signs of being affected. Her cheeks were flushed, her giggles coming more freely as I noticed her "special martini" glass was empty. Was this part of Gabe's plan? It was hard not to wonder.

The two of them were deep in conversation—talking like old friends, laughing at some inside joke. I tried to focus on the noise of the bar, the clinking of glasses, and the occasional murmur of conversations around us. Every so often, I'd pretend to pay attention to one of the TV screens mounted on the wall.

A man sitting across from me caught my eye. He was in his early 60s, with salt-and-pepper hair and a look of quiet confidence about him. Since Ellie and Gabe were still lost in their conversation, I figured I'd make some small talk.

"So, are you a member here?" I asked.

"No, actually," the man said, shifting in his seat. "I'm meeting some friends—a husband and wife. They're running a little late, so I'm just passing the time. I live a ways out of town but we meet occasionally for dinner."

I nodded, trying to keep the conversation going. "Nice," I said, offering a friendly smile. "I'm Rachel," I continued, extending my hand.

"Bennett," he replied, shaking my hand with a firm but kind grip.

"So, what do you do for work?" he asked, the question coming naturally as the conversation began to flow.

"I'm a realtor."

His eyebrows lifted in slight surprise, and he reached into his jacket pocket. "Here's my card," he said, handing it over with a small, knowing smile.

I took the card, raising an eyebrow. "Do people even use business cards anymore?" I said, half-laughing, mostly to cover up the awkwardness of the situation.

"Well, you'd be surprised," he replied, clearly amused.

"So what is this? What do you do?" I asked, trying to figure out the business card he had handed me.

My eyes widened slightly when I read his name and his profession. "Well, I guess they do still exist," I joked, laughing again.

CHAPTER SEVENTEEN

"Are you here with your friend and her husband?" Bennet asked, looking at me with genuine curiosity.

I froze for a second, unsure of how to respond. "Oh no, that's not ... wait. I mean, I am with her, but that man's not exactly who you think. It's a long story. Never mind. Sorry." I felt my face flush in embarrassment.

Bennet chuckled lightly, a reassuring smile on his face. "It's okay. I wasn't trying to dig for details. I was just wondering if you were with them. I noticed you talking with them also."

I glanced over at Ellie and Gabe, who were deep in conversation on the other side of the bar. "Well, I guess I *am* with them," I said, finally feeling a bit more at ease.

"So, what is this? You're a private investigator, right?" I asked casually. "I bet you have a lot of interesting stories. I mean, I have met a lot of bankers, lawyers, and doctors here but never a private investigator."

Bennett's smile widened as he swirled the ice around in

his glass. "You're right. I do have some interesting stories," he said, clearly enjoying the subject.

I shifted in my seat, feeling a little restless. "I'm hoping I can leave soon. My friend and I have been here for hours now." I glanced at my watch. The afternoon had slipped into early evening without me even noticing.

"No offense, and I'm sure you're pleasant to talk to," I added sheepishly, hoping he wouldn't take it the wrong way. "It's just that I'm really starting to feel the fatigue,"

Bennett laughed again, shaking his head. "No harm done, really. I understand."

Just as the conversation seemed to wind down, Ellie leaned in and whispered in my ear, her voice low enough that only I could hear. "Who are you talking to?" she asked, her eyes narrowing playfully.

I turned toward her and whispered back, "He's meeting friends here. I guess he's a private investigator."

Ellie's eyebrows shot up in surprise. "Really? A private investigator?" she asked, her voice filled with intrigue.

"Yeah, kind of funny, right?" I said with a small laugh.

"Well, I am sure he's interesting," Ellie remarked. "I have to meet him."

I turned to Bennett, smiling, and said, "Bennet, this is my friend Ellie. Ellie, meet Bennet."

They exchanged handshakes as I leaned back, giving them space to greet each other. After the pleasantries, I looked back toward the TV, just for something to focus on. In the midst of the small talk, I couldn't help but notice the faint buzz of my phone vibrating in my purse. It wasn't loud enough for anyone else to hear, but I had a feeling the call was from Mark.

I had to get out of here, and quickly.

"I'm going to the ladies' room," I said, standing up and grabbing my purse. "Make sure no one takes my seat," I added with a wink, glancing over at Bennett and Ellie.

Bennett nodded, his tone light and joking. "Go ahead, young lady. I'll keep an eye on your seat."

"Thanks," I said, giving him a grateful smile, before slipping away toward the bathroom.

Inside the bathroom, I quickly pulled out my phone. The call had been from Mark. I smiled as I dialed him back, and we chatted briefly, confessing how much we had missed each other and how excited we were about next week. But as much as I wanted to stay on the phone with him, I didn't want to be caught talking in the bathroom. I tucked my phone back into my purse and stepped out of the stall, heading back toward the bar area.

As I rounded the corner, I saw Bennett handing Ellie a business card. I froze for a second, feeling a twinge of confusion. I had already told Ellie about Bennett's job, so why was he handing her a card now? Maybe she had asked for it.

Another hour went by while I made small talk with my new friend Bennett. Tom was watching the TV above the bar, and Ellie was busy talking to Gabe.

"I'm going back home," I said to Ellie.

"Are you okay to drive?" she asked, her concern genuine.

"I'll call an Uber," I replied, standing up again.

"Tom, it was nice to see you again!" I called over to the bartender, who was busy pouring a beer.

"We'll see you soon, Rachel," he said, giving me a wink.

"And Bennett, it was nice to meet you," I said, leaning in

to shake his hand. "I'll keep your card in case I need any investigating done."

"Nice to meet you, young lady," Bennett said, his tone warm as he shook my hand again.

Stepping outside into the cool evening air, I paused for a moment, considering my options. I couldn't drive, so calling an Uber seemed like the best bet. But then again ... I wondered if Mark might come to pick me up instead. It was dark, and no one would see. Without thinking too much, I dialed his number.

The country club was nestled just beyond our neighborhood, but getting there was no simple stroll. A winding brick path snaked through the trees, leading me on a path that felt far too long for someone in heels. The final stretch took me right through the heart of the neighborhood, passing in front of a handful of houses where curious eyes might be watching. It felt absurd, almost like a walk of shame, as if I were parading past the windows of any neighbor who happened to glance out at the wrong moment.

"Hi again. What a great surprise," Mark answered, his voice making my heart skip a beat.

"Hi," I whispered, not wanting to attract attention.

"Why are you whispering?" he asked, a hint of amusement in his voice.

"I'm outside Blue's. Had a couple of drinks, and I can't drive. Do you think you could come pick me up?" I asked, feeling a little sheepish.

"Who were you with?" Mark asked, his curiosity piqued.

"Ellie."

"Is she still in there?"

"Yeah, she is inside with someone else," I said in a low voice.

"I'm on my way home from drinks with a few friends," Mark said. "Walk to the end of the parking lot and wait where the road curves into the lot. I'll be there in just a few minutes."

"Thank you. I'll see you soon." I hung up and started to walk.

I strolled across the parking lot, glancing over my shoulder to see if anyone was watching. Ellie and Gabe didn't seem in a hurry to leave, so I felt safe. I arrived at the corner where the parking lot ended, just as I saw headlights coming toward me. It was Mark's car.

I hurried over and climbed in. He gave me a quick glance, then did a U-turn to head back out.

"I hope no one sees me. I just don't like to explain things," I said.

"It's dark out, so I think we'll be fine." Mark gave my leg a gentle squeeze.

After driving through the gated entrance of the neighborhood, he suddenly sighed, his mood turning slightly more serious. "There are some people out walking right now."

I groaned. "Ugh, I know. I see them."

"I have an idea," Mark said, squeezing my leg again.

"What's your idea?"

"Just sit tight," he replied with a smirk.

He turned around and went back to the country club. As we pulled into the parking lot, I sat up slightly, looking around. Ellie's car was still there, and Mark parked next to mine.

"We're going to grab your car, and I'll park mine in the

corner so no one will see it. I'll drive you home, and then I'll go back to get mine, so no neighbors wonder why another vehicle is at your house."

"That's so clever," I said, a smile tugging at my lips.

"We need to move fast," he added, his tone now filled with urgency.

After quickly clambering into my car, we returned to the neighborhood.

"I wish I had more time," he said, glancing at me with regret.

"I know," I said, smiling softly. "Thanks for picking me up."

Mark paused before asking, "Where should I leave your key?"

"Just lock the car and leave it under the floor mat. I have my spare key, and I'll grab my car tomorrow," I said with another smile.

I gave him a quick kiss before we parted. I got out of my car quickly as Mark had it pulled up as far as he could to the front of the garage.

CHAPTER EIGHTEEN

As soon as I stepped through the front door, the weight of the night settled heavily on my shoulders. *A quick walk*, I thought—just enough to shake off some of the alcohol still lingering in my system. The air outside would do me good. Jax bounded around me excitedly, ready for his own break from the house. I didn't waste any time; a swift change into something more comfortable, and then I grabbed his leash and opened the door. Slipping into my workout gear or walking clothes would blend me into the night, unlike an awkward and conspicuous midnight march through the neighborhood in heels.

We headed down the driveway, the rhythmic click of Jax's paws keeping time with my thoughts. I wandered aimlessly, not far—just a few houses down—before I turned around, deciding I'd rather avoid any awkward encounters with neighbors at this hour. The evening air was thick with the scent of twilight as the sky dimmed. I could make out the faint glow of headlights cutting through the gathering dark. I didn't bother looking. My mind was too occupied with other things. I kept my eyes fixed ahead, thinking about Ellie. Was she still perched on that barstool beside Gabe? Most likely. It was a thought that didn't sit well with me, but I couldn't shake it.

Back inside, Jax followed me into the living room, plopping down at my feet like a familiar weight, offering a momentary distraction from everything else. I glanced around, then stood up and made my way to the kitchen. Maybe I could find something to nibble on. I opened the fridge, hoping for a hidden gem among the leftovers, but nothing caught my eye. A quick glance at my phone confirmed what I already knew: it would take too long for a takeout to get delivered. Sighing, I grabbed a box of crackers and a bottle of water, resigned to a snack that wouldn't quite hit the spot.

Back in the living room, I let myself sink into the couch and tuned out the world for a bit. My latest binge-worthy series had a way of pulling me in and shutting everything else out. Time slipped by unnoticed until, finally, I rose to head to bed. But just as I was about to turn off the lights, I saw it. Ellie's car—gliding past the window, its headlights flickering briefly in the dark. Hadn't I left her about two hours ago? I could only imagine she had been wrapped up with Gabe all this time.

The shrill sound of my alarm blaring at half-past six shattered the quiet the next morning. I hadn't set it early to work out, knowing full well that a workout wasn't happening today. The alcohol from last night had worn off, but my mind was still too heavy. I headed out of town for a couple of showings. As a realtor, you never really have a day off. The couple I was with didn't rush through the houses—they examined every little detail like they were inspecting a work of art. We spent what felt like hours talking through what they liked and didn't like, discussing the merits and flaws of each property. I didn't mind. Patience was key. I'd learned that much in this job. As long as they knew I wasn't pushing them into a decision, they'd stick with me as their realtor.

By two in the afternoon, I was back in Glen Springs, but I wasn't ready to head home, so I drove to Blue's. It was my go-to escape when I needed to clear my head. I grabbed my bag and laptop and set up shop at one of the large high-top tables in the bar area. It was quiet enough there to get some work done since it was a Sunday afternoon.

As I settled in, Tom came over to drop off a napkin and a glass of water.

"Hi there, what can I get you, Rachel?" he asked, his voice casual but friendly.

"Oh, hey," I said, rummaging through my bag for my charger. "I'll just stick with water for now. But can I get a lunch menu?"

He nodded and walked off, and I finished setting up my laptop. A few minutes later, Tom returned with the menu, but he had something else to add.

"You just missed Ellie," he said, a knowing look in his eyes.

"Really? She was here?" I asked, trying to sound indifferent.

"Yeah, she left about thirty minutes ago," he said, wiping down the high top. "She was here with that guy you were talking to last night, the one who sat next to you at the bar."

My heart did a strange little flip at his words. Something about hearing it confirmed from Tom left me wondering.

"The older guy, right?" I asked, keeping my voice steady.

"Yeah, they didn't sit at the bar, though. They were in one of the corner booths in the dining area. I could see them from here," Tom explained, his gaze flicking over to where they had sat.

I tried to keep my expression neutral, not wanting Tom to think I was fishing for details, though I had a thousand questions running around in my head. Why had Ellie met with the private investigator? What was going on between them? Was there something more to it?

"Oh, nice," I said, glancing down at the menu, pretending I wasn't rattled by the information.

Tom nodded. "I'll be back in a few to take your order."

As he walked away, I felt my stomach lurch. What had Ellie been talking about with the private investigator? The night before, I'd seen him handing her a business card. Why? Was she planning something I didn't know about? Was I the last to know?

The questions gnawed at me, so I texted her.

> Hey, how are you? Do you want to come down to Blue's and meet for a late lunch?

Her reply came almost instantly.

> I can't. I've been doing a lot of cleaning around the house all day. More gardening, too, out back.

> OK. Not a big deal. We'll get together soon.

My response may have been casual, but truthfully, I felt unsettled.

CHAPTER NINETEEN

I spent a few hours at Blue's, trying to focus on work while the hum of the restaurant and the chatter of the TVs created a strange but oddly comforting background noise. It felt effortless, really, as I clicked through documents, responded to emails, scheduled more showings, and typed away at my laptop. The constant buzz around me had a certain rhythm, almost like white noise, that helped me focus, and I could immerse myself in my tasks without distraction. But soon enough, it was time for me to head home. As I packed up my things, I thought about the evening ahead. I had no interest in sticking around while the restaurant got busier with the dinner crowd. A quiet night at home felt like the perfect way to wrap up the week.

When I got home, I unpacked my things into my office space, but it didn't take long for my attention to wander. There was more work to be done, of course, but my mind kept drifting outside. I glanced over at Ellie's house, wondering if she was out in her garden like she said she was. The garden was visibly kept together in the front, with no signs of her out there.

A ping sounded on my phone. It was a message from Mark.

I don't know if I can wait until next week to see you. :)

I felt a flutter in my chest as I quickly typed back, *What are you up to?*

I have to run to work to grab some extra paperwork I left there. Wanna meet me there?

I'll be there soon:) You're the perfect wind-down to my day!

Excitement bubbled up in me—just a couple more days until I left to go out of town with him, but tonight, it was just us again.

I took a long breath and tossed my phone on the couch; I was just going to take a minute for myself before getting ready. The doorbell rang, followed by Jax barking. I walked through the house to the foyer, not sure who it would be. When I peeked through the window, I saw it was Ellie standing at the door.

"Hey, how are you?" I squinted, wondering why she was here. I motioned for her to come inside, though I immediately questioned the impulse. Why had I invited her in? I was going to be running late now. I needed to get her out of here quickly!

"What are you doing tonight? I was hoping maybe we could have drinks later? We can stay here, maybe invite Chloe over?" Ellie asked, her voice soft and apologetic.

"Yeah, that could work," I replied, though my thoughts were racing. "I have to run out for a little bit; I need to get some work together for a closing next week. I'll be back in a couple of hours ... does that work? It's only around five right now, so I'll be back by seven."

I was trying to keep my cool, but inside I was wondering if I should mention I had been at Blue's earlier, where I ran into Tom. I knew Tom had seen Ellie, but I wasn't sure if she had noticed him. It seemed safer to leave that detail out for now.

"Yeah, that's great," Ellie said, pulling out her phone. "I'll text Chloe. She's new around here, our age, and she doesn't have kids yet. I think you may have met her once? Anyway, she always says I should invite her when we do things, but I always forget when we go to Blue's."

"Oh, that sounds great," I said, nodding. I needed to freshen up before leaving for Mark's office, so I hoped the conversation wouldn't drag on for too long.

"All right, I'll text her." Ellie was already typing away, still standing in my foyer. "We will be back in a bit for drinks."

"Oh, she already texted me back," she announced. "She can make it too."

I didn't need to be told twice. I walked toward the door and gave her a little nudge, signaling it was time for her to leave. She caught on and left with a smile, promising to come back later.

I ran upstairs to fix myself up. I didn't want to show up to Mark's office looking like I'd just run a marathon.

Soon, I was driving to his office; it was still light out, but everyone was gone since it was the weekend. I parked in the back and walked through the familiar path of the courtyard.

As I stepped inside, Mark stood up from his chair, a smile spreading across his face. Soon I was lost in his kiss, which felt like it lasted for hours, all the tension from the day melting away.

He walked over to the blinds and lowered them, dimming the lights until the room was just shy of being completely dark. I watched him, intrigued by his sudden mysteriousness, wondering what he was going to do next. His eyes locked with mine, and without saying a word, he pulled me toward him again, guiding me to him on the couch as I slid a leg over him, straddling him. He was dressed in a long-sleeved golf pullover and some casual golf pants, which soon came off. Time seemed to stretch as we moved in slow motion together, and before I knew it, we were both sweaty and breathless.

When it was over, I rolled off him and sat up on the couch. I leaned my head on his shoulder, holding his hand.

"I always miss you when I leave," I whispered.

"I can't wait until we go away together," Mark said in a soft voice as he kissed my hand.

I stood up and smoothed all my clothes back into place, not noticing that my purse fell down when I grabbed my clothes.

"Your purse fell off the chair," Mark said, gathering the scattered contents of my bag. He picked up a business card, holding it up to his eyes with a chuckle. "A private investigator? What's this for?" he asked, clearly amused.

I hesitated, wondering how to explain. It wasn't something I'd planned on telling him, but now seemed as good a time as any. "That's something I need to explain," I said, my voice quieter now.

CHAPTER TWENTY

"I was going to wait until next week, when we were out of town, to tell you, but I'll tell you now." I hesitated, shifting uncomfortably as I spoke. "There was a private investigator who sat at the bar with Ellie and me at Blue's a couple of days ago. He gave me his business card, and when I went to the bathroom, I came back to see him handing one to Ellie too," I said, almost reluctantly.

Mark's brow furrowed as he processed my words. "She didn't say anything to you about it?" he asked, curiosity and concern mixing in his voice.

"No," I answered quickly, the unease lingering in my chest.

"But there's more," I added in a low voice.

Mark's eyes narrowed. "What do you mean?"

I swallowed, my stomach turning as I continued. "When I was at Blue's this afternoon for lunch, Tom, the bartender, told me he saw Ellie in there, meeting the same private investigator. They were sitting together in a booth in the dining area." My voice trembled as I spoke.

Mark's face turned thoughtful, but then a look of worry flashed across it. He began pacing the floor, his mind clearly racing. "Do you think she knows about us?" he asked, his steps quick, almost frantic.

"I don't think so," I replied, though my voice lacked certainty. "She still seems like her normal self toward me. I am supposed to have drinks with her and Chloe tonight."

Mark stopped pacing for a moment, his eyes narrowing as if evaluating something I couldn't see. "You don't know what she's really like," he said, his tone laced with a sharpness that caught me off guard. "She's an evil person."

I blinked in confusion. "What are you talking about? I mean, I know at times she seems a little odd, and lately, her stories have not been adding up." I sensed there was something more he wasn't saying. "What makes you say that?"

Mark paused, clearly holding something back, and I could see the tension in his posture, like a pressure building inside him. "I guess you don't really know her like I do," he muttered, his voice distant.

I could feel the urgency in his words. "I feel bad for what we're doing," I admitted softly, torn by the guilt gnawing at me. "She's one of my good friends, but ... what do you mean by 'evil'? What's going on?"

Mark let out a frustrated breath, his pacing picking up again as he ran a hand through his hair. "There's just ... more to it," he said. I could tell he was getting more worked up by the second, and the last thing I wanted to do was push him further.

"I'll see if I can get some more information out of her tonight," I said, hoping to steer the conversation away from the mounting tension. "Since we are having drinks, maybe she will start talking about why she met the private investigator."

Mark's eyes softened for a brief moment, and he leaned in, pulling me close. "Yeah, see if she says anything else," he murmured, his voice low, almost reluctant.

He held me tight, pressing his lips against my forehead. "I don't want to let you go," he whispered, his breath warm against my skin.

I sighed, resting my head on his shoulder, trying to steady my own racing heart. "I can't wait until we have some days away alone," I said softly, my mind still racing with all the chaos.

After a long moment, I pulled away reluctantly, giving him a quick kiss. "Don't forget to wipe the lip gloss off," I said with a playful wink.

"I will," he said with a grin, turning toward his desk to grab a tissue, probably to remove any trace of me that lingered behind.

I made my way through the courtyard, glancing around cautiously even though I knew more than likely no one would be there since it was the weekend. Off in the distance, I saw the familiar sight of some cars lined up— probably a weekend cleaning crew. I let out a quiet breath, grateful to be unnoticed, but my mind kept racing.

As I drove home, Mark's warning about Ellie being "evil" echoed in my mind. What did he really mean by that? I had been so focused on the private investigator situation that I hadn't even asked Mark about the strange yelling I'd heard from their house. Maybe it was for the best, though. He'd been so stressed already, and I wasn't sure I wanted to bring up more questions, especially not when everything felt so tangled. His home life was typically a subject that was always off the table ... something we never spoke about.

When I finally pulled into my driveway, I quickly sent Ellie a text, trying to act normal.

> I'm home. You and Chloe can come over anytime :)

OK, be over in 10.

I sighed, trying to calm the nerves rattling through me, and walked through the garage door. I flipped on the outside light and unlocked the front door, knowing they would be here soon. As I passed by the half bath, I paused, suddenly aware of how I might look. The mixture of my perfume and Mark's cologne clung to me, and I could tell I didn't exactly look like I'd just come from a quick run to the office. My hair was a little messier than usual.

I dashed upstairs to my bedroom and quickly stripped off my clothes, tossing them on the floor. My heels came off next as I rushed into the bathroom. I grabbed a hand towel, ran it under the faucet, pumped some soap on it, and wiped down my neck and wrists, trying to rid myself of any trace of the perfume or cologne I might have shared with Mark. After that, I ran a brush through my hair, gathering it up in a quick twist and securing it with a clip.

A pair of jeans and a simple shirt were next, and I took one last look in the mirror. Everything seemed in place. My pulse quickened, and just as I started heading down the stairs, the doorbell rang.

CHAPTER TWENTY-ONE

"Hey ladies, come on in!" I called out warmly, waving my arm in a welcoming gesture as Ellie and Chloe stepped inside. Jax bounded over to greet them, too, his tail wagging in excitement. He wasn't really familiar with Chloe, so he kept jumping up at her and sniffing her until he approved of her.

"We brought drinks!" Chloe announced cheerfully as she walked in behind Ellie, holding a bottle of wine in each hand, her smile wide and full of energy. Ellie followed closely, her hands occupied with a bulky reusable plastic bag that caught my attention—something about its heavy, almost sloshing sound made me glance down. The bag looked like it was filled with a collection of hard liquor.

Chloe and her husband were relatively new to the neighborhood, having moved in just a few months ago. They lived only a couple of houses down from Ellie. I had only met Chloe once before, a brief encounter while I was walking Jax one afternoon. I had stopped to chat with her and Ellie, who were catching up on the sidewalk. Since then, I'd noticed them hanging out more often, usually on Chloe's front lawn. Chloe stood at around 5'10". Her short black hair was styled in spiky, sleek layers that framed her face, and she wore more jewelry than anyone I knew —gold hoop earrings that almost reached her shoulders, several layered necklaces that gleamed in the light, and an arm full of clinking bracelets. I had never been formally introduced to Chloe's husband and had just glimpsed him from afar now and then, usually while he was outside.

Ellie and Chloe kicked off their shoes and headed toward the kitchen, setting down the drinks on the counter. It was a cozy moment, with the house feeling warmer now that they were both here.

"So, what should we start with?" I asked, eager to get things rolling.

Ellie grinned and replied, "Oh, I don't know, but definitely make mine a double to start." She was already pulling out the bottles from her bag, an array of colorful liquors that made me raise an eyebrow.

I laughed, raising my hand in mock sympathy. "Wow, sounds like it's been a stressful day." As I grabbed the bottles, I couldn't help but wonder what had Ellie so worked up, but I didn't press her—yet.

"How about a mojito?" I suggested, glancing up at her. She gave a nod of approval, a smile dancing on her lips.

Chloe, who had been quietly watching the exchange, shook her head with a chuckle. "No way, I wouldn't even be able to walk home if I drank that. I'll just stick with the wine I brought."

"Smart choice," I said, before grabbing a bottle of wine for myself. My plan, though, was to keep Ellie's drinks flowing—if I could get her tipsy enough, maybe she'd let slip why she had met with a private investigator.

Drinks in hand, we made our way to the living room, and Chloe began telling us about how she and her husband had moved back to town from California to be closer to family. They were hoping to start a family soon; they wanted their kids to grow up with the same family connections they'd had growing up.

"Where in California are you from?" I asked, a spark of curiosity in my voice. "That's actually where I grew up."

"Northern California," Chloe replied. "A little town just north of San Francisco."

I let out a soft laugh. "Ah, got it. So, not exactly neighbors then—not even close, actually."

"Are you working right now?" I continued, taking a small sip of my wine. I didn't want to come off as too nosy, but I was genuinely curious.

"Yes, I'm a marketing consultant," Chloe replied with a nod. "That's what I went to school for."

I didn't want to dig too deep into her job—honestly, I was more interested in what Ellie had been up to lately. I noticed that Ellie had already knocked back most of her drink, and I caught myself glancing at her empty glass.

"That was great! Whatever you did to make that drink, I need the recipe!" Ellie exclaimed as she stood up, holding out her empty glass for me to see.

"Another round?" I asked, already knowing the answer. "I added a freshly squeezed lime to it also … with a little tahini on the rim."

"Yes, please!" Ellie grinned, heading toward the kitchen as I followed behind her.

"Chloe, do you need anything?" I called, even though I

knew she didn't. It was more of a polite offer than anything. I quickly grabbed some cheese and salami from the fridge, arranging them neatly on the counter as I made Ellie's next drink—just as she had requested.

We returned to the living room, Ellie holding her new drink with a smile. After this one, I figured she'd be tipsy enough to give me something useful about the investigator. But then, a thought hit me: Should I even ask in front of Chloe? It was something to consider. But then again, I didn't even know if Ellie had actually *hired* him—maybe the meeting had been about something completely innocent.

I wandered back to the kitchen to grab the snacks. I returned and set the cheese and salami on the coffee table, hoping it would distract everyone for a moment.

Nibbling on a few pieces of smoked Gouda, Chloe grinned and said, "Ugh, I love cheese, but it doesn't always love me. I just can't resist it when it's in front of me." She sighed dramatically. "How's that second drink treating you, Ellie?" she asked, eyeing her glass.

"So good," Ellie replied, her voice slightly slurred, but in a pleasant way. She took another sip, clearly enjoying herself.

The conversation shifted to me as Chloe asked what I did for work. I told her a little about my job, and then she asked, almost casually, if I was married. It was a question I'd been dreading. But I answered with a tight smile, telling her how I'd lost Steven last year. It was hard, but talking about it felt almost like a release.

As I spoke, I noticed Ellie kept sipping her drink again— she was downing it much faster than I expected. Chloe didn't seem to notice, but I did, and a small part of me hoped I was getting closer to what I wanted to know.

"Oh no," Chloe suddenly groaned, holding her stomach. "I think it's the cheese. I really need to learn to say no to it. My stomach feels so upset."

"You okay?" I asked, concerned.

"I'm going to head home," she said with a small laugh. "I have some stomach pills at home that will help. I'll see you ladies next time. Rachel, thank you for having me. I can see myself to the door."

"Well, I guess that's the end of the party for now," Ellie said, tipping her head back and finishing the last of her drink. She set the glass down a little too hard on the table.

I chuckled, grabbing her glass. "I think you've probably had enough anyway. Let's head to the kitchen. We can just sit in there."

She followed me to the kitchen, sitting down at one of the barstools as I wiped down the counters. I took a moment to gather my thoughts, trying to figure out how to bring up the investigator without pushing Ellie too much. Now that Chloe was gone, I had a window of opportunity.

I turned to Ellie as I kept wiping. "I had such a busy day today. It's nice to unwind like this. By the way, I stopped in at Blue's earlier. Tom mentioned he saw you there."

Ellie stiffened slightly, and I could tell she was already anticipating where the conversation was heading. I leaned casually against the counter. "He said he saw you with the private investigator—the one who was sitting between us at the bar that day."

Ellie froze, her eyes widening just for a moment. But I kept my voice light, trying not to pressure her too much.

Ellie hesitated, but then she answered quickly, "Oh, I

actually just ran into him when I arrived to grab a quick bite. He offered to buy me lunch and suggested we sit in the dining area."

I hadn't asked where they were sitting, so that extra detail struck me as odd. But I didn't push. I kept my tone friendly and nonchalant.

"Oh, nice. He seemed like a really nice guy." I smiled, but I was mentally filing away everything she had said. I couldn't help but replay the moment in my mind—how, when I invited her to lunch earlier, she had never once brought up that she had been there earlier.

And just like that, I had what I needed. Ellie had met with him, but she said it wasn't about anything specific. Or at least, that's what she wanted me to think.

CHAPTER TWENTY-TWO

Chloe texted that she wasn't feeling any better and wouldn't be coming back over. I wasn't surprised. The night had taken an unexpected turn, and I understood that she just wanted to stay home.

Ellie, however, was still very much in the mood to unwind. "I'll have one more of those mojitos if you don't mind?" she asked, a slight smirk tugging at her lips.

"Sure thing," I said, grabbing the liquor from the counter. As I started mixing yet another drink, we chatted casually about Chloe. She'd really been a pleasant surprise tonight, and I was genuinely glad she had come over. A part of me was still wondering about the whole private investigator situation. Instead, I leaned over the counter, watching Ellie take a sip of her drink and wondering if she was hiding something. Should I bring it up? Should I dig a little deeper? In the end, I decided against it.

"So, what did you end up eating for lunch at Blue's? I heard they have a bunch of new items on the menu," I asked, trying to keep things light as I bagged up the leftover meat and cheese from earlier.

Ellie didn't seem to mind the change in subject. "I had the chicken pesto sandwich," she replied in a casual voice. But I noticed her shifting in her seat. She was definitely squirming. Something about her response seemed off, as if I'd just triggered some memory or thought. I couldn't quite put my finger on it.

I considered pushing her further, trying to catch a little more of her body language, but I held back. Instead, I decided to try another question to throw her off.

"How's that drink?" I asked, glancing at her glass. She'd already made a good dent in her next drink.

"It's delicious," she said, her smile a little wider, a little more relaxed now that we weren't talking about private investigators anymore.

I smiled back, glad the tension had eased. But I was still curious. "Did you do any gardening today?" I asked, trying to throw her off guard again.

"No, why?" she asked, raising an eyebrow as if she couldn't quite figure out where I was going with the question.

It was then that I realized I might have caught her off guard. She had told me before that she was busy gardening today.

"Oh, just wondering, seems like you have been doing a lot of gardening lately," I said casually, hoping I wouldn't seem too pushy.

Ellie looked a little flustered. "Oh, I mean not today," she quickly corrected herself, as if trying to cover up a slip-up. "But I did a bunch the other day. I find it really relaxing."

I nodded along. "I see. I was just wondering how your garden was coming along."

The conversation died there, and I decided to move on. "Do you want me to get the snacks out again?"

"I don't know ... I am only walking home, but I've had a lot to drink.

"Might help to have a little something in your stomach," I added, a hint of concern in my voice.

"Oh, maybe," she murmured. The effects of the alcohol were working overtime.

As I reached for the box of crackers, I threw another question her way. "So how's everything else going? You know, with life?"

"Oh, you know ..." Ellie said, a vague answer that only seemed to make me more curious.

"Yeah, but what do you mean by 'you know'?" I pressed, genuinely interested, giggling.

She giggled back awkwardly. "Just ... home life. It's, like ... I don't know ..." she trailed off, leaving me more confused than before.

I had no idea if she meant it was going badly, or if there was something else she wasn't saying. Before I could press further, both of our phones chimed at the same time, signaling a new text. It was from Chloe.

> Had a great time with both of you girls.
> Hopefully, we can do it again soon. I
> promise I won't get sick, so I don't have to
> leave so soon!

I read the message aloud, laughing softly at Chloe's lighthearted comment.

"I hope you don't mind, but I gave Chloe your number,"

Ellie admitted as she slurred her words, looking at me with a mix of apology and uncertainty.

"Yeah, that's fine. Not a big deal," I reassured her with a smile. "I'll text her back." I typed out a quick reply:

> Not a big deal at all. We'll get together again soon :)

I also saved Chloe's number. "So, as you were saying ... what's going on at home?" I asked, trying to ease Ellie into more conversation, though I could tell she was holding something back.

"Oh, you know ..." she repeated, snatching another cracker. Clearly, she was avoiding something.

Ellie glanced at the clock, her eyes widening as she suddenly seemed to realize how late it had gotten. "Wow, I should get going," she said, standing up unsteadily and stumbling a little.

"Eat a couple more crackers, and I'll walk you home, okay?" I suggested, concerned that she might be too tipsy to walk on her own.

She agreed, nibbling on a few more crackers as I handed her a bottle of water. "Let's get you home," I said, guiding her toward the front door.

After she quickly slipped into her shoes, we stepped outside into the warm night air. Ellie linked her arm through mine as we walked down my front pathway toward the street. As we crossed the road toward her house, I noticed that her garage door was open.

Mark had probably left it that way for her.

When we stepped into her garage, the motion sensor light flicked on, illuminating the perfectly organized space. I hadn't realized until now how pristine everything was.

Not a single item was out of place. On the far side, there were two bikes and some neatly arranged golf clubs, while a small bench nearby held gardening tools. But there was something odd: As I passed by, I noticed a faint layer of dust on all the gardening tools, almost as if the tools hadn't been touched in years.

Ellie's arm was still looped through mine as we approached the door leading into the house. I knocked gently, and Mark opened it almost immediately.

"Here she is. Looks like she had a bit too much to drink," I said, holding back a laugh as Ellie swayed slightly, trying to regain her balance.

"Oh, wow," Mark said, a smile tugging at his lips as he motioned for Ellie to come inside. "Thanks for walking her back."

"I can get in by myself," Ellie mumbled, trying to sound more in control than she probably was.

"No problem," I said with a smile, giving Mark a nod before turning to leave.

As I headed back toward the street, I noticed Mark starting to shut the garage door, the light still glowing softly behind me. The garage, pristine and orderly, seemed almost too perfect. I couldn't help but feel a little curious about the dust on those gardening tools. It was a strange little detail.

CHAPTER TWENTY-THREE

Today had arrived—the day I had been waiting for, the day Mark and I were finally going to meet out of town in Syracuse. I had been anticipating this moment for a while, and now that it was here, I could barely contain my excitement. I woke up early to get a head start on the day. As the sun barely kissed the horizon, I was already at my desk at home, making sure everything was in order before I left. My bag was packed with clothes, and I'd already arranged for Jax to be dropped off at the kennel early in the morning. A neighborhood kid coming over to let him out would look suspicious, and I wanted to avoid that.

I stood over my desk, organizing the last few things into my work bag, when my phone buzzed. It was a message from Mark.

Today's the day!

I can't wait! I wrote back.

I'll send you the hotel details soon, Mark replied. *I am on my way there right now. Let me know when you're getting close.*

A warm, fluttery feeling spread across my chest, and I

felt giddy. The anticipation of seeing him again was enough to make me feel like I was walking on air. I grabbed my keys and made my way out to the car, glancing at my packed bag on the back seat and Jax in the other seat. The butterflies in my stomach fluttered again.

About an hour later, I arrived at the hotel. There was something luxurious about it, with its tall glass windows in the front. I pulled into the back parking lot, far from the entrance, to keep things discreet. When I texted Mark to let him know I had arrived, he sent me the code for the back door of the hotel.

I entered through the back, the quiet hum of the building filling the air as I made my way to the elevator just inside the door. The ride to the seventh floor was quick, and I felt my excitement build as I walked down the hallway toward room 741. The modern gray carpet under-foot and the chic, white wall panels gave the hotel an upscale, contemporary vibe. I had no doubt that staying here came with a hefty price tag—at least $700 a night, if not more. It was the kind of place where elegance dripped from every polished surface, where even the air smelled expensive. Crystal chandeliers hung every twenty feet or so down the hallway, casting a soft, inviting glow. When I reached the door, I noticed it was propped open by the safety latch. I smiled to myself—Mark had clearly been expecting me.

I stepped inside quietly, placing my things down as I locked the door behind me. Mark was seated at the desk, typing on his computer, but when he heard the door, he stopped immediately and turned to look at me. His smile was warm. Without saying a word, he stood up, closed the laptop with a soft click, and turned off the TV, which had been playing quietly in the background. Then, with an air of confidence, he crossed the room toward me.

He pulled me close, his arms wrapping around my body, and I could feel the heat of his chest against mine.

"It's just us now," he whispered.

His hand slid to my back, urging me closer, and I looked up into his eyes. He closed them for a moment and kissed me—slow, soft, and lingering. It was as if he was savoring the moment, just as I was. He pulled away slightly as his hands continued to move over my back. Then, as if unable to resist, he kissed me again, even more slowly this time.

"I have to go to a conference and some meetings," he whispered softly, his breath warm against my ear. "Then I'm going to get out of the work dinner, and I'll come back to pick you up for a late dinner. I have a special time planned for us."

I nodded, feeling a warmth spread across my skin as he kissed me again, slow and deliberate, as though time had stopped. I wanted to say something, but he pulled away just enough to leave me breathless.

"Let me know when I should be ready," I murmured, still feeling the softness of his kiss on my lips.

Even though Mark had a conference and meetings, I was just so excited to be here with him. This was our space now. I had planned on working from the hotel room during his meetings. Just being with him was a nice getaway.

Mark was dressed to impress in navy blue dress pants, a white button-down shirt, and a blue-and-gray striped tie. I admired the way his clothes fit him perfectly, the way his posture exuded effortless elegance. I, too, had dressed carefully—in a light grey button-down blouse, a black flounce skirt, and strappy heels. As I ran my hands down his back, feeling the fabric of his shirt, I couldn't help but tug at its hem, wanting to pull him closer. But Mark gently pulled back, a smile curling at the corners of his lips.

"Let's wait until after dinner, okay?" he said, his tone playful yet reassuring, as he cupped the side of my face with one hand. His smile made my heart race.

As he stepped out of the room, I let the silence settle around me and took it all in. The king-sized bed caught my attention, its frame set against a sleek wooden accent wall that gave off a quiet, modern charm. I let my fingers trail across the bedding—smooth, cool, and undeniably luxurious.

I spent the next several hours taking care of some work things—calling clients, tying up loose ends—but my thoughts kept drifting back to Ellie and her meeting with the private investigator. I couldn't help but wonder what was going on. After finishing another phone call, I stood up, walked over to my purse, and retrieved the business card of the private investigator. I had kept it with me only because he had handed it to me, not knowing that I might need it at some point. I tucked it safely into the side pocket of my purse and returned to my seat.

Several hours later, my phone buzzed. It was a message from Mark.

I'll be up to get you in 20 minutes.

I texted back.

Great :)

I couldn't help but smile as I put my phone down. I freshened up in the bathroom, applying a little lotion to my arms and legs to give them a smooth, polished look. I also added a delicate gold necklace to complement my outfit and a fresh spray of perfume. A few minutes later, I heard the door unlock, and Mark stepped inside.

"Ready?" he asked with a playful smile. The look in his eyes made my pulse race.

I smiled back, knowing he understood exactly how happy I was to be here with him.

"I've reserved a nice table for us for dinner," he said, extending his hand.

"Where are we going?"

"I can't tell you. It's a surprise," he replied with a wink.

Taking his hand, I felt a warmth spread through me. We walked down the hallway toward the elevator. As the doors closed, Mark held my hand and squeezed it gently, his gaze never leaving mine. His expression softened, and for a moment, I could see a hint of something more behind his eyes—sadness, perhaps? Was he feeling guilty or possibly sad about something?

"I'm really looking forward to this time with you," he said quietly, throwing me off guard.

His words hung in the air, and I wasn't sure if they were just for me or if there was something deeper behind them. Regardless, I squeezed his hand in return, offering him a smile of reassurance.

We drove about five miles to the downtown part. The air was humid, a perfect summer night. As Mark pulled up to a small restaurant, its dimly lit windows exuding a sense of intimacy, a valet opened my door, and another opened Mark's. It was still light outside as we were still in the summer months, and I felt a wave of excitement wash over me. The night was young, and it felt like nothing could interrupt our time together.

Inside, the restaurant smelled rich and sophisticated. The dim lighting created a cozy, elegant atmosphere, with candles flickering softly on every table, casting a warm glow over the fine linens. We were escorted to our table by a hostess, who led us to a quiet spot near the back of the restaurant. The view from our table was breathtaking—a large inland lake in the distance, with sparkling lights along the shoreline, waiting for night to settle in. Mark pulled my chair out for me; his unbuttoned suit jacket gave him a relaxed yet polished look.

We ordered a bottle of fine red wine and sipped it slowly, talking about everything and nothing at the same time. As we enjoyed our meal, Mark reached under the table and gently placed his hand on my leg. It wasn't flirtatious but comfortable, reassuring, and intimate in the most natural way. I liked it—I liked how easy it felt to be close to him, to let him touch me in a way that wasn't rushed or forced.

"So, what do you think about all this?" Mark asked, his eyes lingering on mine as we sipped our wine, the soft clink of glasses and hum of the restaurant settling around us.

"What do you mean?" I laughed lightly. "The dinner? It was perfect," I said, smiling warmly.

"No," he said, leaning in slightly. "I mean *this*—you and me, out together like it's just another ordinary evening. Like this could be normal."

I traced the rim of my glass slowly, my gaze locked on

his. "It feels ... really good," I said softly. "Like something I didn't even realize I was missing until now."

We leaned in toward each other, and the world outside the restaurant seemed to disappear.

After dinner, Mark looked at me with a playful glint in his eye. "Shall we leave?" he asked in an inviting voice.

He stood up and offered me his hand, and as we walked out of the restaurant, I couldn't help but notice how free and at ease he seemed now. Holding my hand in his, he looked more relaxed than I had seen him in a long time. It was as if, for tonight, there was nothing to hide.

CHAPTER TWENTY-FOUR

The ride back to the hotel was quiet but comfortable. Mark's hand rested in mine the entire time, his fingers warm against my skin, and even though the car hummed steadily along the road, the atmosphere between us was peaceful. There were moments where the conversation would taper off, the world outside speeding by, but it never felt awkward—just natural. The quiet was companionable, like we both knew we were sharing something special, and the stillness only seemed to make it feel more intimate.

When we finally arrived back at the hotel, the evening sky had darkened. We went up to our room, and as we entered, Mark immediately pulled his phone from his pocket. There was a moment of hesitation as he sat down on the edge of the bed, a slight laugh escaping his lips.

"Give me just a minute," he said, a touch of amusement in his voice, as he settled in. "I want this to be just right." His words were soft, but there was an undercurrent of sincerity in them, as if he was trying to create the perfect moment.

"It already is," I replied, my voice soft, genuine. I didn't need him to do anything more for it to be perfect—it already felt that way to me. I walked over to the sliding glass door that led to the balcony and tugged the curtain back slightly, then slid the door open, stepping out onto the balcony. The cool night air rushed in, and I paused to admire the hotel's outdoor eating area below. The scene was peaceful, almost like something out of a movie—lush, green trees surrounded by modern paths, soft lights illuminating the scene in a gentle glow. The busy city was off in the faint distance.

"It almost feels like it has warmed up a little since we left earlier," I said, glancing over my shoulder at Mark. I was trying to break the silence, to fill the space with a little more conversation.

Still fiddling with his phone, Mark didn't look up right away but responded, "It's supposed to be really hot tomorrow, so yeah, it probably has warmed up." His voice was distant, and he was absorbed in whatever he was doing, but I could tell that he wasn't entirely disconnected from the moment.

I looked out again, the trees below catching my attention as the wind picked up slightly. I watched as their leaves rustled gently, creating a soft, soothing melody that mixed with the sounds of the city in the distance.

"Okay, I got it!" Mark's voice broke through my thoughts, and I turned to find him laughing softly as he set his phone on the dresser.

As I started to turn back toward the room, a gust of wind blew through the slightly open door, sending the white sheer curtain fluttering in front of me. I turned around, pushing the door back slightly, leaving it just cracked enough for the warm wind to continue flowing through the room. The curtain danced in the breeze, flowing with a quiet elegance that almost seemed to mirror the mood between us.

I caught a faint hum of music from Mark's phone, the soft, familiar notes filling the space with an intimate energy.

"Is this okay?" he asked, his tone more serious as he flicked the light switch to darken the room. He glanced over at me, his face still partially illuminated by the faint glow from the balcony.

I smiled and walked closer to him. He reached up to loosen the knot of his tie. The fabric slid easily from his neck, and he pulled it off, tossing it aside with a casual ease that was both charming and intimate. There was something about the way he did it that made me smile inside.

He moved toward me as a love song filled the room. The lyrics sounded like they had been written for moments just like this. Mark reached for me, his fingers gently gliding down the outer curve of my arm, a soft, almost imperceptible touch that sent a shiver through me. The scent of his cologne drifted toward me, a fresh mixture of something warm and comforting. I closed my eyes for a moment, breathing him in.

His hand moved slowly, almost as if he was taking his time to savor the moment. He slipped his fingers between my arm and side, his touch smooth and deliberate, sending a wave of warmth through me. I could feel him move closer, his chest brushing against mine as he took me in, his eyes dark and intent. My heart beat just a little faster, the proximity, the music, and the warmth of the room all coming together in a heady rush of anticipation.

Out of the corner of my eye, I saw the wind stir the curtain again, the sheer fabric swaying in the air, casting a soft, ethereal glow over us. There was no need for words—everything we needed to say was already understood.

We swayed together, our bodies pressed close as we moved to the soft melodies issuing from his phone. Our hands explored, trembling with both excitement and restraint, peeling away our clothing. Every moment stretched, suspended in time, as we savored the anticipation humming between us.

But just as he began to lead me toward the bed, he stopped and hesitated. His breath hitched, and he looked away, his expression shifting into something hesitant, almost vulnerable. "I can't," he whispered, his voice barely audible over the music. "I don't want you to see me."

His words stopped me cold. I had seen his body so many times before. I pulled back slightly, searching his face, my heart tightening as confusion flickered through me. "What do you mean?" I asked gently. But he wouldn't look at me. His shoulders tensed, his hands retreating as if he were suddenly exposed.

CHAPTER TWENTY-FIVE

My concern began to deepen as I took in the way his shoulders tensed, something unreadable flickering in his eyes. "What's wrong? You can tell me," I asked softly, tilting my head as I tried to meet his gaze.

He exhaled, his jaw tightening. "You don't wanna know," he muttered, shaking his head as if trying to push away the thoughts gnawing at him.

That only made my worry grow. I reached for him instinctively, running my fingers along his arm in slow, soothing strokes. "Are you okay?" My voice was quieter now, laced with the kind of patience that I hoped would make him feel safe enough to tell me whatever was weighing on his mind.

He hesitated, then let out a bitter chuckle—one without humor, one that sounded almost exhausted. "Yeah ... you just have no idea what it's like living with her." His voice turned heavy, laced with something close to resentment. "She is evil."

I frowned at his words. His tone was raw, but considering what we'd been doing only moments before, I wasn't sure how much weight to give it. Although something about the way he said the words made me pause.

"What do you mean?" I asked carefully, making sure to give him the space to answer on his own terms.

Mark didn't respond right away. Instead, he inhaled deeply, as if bracing himself, and then turned around on the bed. "Look," he said quietly. His voice had lost its sharpness, replaced by something almost hesitant. "Look down."

I did. And what I saw made my breath catch in my throat.

His lower back was a mess of angry red scratches and cuts, some fresh, others older but still visible—layer upon layer of claw marks and cuts covering more skin than not. It looked raw, painful, like he'd been attacked over and over again.

"Oh my god ..." The words barely escaped my lips as I lifted my hands to my mouth to stifle my shock. But it was too late. The look on my face had already given me away. I hadn't meant to react so strongly—I didn't want him to feel ashamed—but I couldn't help it. The mood had changed drastically, although this would bring us closer and also let him know he could trust me.

Mark tensed at my reaction, his head dipping slightly.

"Wow ... it's definitely not what I would have ever expected," I managed, my voice barely above a whisper. My mind was reeling, trying to piece together what this meant, trying to make sense of it.

"I have so many questions," I added after a moment, my voice softer now, more careful.

Mark turned back toward me, his eyes serious, almost pleading. "I have never laid a hand on her. I really haven't. I promise you I have never touched her in an abusive way." His voice was firm, but I could see the desperation beneath it, the fear that I might think otherwise.

The thought hadn't even crossed my mind. Somehow, I knew—deep down—I didn't need an explanation to believe him. He just wasn't the type.

"I know," I said simply.

I reached out hesitantly, my fingers brushing over a few of the fresher scratches, the ones that were still a deep, irritated red. "Do they hurt?" I asked, my touch featherlight, barely skimming his skin.

Mark let out a breath. "Not really, not anymore." He looked down, his expression touched with something close to embarrassment, as if he was ashamed of the marks, of the situation, of himself.

I swallowed the lump in my throat, my heart aching for him. "I'm so sorry. Really, I am." Without thinking, I leaned forward, resting my head gently against his shoulder, hoping he could feel the sincerity in my words.

For a few moments, we just sat there in silence, holding hands.

Then something clicked in my mind. "So ... is this about the noises I've been hearing from your house lately?" My voice was cautious, almost afraid of the answer.

Mark hesitated for only a second before nodding. "Yeah, it is. I always wondered if other people could hear her."

I felt my stomach twist, anger bubbling under my skin. *Ellie.* My mind raced, piecing things together in a way that made my blood simmer. Now I understood why her nails were always chipped, why they always looked scraped up.

Mark sighed, running a hand through his hair before turning to me again. "She would tear through things in the house. Pick things up and throw them ... either at me or just at the wall. She would tear through my clothes to get to my skin and gouge it with her nails. I know this is a lot to tell you," he said, rubbing his forehead before continuing, "Let's just move on with the night. I'm sorry—I should've told you earlier, just to get it over with. I knew it would be awkward."

I shook my head. "It's okay." Reaching out, I cupped his cheek gently. I didn't care about the awkwardness—I only cared that he was okay, that he knew he wasn't alone in this. I was still trying to make sense of his words. They echoed in my mind, tumbling over each other as I tried to grasp their full meaning. A part of me wanted to retreat inward, to sit with those words, analyze them, and untangle the web of emotion they stirred up inside me. But I knew this wasn't the moment for that. This wasn't about me. So I gently placed my own feelings on a quiet shelf inside, promising myself I'd return to them later—when the storm of this moment had passed. For now, I needed to stay present with Mark, to offer him the steady support he so clearly needed. Whatever processing I had to do could wait; he couldn't.

His eyes softened, and for the first time since this conversation started, he looked relieved. "I'm so glad to be here with you," he murmured, his fingers reaching up to cradle my face the same way I had his.

I placed my hand over his, letting the warmth of his touch settle me. "Me too."

I felt another gust of warm breeze flow through the room. I stood up in front of Mark as he was now sitting on the side of the bed, still looking sad.

"Let's pick up where we left off," he said.

I woke up the next morning to the sound of the shower. From the bed, I could see Mark showering through the clear shower doors. My eyes were locked on his lower back. I had so many questions. How long had this been going on? What was setting her off now?

The only thing I knew was that I had another good view of everything Ellie had done to his back.

CHAPTER TWENTY-SIX

I slowly sat up, the warm white sheets pooling around my waist as I slid to the edge of the bed. My body still felt heavy with sleep, but my mind was already awake, still fixated on the sight of Mark through the glass of the shower. Steam curled upward, moving against the transparent barrier, softening his silhouette. He stood with his back to me, the water cascading down his toned shoulders, his posture relaxed but somehow weighted.

I reached over to the nightstand, tapping the top of my phone. The screen lit up—8:42 AM.

A deep breath filled my lungs before I made my way toward the bathroom. The sound of running water filled the space, mingling with the faint scent of soap and fresh morning air. Mark had just turned around, rubbing the slick lather over his chest, his muscles flexing beneath his skin. For someone constantly wrapped up in the demands of his job, he was in remarkable shape, every line of his body defined by strength and discipline.

Without hesitation, I stepped forward and opened the

shower door, letting myself in. The steam wrapped around me instantly. I gently smiled and then reached for the soap, filling my palm with the same lather he had just been using. Then I pressed my hands against his chest, rubbing slow, deliberate circles over his skin. His eyes fluttered closed, his body sinking into my touch.

"That feels so good," he murmured in a hushed voice, almost as if the warmth of the water and the softness of the moment had lulled him into a trance.

As the suds built up across his chest, I stepped behind him, trailing my hands over his shoulders, his upper back, avoiding the lower portion that was freshly wounded. But as my fingers ghosted over the ridges of his muscles, my eyes fell on something new—a deep gash along the back of his arm, the cut still raw, mirroring the ones that marked his lower back.

A knot formed in my stomach, knowing this was part of Ellie's doing.

It wasn't just the injuries themselves. It was the pattern. The depth. My jaw tightened as I forced myself to look away, while my hands continued their gentle motions. I didn't want my disgust to show—not disgust toward him, but toward what had been done to him.

For a brief second, a small voice in my head asked, *Is there another side to this story?* But the thought disappeared as quickly as it came. *Why didn't he try to defend himself somehow?* I decided to ask that question later. I could only go off the man I knew now—the one standing here with me, vulnerable and strong all at once.

I moved back to his front, forcing myself to focus on the present, on him, not on the marks left behind by someone else. I reached for the clean washcloth to help him rinse. As

I set it back in place, I stepped forward, pressing my cheek against his chest, leaning my body against him. His arms wrapped around me, holding me there, our bare, wet skin molding together under the steady stream of water running down his back.

For a while, we just stood there, letting the warmth seep into us.

By the time we stepped out and toweled off, we were both slipping back into the reality of the day ahead. I dried my hair, applied my makeup, got dressed, and packed up my bag while Mark finished getting dressed and gathered his things.

"I wish you could have ridden here with me," he said as he zipped up his computer bag. "I feel bad you have to drive back an hour by yourself."

I smiled at him over my shoulder. "I don't mind," I replied in a teasing voice, throwing him a playful wink as I folded the last of my belongings into my tote.

Mark slung his bag over his shoulder and gave me a look that was both hopeful and expectant. "Can I see you again this week?" His tone was casual, but I could tell it wasn't just a polite question. He genuinely wanted to know when he would see me next.

I glanced at my phone, running through my mental schedule. "Tomorrow?"

A slow smile spread across his lips. "That's perfect."

He stepped closer, his hand finding my lower back, pulling me against him in that effortless way. His lips met mine in a lingering kiss, one that made me forget about everything else for a moment.

When we were both fully ready to leave, Mark picked up my bag as we headed toward the elevator.

"Do you want to leave a few minutes before me?" he asked as the doors slid shut. "Just so we don't get back into town at the same time?"

I nodded. "Yeah, good idea." Another wink. He smirked.

As the elevator hummed downward, I shifted my bag higher on my shoulder and turned toward him. "I'm going to set up a meeting with the private investigator," I said. "I want to see if I can find out what Ellie was really up to."

Mark exhaled, shaking his head. "I would like to know what she's up to with him."

"I agree."

The elevator dinged, and the doors slid open. We walked through the lobby together, but before stepping outside, we exchanged one final glance—silent understanding passing between us. Then, with a quick goodbye, we went our separate ways as I headed toward the back door of the hotel, and Mark stopped at the coffee station off to the side.

The moment I pulled into the office parking lot, I exhaled. Even though being a realtor meant I was constantly in and out, working between showings and meetings, I didn't want to take any chances with Ellie showing up at my house unannounced. The office felt like a safer place to regroup.

Inside, I settled at my desk, unpacking my laptop and folders. The space was small but modern.

I opened my desk drawer, retrieving a small mirror to check my hair and makeup. As I rummaged through my purse for lipstick, my fingers came across the private investigator's business card.

I pulled it out, staring at the first name printed in bold letters: **Bennett.** The private investigator. The man I met that night at Blue's. The man Ellie met with again the day after.

Slipping the card under my desk calendar—out of immediate sight—I focused on work for about an hour before finally reaching for it again. With a steady breath, I dialed the number.

He answered on the second ring.

"Hi, is this Bennett?" I asked, my voice more confident than I felt.

After brief introductions, we settled on meeting for a later lunch that afternoon.

"How about Jake's?" I suggested. "I'll text you the address." I made sure to choose a spot on the other side of town—away from Blue's, away from familiar faces.

"That works just fine, young lady," he said with a chuckle. "I'll see you then."

We agreed on half-past two, a time when the lunch crowd would have already thinned out, ensuring we could talk in peace, with fewer people around.

After ending the call, I sat back in my chair, exhaling slowly.

This wasn't just about curiosity anymore.

It was time to get answers.

CHAPTER TWENTY-SEVEN

I kept checking the time on my phone over and over as the minutes slowly ticked by, knowing exactly when I needed to leave to meet Bennett. A few minutes before two, I finally decided it was time to pack up and head out. I slid open my desk drawer and tucked a crisp white envelope into my purse. The sight of it sparked a quick reminder—an extra minute was all I'd need to swing by the bank. I gathered my things, stuffed my phone into my bag, and walked out the door, feeling the warm air against my skin as I walked to the car.

The drive across to the other end of town felt long. Finally, I ended up at Jake's—an unassuming little hole-in-the-wall bar, hidden from the main road, like it didn't want to be found.

Jake's was a relic, an old gray cement building that seemed to have been forgotten by time, its narrow windows blocking out most of the daylight and giving the place an almost secretive feel. The parking lot was a dusty gravel lot, with a few scattered vehicles and a rusted chain-link fence running along the back. I pulled around to the rear and parked near the back of the bar, grabbing my purse from the passenger seat before heading toward the side door.

The interior was dimly lit, with a grim, moody ambiance. I slid into a booth in the back corner, facing the back wall. Overhead, small, hanging lights barely illuminated the booths, casting a soft, golden glow over everything. I leaned back, taking a deep breath as I waited. A few moments passed, and the door swung open, the bell chiming faintly. I leaned forward, craning my neck toward the front of the bar to see who it was—an older man, probably in his seventies, shuffling in slowly. Dressed in an old, worn flannel shirt, he made his way to the bar, looking like he had probably been coming here for years.

Just as I was about to settle back into my seat, the door opened again. This time, Bennett stepped inside. I immediately caught his eye and gave a small, almost imperceptible wave. He acknowledged me with a quick nod and made his way to the booth where I sat, sliding into the seat across from me and facing the front of the bar. The decision was more about instinct than logic—if anyone were to walk in and see us, I figured it'd be less likely they'd recognize him first.

"Well, this is a little different from the country club vibe from the other night," Bennett said with a dry chuckle.

"I know," I replied, my voice low and serious. "It's more … hidden. More out of sight."

He nodded in understanding. "I get it."

The waitress arrived to take our drink orders. She came back and set down two drinks: an iced tea for me and a soda for him. We exchanged pleasantries for a few moments, talking briefly about where he grew up, the usual small talk you make when you're just getting to know someone. But I had something more pressing on my mind.

I shifted in my seat, my thoughts turning darker. I couldn't just let it go any longer.

"Well," Bennett said, looking at me with a slightly amused expression, "I'm sure you didn't bring me out here just to ask about my childhood."

I met his gaze. "No, not exactly," I said, taking a steadying breath. "The girl I was with the other night— Ellie. She met you at Blue's, right? You two had a conversation there. What was that about?"

Bennett's expression hardened, and he sat back in the booth, his demeanor shifting to something more guarded. "Oh, ma'am," he said, his voice taking on a steely edge, "in my line of work, that information is confidential. I can't talk about that."

I held his gaze, undeterred. "I know. But I really need to know." I leaned in to emphasize just how much I needed to know.

He didn't say anything. We stared at each other for a long moment. I could feel the tension mounting, but I wasn't backing down.

I glanced down at my purse, my fingers brushing the edge of its opening. From inside, I pulled out the white envelope and slid it across the table toward him. I had come prepared, not even knowing if I would need to.

"Will this help?" I asked, my voice low and calm, but with an edge to it now. He immediately knew what was inside the envelope, his fingers brushing over it as if he were trying to hide it from view.

"Why is this so important to you?" Bennett leaned in

closer, his voice dropping even lower, as if he was trying to get a read on me.

I took a slow breath. "It's complicated," I said, the words coming out quietly but with an intensity that matched his. "But before I tell you anything, I need to know that what I'm offering you is going to buy you out of whatever she's asking you to do."

He hesitated, then reached for the envelope, slowly opening it to reveal the stack of bills inside. He fanned them out, the crisp bills catching the dim light.

"That's a lot of money," Bennett said, his voice sounding almost strangled as he spoke.

"There's more where that came from," I replied, not breaking eye contact. "I need you to work for me. I'll match whatever she's paying you and throw in a lot of extra for your trouble."

He slid the envelope into his jacket pocket with a practiced move, his fingers lingering there for a moment. "I have to say ... she was a really odd lady when I met her."

"Odd?" I asked, my curiosity piqued.

"Yeah," Bennett continued, leaning back in his seat and taking a sip of his soda. "I've met a lot of people over the years, a lot of clients, but there was something about her. Something strange. Just ... off."

I waited for him to elaborate. And when he didn't, I asked, "What did she hire you for?"

He looked at me with an almost detached expression, his voice becoming more measured. "She wanted me to investigate her husband. She thinks he's cheating on her."

I froze for a moment. I didn't say anything. I just stared at him, feeling the words settle over me like a heavy fog.

"So I guess this might have something to do with you?" Bennett asked, his tone more serious now.

"No ... maybe," I said quickly, trying to regain some control over the conversation. "It's just ... confusing. I'm trying to make sense of it. Something more is going on with her, like you said."

Bennett paused, studying me carefully. "The more she drank, the more she started talking. Maybe I was a safe place for her. After about four drinks, she started saying things like 'If you only knew.' That's usually when you know there's more to the story."

I took a breath, my mind racing. "I need you to buy some time. Tell her you're watching her husband, but that you're not finding anything. Just keep her occupied for a while."

He gave a slight nod, his eyes narrowing as he thought it through. "All right," he said in a thoughtful voice. "I can do that."

"Can you meet her again? See if you can find out anything more? Anything at all? I'm serious. I'll cover all of your costs and then some," I said, my voice steady but with an undercurrent of urgency.

Bennett looked at me, his eyes narrowing slightly as he processed what I was asking. "I'll get you whatever info you need," he replied, his tone firm, no hesitation in his words.

"Okay," I said, leaning back slightly in the booth and letting out a quiet breath. "We will be in touch."

He nodded, his gaze unwavering as we both stood up.

"I'm going to leave now, but wait about five minutes before you head out, all right?" I said, already turning to head toward the door.

Bennett gave a small nod in agreement, his posture relaxed but with a slight edge.

As I walked back to my car, I couldn't help but think about Mark. Should I call him now and tell him everything, or wait until I see him next? The thought of unloading this on him over the phone didn't sit right with me. I wanted to tell him face-to-face. So, I decided to hold off and wait until I see him next.

I drove back to my office, the conversation with Bennett still lingering in my mind. After a brief stop to organize my work, I left again to go to my showings—again for a couple with very particular tastes. I'd been running them through a slew of homes lately, and it had been eating up a ton of my time.

I was wrapping up my last showing when my phone buzzed in my pocket. The couple asked for one last stroll through the master suite—so I wandered back to the kitchen, letting them have a quiet moment to imagine the space as their own.

It was a message from Ellie:

> Do you want to grab dinner tonight at Blue's? I'm starving.

I smiled as I read her message and then quickly typed a response:

> Yes! Do you want to try somewhere else? That seems like the only place we go to lately, lol.

> I was really hoping for Blue's. Do you mind?

I sighed.

> I'm at a showing now, but I'll meet you there in an hour. Does that work?

She agreed.

I had added the extra time because I remembered I needed to swing by the kennel to pick up Jax and get my overnight bag back in the house. It wasn't a long detour, but I didn't want to feel rushed.

I got Jax settled back at home and then changed into something more casual—capris and a short-sleeved light sweater. As I stood in front of the mirror, I realized just how hungry I was. It had been a long day, and I hadn't had much to eat. I went back downstairs, grabbed my phone from the kitchen island to check the time, and noticed a text from Mark.

> Do you want to come by my office tomorrow at 6:30? I'm working late.

I responded immediately.

> Yes :)

> I can't wait to see you! I have more info for you, too. About what we discussed earlier.

I knew I would have to tell him about the private investigator and his meeting with Ellie.

As I walked into the bar, I spotted Ellie sitting at one of the high-top tables near the outer edge. She waved enthusiastically as soon as she saw me.

I walked over and gave her a quick hug.

"I just sat down right before you got here," Ellie said with a grin.

Before I could even settle into the seat across from her, Gabe was already at our table, ready to take our drink orders. I noticed Ellie's eyes lingering on him a little longer than usual. It was subtle, but it was there.

As soon as he left to fill our drink orders, I leaned in with a teasing smile. "So, what's going on with you two?" I asked, raising an eyebrow as if I already knew the answer.

She rolled her eyes but smiled, playing along. "Come on. Spill it," I insisted.

"Nothing, really," Ellie said, straightening up a little, trying to compose herself. "I just think he's cute. That's all," she added, twirling the straw in her water, but I could tell there was more to the story.

Gabe returned with our drinks. As he set them down, I noticed he gave Ellie another flirtatious smile.

Ellie took a sip of her drink, grimacing slightly. "Wow, he made this strong," she commented, setting the glass down.

I chuckled to myself. I was sure Gabe had made it strong on purpose.

We chatted for a few minutes about the houses I'd shown earlier, but I couldn't help noticing Ellie's gaze flicking back to Gabe, who was working the bar. She was definitely more interested in him than she had led me to believe.

"Hey, there are two seats opening up at the bar. Want to move up there?" she asked, practically bouncing out of her seat.

"Oh, yeah, sure, I guess," I said, grabbing my things as she practically dragged me over to the bar.

As soon as we sat down, I could tell she was in her

element. She was right in the thick of things now, and her smile became more flirtatious as Gabe came over to check on us. I noticed Tom, the other bartender, was also working. He was handing drinks to an elderly couple dressed in fine golf attire when his eyes met mine. Without missing a beat, he gave me an innocent wink, and I couldn't help but smile back.

Tom came over to our side, and we chatted for a few minutes. I made sure to subtly whisper to him, "Don't say anything about the private investigator. Ellie's too distracted with Gabe." He gave me a knowing smile and a nod, agreeing to keep quiet.

As Tom turned to check on another couple, I turned my attention back to Ellie. She was so absorbed in Gabe that she had forgotten I was there. I watched her laugh at something Gabe said, and I couldn't help but wonder just how much she was hiding beneath that smile of hers.

"Would you ladies like to do a shot with me?" Gabe asked. I was quite surprised because, given how classy Blue's was, I wouldn't have expected the bartender would be doing shots with the customers.

"Yeah, bring it on over," replied Ellie.

"Oh, none for me," I said. "I am just going to stick with my drink."

Tom stood frozen for a moment, eyebrows lifted and mouth slightly ajar, as if his brain needed an extra beat to process what he'd just witnessed—Gabe and Ellie tossing back a shot. After the shots, Gabe kept coming over and talking to Ellie as we ate dinner. He was checking if our food tasted good, and he stayed longer than normal. He also kept offering Ellie drink after drink. By the time we finished eating, she had three drinks plus the one shot. I think Tom could tell I was bored. He looked over at me one time while we were eating and kind of laughed at me.

Tom kept working at the bar outside, on the deck, and the bar in here, stocking items and making drinks. When he came in the last time, he spent a few minutes behind the bar and then casually made his way over to me.

"Have you seen the new addition they made to the bar outside?" he asked very quietly, winking. "No, not really," I said.

"They added some really neat outdoor string lights and a couple of really neat modern high tops off to the side," he replied. Then he slowly moved about to get some men their drinks.

"I am going to the ladies' room," I said, getting up and setting my napkin on the bar in front of me.

"Oh, okay," Ellie said as she waved my way. I probably could have left the restaurant, and she wouldn't have known.

I walked toward the back of Blue's, toward the wall of windows near the deck Tom was referring to. The ladies' room was down the back hallway. I looked out of the window to the outside bar, and Mark was out there, sitting at the bar with a few other men.

I turned around and looked over my shoulder to see Ellie at the bar area with Gabe, then I turned around again to see Mark out the window.

I took another look at Ellie. The way Gabe was leaning over the bar and how Ellie was lightly running her fingers over his hand was more than how friends would behave. I had to think quickly.

I went into the bathroom and pulled my phone out of my purse, and sent a text to Mark.

> I am at Blue's. I see you out the window on the back deck. Ellie is at the bar. Go to the bathroom and subtly look in the bar area at her. I am going back to my seat now. I will check my texts later.

He replied instantly.

> OK.

On my way back to my seat, I saw Mark out of the corner of my eye; he was coming in the back door of the deck to go to the bathroom. I subtly noticed him walking slowly and glaring at Ellie as she was caressing Gabe's arm with her fingers.

Neither of them noticed Mark.

CHAPTER TWENTY-EIGHT

It wasn't long before I decided it was time to head out. The day had dragged on, and the exhaustion had finally caught up to me. I stood up, ready to make my exit. Gabe was still hovering over Ellie, his attention entirely focused on her.

I caught his eye, trying to signal it was time for me to pay and leave. "Hi, can I get my bill, please?" I asked.

He waved his hand casually at Tom, gesturing for him to take care of it, but Tom's face showed an exaggerated expression of disbelief, as if he couldn't believe Gabe had left him to handle this. I couldn't help but chuckle to myself.

As I was leaving, I stopped at the large white marble entryway, where the hostess stood. She was a younger girl, one I saw fairly often, and she had mentioned in the past that she wanted to work in real estate. We chatted about how her summer classes were going.

After several minutes, I finally made my way out the front door, stepping into the evening air. The walkway curved gently toward the parking lot, the soft rustling of leaves filling the space with a quiet calm. As I neared my car, I reached into my pockets and immediately realized I'd forgotten my key fob on the bar.

"Oh no," I muttered, turning back without hesitation. I started walking quickly toward the restaurant. But halfway back, I spotted Tom striding toward me with a grin on his face, the key fob in his hand.

"I have it for you!" he called out with a wide smile.

I laughed, relieved. "Oh, thank you!"

He handed it over, then gave a subtle nod toward the side of the parking lot.

"What's that?" I asked, curiosity piqued.

"Over there." He nodded again, more emphatically this time.

I glanced in the direction he was pointing and saw Ellie and Gabe at Ellie's car. They'd parked in the overflow lot, which was usually a bit quieter than the main lot.

I frowned, piecing it together. "They must have slipped out a side or back door right after I left," I said, trying to make sense of it all.

Tom shrugged, shaking his head slightly. "They went out the banquet door, I think. Probably so no one would notice them."

"You know," Tom remarked next, his eyes fixed on them with a look that bordered on wary, "whatever's going on between those two ... it's been happening a lot longer than you think. I don't trust her. I don't trust either of them. There's just something off—like the air shifts when they walk into a room."

He hesitated, lowering his voice. "Please don't say

anything. I mean it. I try to stay out of their way, keep to myself. But they're always ... circling. Like they've got something to hide."

"You don't have to worry," I said, giving him a steady, knowing look. "Your secret's safe with me. And for what it's worth—I feel the same. There's something slippery about them. Always has been."

My mind immediately started racing. There was so much to fill Mark in on. I couldn't help but wonder if he would be surprised by what was happening right now.

I didn't say much more, but my thoughts were buzzing. I didn't want to seem obvious, but my curiosity was getting the best of me.

"I'd better get going, before they see me staring, but thanks, Tom," I added with a forced casualness.

I started walking back toward my car, but I couldn't resist glancing over my shoulder, just slightly. Ellie and Gabe were still standing by her car, talking closely. He leaned in, and I could see his lips move toward hers. She didn't pull away. I tried not to stare, but the temptation was too much.

As I slid into my car, I gave them one last look before I drove forward a few inches to see more clearly. From a distance, between the rows of parked cars, I could still make out their figures. My eyes squinted as I tried to focus, my heart hammering in my chest. What was going on here? Was Ellie really doing this while Mark was inside? I wondered for a moment if she even knew he was there?

They kept kissing, and there were occasional pauses as they spoke to each other. She eventually got into her car, and Gabe headed toward the back of the restaurant, as though nothing out of the ordinary had occurred.

Ellie drove off, leaving me behind. I lingered for a few minutes, not wanting to follow too closely, but not wanting to be too far behind her either. As I drove home, I tried to push the intrusive, confusing thoughts out of my head. When I pulled into my driveway, I glanced over at Ellie's house. Her garage door was still open, likely waiting for Mark to come home.

Just as I was about to walk into the house, my phone rang. It was Mark. I figured he must've been finishing up at Blue's.

"Did you see my wink?" he asked, his voice full of humor.

I couldn't help but giggle. "You're so cute," I said, smiling into the phone.

"You will have to fill me in on Ellie and the bartender guy, but I wanted to call and say hi quickly."

"I will," I replied.

His tone shifted slightly. "I really miss you. I only have a couple more minutes before I turn onto our street."

"It's okay," I replied softly, my voice warm. "I'll see you tomorrow, and I can fill you in then."

There was a pause before he responded, his words laced with affection. "Yeah, I can't wait ... to see you, I mean."

And as I hung up, I couldn't shake the strange feeling in my chest. There was so much going on, and so much left unsaid.

The next morning, I decided to stay and work from home, knowing it would give me the privacy I needed for an important phone call. It was the perfect setup. My first showing wasn't until eleven, so I'd have plenty of time to call Bennett before leaving. I knew I'd need every second of that time, especially with the busy day I had ahead. I was hoping—no, *praying*—that today's showing would bring in an offer. The pressure of it all was starting to weigh on me, and I could feel the tension creeping into my chest. There was just so much on my plate, and I hadn't even really begun yet.

As I sat in my office, I glanced at the time. It was nearly ten. I reached up to turn off the TV, ensuring there'd be no unwanted noise in the background while I spoke. My fingers hovered over the phone, and then I dialed his number. The conversation started casually, but I could hear the slight tension in his voice. He told me that he and Ellie had made plans to meet up that evening at seven in a coffee shop tucked away inside a grocery store on the other side of town. I nodded as I listened, picturing the location in my mind—it was the same general area where I'd met him the day before.

We confirmed the details of his plan, and he told me that he'd call me again at nine in the evening to fill me in on what had happened. I knew I had to hold it together until then.

Once our conversation ended, I refocused on the day ahead. My showing was close, and it was the second showing of a house the couple had already walked through. I was determined to make it go smoothly. The couple I'd been working with—particularly the husband, who had a reputation for being impossible to please—had finally agreed on a house. And not just any house, but one they had been eyeing for a while. They'd gone over their budget by a pretty significant margin, but it was clear they were in love with the place and wanted to walk through it one more time.

Their final offer came in at a whopping $2.4 million, which was much higher than I'd anticipated, especially given how picky they had been. The house itself was situated in another upscale gated community, just down the road from where I lived. My emotions were a whirlwind after that, and I couldn't wait to share the good news with Mark tonight.

I parked in my usual spot outside Mark's office around half-past six in the evening, after which I tried to steady my nerves. This was the calm before the storm, the quiet moment before everything got a lot more complicated. After taking a breath, I got out of my car and made my way up to his door, tapping lightly before entering. As soon as I stepped inside, my heart skipped a beat. Mark was sitting at his desk, his presence commanding as always. But tonight, he looked different—more relaxed. His shirt was untucked, the buttons left carelessly open, and his tie was lying lazily across his desk, as though he'd just shrugged it off in the middle of work.

For a moment, I was lost in the sight of him—his posture, the way his sleeves were rolled up just enough to show the muscles in his forearms. My mind instantly went back to all the times we'd been together, the sparks between us impossible to ignore. I'd had a million things to think about today, but now, as I stood there in the doorway, it was as if all my thoughts were overtaken by him. His presence alone was enough to make my heart race.

"Hey, there," I said, my voice soft but full of emotion.

He looked up from his computer, a smile lighting his eyes. But even though he was right there, I couldn't help but feel distracted by everything that had already happened recently. The real world—full of deals and secrets and the things I needed to sort out—was closing in on me, but at that moment, all I could think about was how much I wanted to be with him.

CHAPTER TWENTY-NINE

I wasn't about to let the moment slip by unnoticed. Walking over to his desk, I leaned casually against it, positioning myself in a way that was both seductive and mysterious. Today, there was too much to talk about.

"I have a lot of information for you," I said, my tone deliberately serious, as I watched him intently.

He didn't stop typing.

I felt a surge of determination welling up inside me. This wasn't the time for games or veiled hints. I needed to get straight to the point.

"I have a lot of information from the private investigator about Ellie," I said, my voice steady but firm, making sure he understood the import of what I was about to say.

That caught his attention. He stopped typing midsentence, his posture shifting from casual to alert. His eyes were now fixed on me, his brows furrowing in curiosity.

Without hesitation, I plunged forward. "I met with the private investigator. He told me that Ellie had hired him because she suspected you might be cheating on her."

The words hung in the air for a moment. Mark stood up abruptly, his face flushing with a mix of anxiety and disbelief. He looked like a man who'd been caught in the middle of a storm, and it was written all over his face.

"WHAT?" His voice had a nervous edge, the reality of being exposed clearly sinking in.

I took a steadying breath, moving closer to him. "It's okay," I reassured him softly, trying to ease his panic. "I talked to the investigator and told him I would match whatever Ellie was paying him, and then I offered him more on top of that. A *lot* more."

I reached out to place a hand gently on his arm, hoping to offer some comfort. His shoulders began to relax, and he sighed deeply in relief.

"I mean, I know she's a horrible person," he said, pacing now, his steps quick and restless. "But I just don't want any of this to come out. I'd rather end the marriage quietly, without anyone knowing about this."

I nodded, understanding the gravity of his concerns. I'd seen the toll Ellie's behavior had taken on him. "I know," I said, my voice calm and assuring. "Trust me, we are fine."

But then, I couldn't help but add, "There's more."

Mark stopped pacing, his eyes narrowing with apprehension. He was trying to brace himself.

"What?" he asked, his voice edged with worry.

I could see the wheels turning in his mind, so I delivered the next part with precision. "There are two things. First, Ellie's meeting with him again tonight. The investigator is going to dig deeper into what she's really up to. He said that when they had first met, she was drinking heavily and acting really odd. She kept alluding to some hidden secret.'"

I paused for a moment, letting the words sink in. "It seems like he thought she was acting ... bizarre," I added, my tone a little hesitant.

The atmosphere in the room shifted. The romantic energy that had once existed between us was now replaced with a tension I couldn't ignore. The intimacy of the moment had faded into something much more serious, a reminder that this was real life—and real lives were at stake.

"He's going to call me tonight to let me know what happens during their conversation. Trust me, I'm paying him well," I continued, trying to diffuse the tension.

Mark's eyes narrowed, and he crossed his arms. "How do you know you can trust him?" he asked, his voice still filled with doubt.

"I can trust him," I replied confidently. "I had a good feeling about him. I know that doesn't sound like much, but I could tell he liked me. He seemed genuine."

Mark took a long, deep breath, his hands moving to his hips as he stood still, staring off into the distance. His mind seemed to be racing in a hundred different directions, and I could see the conflict within him.

"I don't get it," I said, my voice softer now, trying to reach him. "Look at you. Look at what she's done to you. This is horrible."

I moved closer to him, my voice quiet but insistent as I continued. "I know what she has done is horrible, but I don't want to get caught."

Mark looked at me, his face filled with frustration and fear. "Trust me, I don't want to get caught either," he admitted. "But you're right. She's horrible."

"We just can't have this coming out like that," he

added, walking over to me, his expression pained. "My job, your job, our reputation in this town ... I would feel horrible if all this came spilling out. People would start talking. And I just ... I don't want that kind of stress."

I nodded, understanding his concerns all too well. "I know," I said, my voice steady but filled with empathy. "We need to figure out a way to make this work—the right way."

Mark seemed lost in thought for a moment, his eyes distant. "Should I talk with the investigator too? I mean, I can offer him even more money," he asked, rubbing his chin.

"If you want to," I replied, my gaze meeting his. "But I've given you a lot of information so far. I'm going to wait for his call, and then I'll set up a time for us all to meet. This whole thing is just ... bizarre. Why would she bring Bennett on board while physically doing this to you? The only explanation I can come up with is that, in some twisted way, she's trying to justify it to herself—like if she balances one wrong with a 'right,' it somehow makes it all okay in her mind."

"Oh, baby," Mark said, his voice filled with a mix of exhaustion and frustration. He walked over to me, his hands gently massaging the top of my shoulders as I sat perched on the edge of his desk. "I feel like this is a lot to take in. Not exactly the most romantic thing to talk about."

I smiled softly, my heart aching for him. "It's okay," I reassured him, my voice warm. "We'll get through this. Together."

Despite the heaviness of the conversation, I could still feel the pull between us. This moment, though filled with tension, was ours to navigate, and I had no doubt we'd face whatever came next—together.

"I need to figure out a way to handle this, to do it the right way," he added, his voice filled with determination. It was clear he was wrestling with the need to make the right decisions, both for his own peace of mind and for any future life we could have together.

Mark's eyes softened, his expression shifting as he offered me his hand. "Come on," he said gently. "Let's go sit on the couch. Do you want a glass of wine? I think we could both use something to take the edge off."

I nodded gratefully. "Yeah, that would be great."

We moved near the couch, and I took a moment to light the fireplace. The warmth of the flames was soothing in his cool office. I didn't even really care about the heat it provided as much as I cared about the ambiance it created —the soft glow of the fire flickering in the dimly lit room, the crackling sound a welcome distraction from the chaos in our minds.

Mark poured the wine with a practiced hand, the crystal glass catching the light just right as he handed it to me. "Here, baby," he said, his voice softer now.

I took the glass from him, appreciating the gesture. "Thank you," I said, my eyes meeting his as I sipped the wine. The warmth of it slid down my throat, helping me feel a little more at ease in the moment.

"The fire is really nice," he commented, sitting down in the corner of the couch. "I'm glad you lit it. It makes everything feel ... calmer, more relaxed."

I smiled, settling in closer to the spot next to him. I leaned my head on his chest, feeling his heartbeat beneath my ear, and for a moment, everything seemed to fade into the background. We were here together, and that's what mattered most to me.

But the silence that stretched between us felt heavy. The conversation we just had wasn't something we could just let go of—it was still lingering, unfinished. And something else had been bothering me, something I couldn't shake.

"Another horrible thing to bring up," I said softly, my voice hesitant as I pulled away slightly to look at him. "But did you realize … we didn't even talk about the other thing?"

Mark's gaze shifted to mine, the realization dawning on him. "I did," he said, his tone serious. "But right now, it feels like everything else is already so overwhelming. I'm just trying to keep it together."

I could see the conflict in his eyes, the tension still there. This was real life—no romantic getaway, no simple solution. We had each other, but we were also tangled in a mess that needed sorting out. And the "other thing" between us had been pushed aside, too complicated to address just yet.

But even as we sat there, with the fire crackling softly and the wine mellowing our nerves, I knew one thing for sure: I was happy to be here with him.

CHAPTER THIRTY

I let out a slow breath, savoring the quiet warmth of Mark's embrace before finally pushing myself upright. His chest had been a steady, comforting place to rest, but now, reality was creeping back in.

"The guy at the bar she was with ..." I began, my voice soft but steady.

Mark took a slow sip of his wine, his eyes still fixed on the flickering flames. "Who is he?" he asked, his tone unreadable.

I exhaled, choosing my words carefully. "He works there. His name is Gabe. You probably noticed when you saw her flirting with him behind the bar." I paused for a moment, searching his face for any reaction, but he simply swished around the deep red liquid in his glass.

"Not too long ago, when we were out by the pool, I saw them together after I left. As time went on, it seemed innocent at first—just harmless talking, then it became little glances, a brushing of hands here and there. But last night ... last night was different." I swallowed, the memory sharp in my mind. "I saw the way she touched him. It wasn't just flirting anymore. She was rubbing his arm, getting too close. That's when I texted you. I wanted you to see it too."

I hesitated, knowing what I was about to say would only twist the knife deeper. "I stopped to talk to the hostess for a little while. When I finally headed out to the parking lot, they must have slipped out the side door together. And that's when I saw it in the parking lot." I was nervous to say the words out loud. "They were in the side lot, by her car. Kissing."

Mark let out a long exhale, tilting his head back against the couch. His expression was hard to read—he wasn't shocked, but he wasn't unaffected either.

"Huh," he finally muttered.

Then, after a moment of silence, he straightened up and murmured, almost to himself, "I need to figure out what to do next."

I frowned. "What do you mean?"

His eyes found mine, and despite the turmoil I knew was brewing inside him, he gave my hand a reassuring squeeze. "Don't worry, baby," he said gently, offering a small smile that didn't quite reach his eyes.

He stood up, leaving his empty wine glass behind. "Another glass?" he asked over his shoulder.

I shook my head. "No, I'm good. I have to drive."

He nodded absentmindedly, but instead of pouring more wine, he reached for the bourbon, opting for something much stronger. I watched as he filled a bourbon glass with ice, then poured a generous amount of amber liquid over it. The weight of what I'd just told him was sinking in, and he needed something to brace himself against it.

"Do you want to ... take a break ... from us?" I asked

hesitantly, not sure if he was having second thoughts about everything.

His answer was immediate. "No, no," he said, shaking his head. "I don't."

But there was something else behind his eyes. He walked back to the couch, his bourbon in hand, and sat down beside me. "I just have to figure out how to get us out of this," he murmured, staring into his glass.

I could feel the news pressing down on him. "I know I want to be with you," he continued, shifting his gaze back to me. "I'm just ... figuring out how to make this work."

I squeezed his hand.

But then his expression darkened. He hesitated for a long moment before speaking again. "Like I said ... you don't know her." His voice was lower now, almost hollow. "She's evil."

The word sent a shiver through me.

He took another sip of bourbon before setting the glass down. "She wasn't always like this. I found out a lot of things after we got married. But she ... she went through things. Horrible things." He exhaled, his fingers running through his hair. "Her dad. Her uncle. Her grandpa."

I froze. "What?" My breath hitched.

He nodded grimly. "It was bad. The only real confirmation I ever had was from her cousin. I got to know her at some out-of-town holiday gathering. A couple of years ago, at Thanksgiving, Ellie's cousin got drunk—too drunk to keep the family secrets. She let it slip."

I swallowed hard, not sure I wanted to hear what came next.

"There was a huge uproar," Mark continued, his voice quiet but steady. "But her cousin's story lined up exactly with what Ellie had told me in the past. It all happened in a camper, parked in the grandpa's driveway. He would abuse them. And then their dads would, too."

I felt my stomach twist. "That's horrible ..." I whispered.

Mark sighed, rubbing his temple. "It doesn't excuse everything. But it explains a lot."

For the first time, I saw something in his eyes I hadn't expected—pity. A flicker of understanding for a woman who had caused him so much pain.

But even with that, I knew one thing for certain. This wasn't over. Not yet.

My gaze drifted to the wall as I tried to process everything he had just told me. My mind was spinning, struggling to find the right words.

"I mean, it explains her aggressiveness, but ..." I trailed off, shaking my head.

Mark let out a slow breath, then lifted the hem of his shirt slightly, revealing faint bruises along his arm and scratches that trailed over his skin. "I know. I can't live like this," he said simply, his voice weighted with exhaustion. "Look at my back. My arms."

I swallowed hard, my chest tightening at the sight. I had known things were bad, but seeing the marks made it feel all too real.

"I begged her to get help," he continued, stepping away from me and heading toward the bar cart. "She wouldn't." His movements were slow, deliberate as he walked over to pour himself another bourbon. The ice clinked softly against the glass, the sound sharp in the quiet room.

I could see the tension in his shoulders, the distant look in his eyes. He was trying to hold everything together, but I could feel him unraveling.

"I can go," I offered gently, not wanting to overwhelm him any more than he already was. "It's been a lot. Do you need space?"

Mark turned sharply, setting his drink down with a soft thud and nestling back into the couch. "No." His voice was firm, almost desperate. He reached for my hand, his fingers wrapping around mine, his grip warm and steady. "Please, don't go. You're the only thing right in my life."

The sincerity in his eyes made my heart ache. I let out a breath and leaned back into him, letting his warmth surround me.

"I loved being out of town with you," he murmured, pressing a soft kiss to my hair. "Holding you in bed, waking up with you next to me. It felt ... real." He hesitated, then added in a whisper, "You know, I really mean it when I say I love you."

I looked up at him, my chest tightening at the vulnerability in his voice. "I know you do," I said softly. "I love you too."

Mark exhaled, his expression relaxing for the first time all evening. "Today was a lot," he admitted.

"It was," I agreed.

He glanced at the fire, his thumb tracing slow circles against the back of my hand. "This," he said after a long pause, "is nice. Just sitting here with you. Just us."

I nodded, sinking further into him. "I wish I could just fall asleep right here," he murmured. "Even if it's just on the couch with you." We lingered there for a long while, wrapped in the quiet hush between us, trying to let the stillness settle our minds.

His words made my heart ache for him. The thought of

him lying awake at night, carrying all this weight alone, made me want to hold him tighter.

"I wonder if we should meet somewhere else for a while?" I asked hesitantly, the thought suddenly gnawing at me. "Just to be safe. I mean ... what if Ellie even showed up here?"

Mark tensed slightly at the thought but nodded. "Yeah, we can do that." He took a sip of his drink, his jaw tightening for a moment before he spoke again. "I don't think she would, though. She hates my job. She hates my office, my coworkers, and everything about what I do. She's always looked down on it, made snide comments, and refused to come to work events." He let out a dry, humorless chuckle. "I'm sure she acted differently in front of you, though. Played the supportive wife."

I raised my brows, surprised. "Wow. I had no idea."

Mark exhaled. "Yeah. She never had anything good to say. Not to me, at least."

"I still think it's a good idea to lay low for a while," I said, absentmindedly toying with the hem of his shirt. "Just until things settle."

He nodded again. "I'll have to think of a spot where we can meet."

I sighed, glancing at the clock. "I should get going." Mark's expression softened as he turned toward me.

"Oh, before I forget," I added, "I didn't even tell you my good news." I sat up a little, a proud smile tugging at my lips. "I sold a house today."

His face lit up, his mood instantly shifting. "Yeah?"

"Two point four million," I said, grinning.

Mark let out an impressed whistle and raised his hand for a high five. I laughed and met it with my own.

"That is some good news I needed to hear," he said, his smile finally reaching his eyes. "I'm really happy for you."

The warmth in his voice made me feel lighter, even after everything we had talked about. Time had slipped away, and I was cautiously watching the clock, knowing Bennett would be calling soon.

As I drove home, the hum of the road beneath my tires was the only sound filling the quiet car. My mind was still buzzing with everything that had happened tonight—especially Mark's pain.

Then, my phone rang.

I glanced at the screen before answering.

"I'm calling with an update," said Bennett.

CHAPTER THIRTY-ONE

"Well, thanks for calling," I said. As I was driving through the nearly dark streets, I was listening intently, every muscle tense, waiting for Bennett to say whatever was on his mind.

"We need to talk," Bennett's voice came through the phone, urgent but controlled, like he was trying to sound calm but couldn't quite manage it. His tone made my stomach do a little flip.

"I've got a closing in the morning, but I can meet you at eleven if that works," I replied quickly, glancing at the clock on the dashboard. My schedule was packed, but this felt important.

"Same place?" I asked, knowing he would know exactly which place I meant.

"Yes," he answered, but there was a pause before he added, "That's in the same area of town where I met Ellie. Are you sure you want to meet there?"

I thought about it for a moment. "Yeah, I don't think

anyone's even going to be there. I'm not worried about running into anyone I know." I felt sure about this. My gut said I would be fine. The place was small, quiet, and out of the way—nothing to worry about.

Bennett let out a small sigh, as if relieved I wasn't having second thoughts. "Ellie and I actually had to move to another spot when I met her," he said, his voice sounding more serious now.

"What? What happened?" I asked, my curiosity piqued. This didn't sound like something I expected.

"We were at a little coffee shop inside the bookstore in the same area," he said. "But then Ellie saw someone she recognized from her neighborhood. She didn't hesitate—got up in a hurry and told me we needed to meet at a new spot." He trailed off.

"Wait—where?" I interrupted, eager for more details.

"Uh ... somewhere north. I can't remember the name exactly, but we left quickly," he explained.

"Well, trust me, I'm not worried about running into anyone we know where you and I are meeting. There's no way. That place is so low-key, nobody's even going to know we're there," I assured him. I had no reservations about our spot.

Bennett seemed to relax at that, his voice taking on a more casual tone. "All right, I'll meet you there. Let's aim for the same booth as before, yeah?"

I smiled a little, appreciating the familiarity of our routine. "Same booth."

After ending the call with Bennett, I immediately dialed Mark's number, knowing I still had a few more minutes until he was home. As soon as he answered, I jumped into the update. "I'm meeting with Bennett tomorrow morning. The private investigator. He just called me."

"Oh, okay," Mark responded; it sounded like he was in his car. "Do you want me to come with you?"

I hesitated for a split second before answering. "You can, if you want," I said, my mind already moving in a million directions at once.

"I'll check my calendar and let you know in the morning if I've got any meetings," he said.

"Sounds good," I replied, trying to sound casual, though the tightness in my chest told me I wasn't feeling all that calm. I was anxious about everything—Bennett's worried tone, the meeting tomorrow, and the way my life was feeling a little too out of control lately.

"By the way," I said, blowing out a breath like I was preparing to dive into a difficult conversation, "I'll probably have to bring Bennett more money."

"Yeah, I know," Mark said. "Let me know how much you give him, and I'll pay you back."

I could hear the slight frustration in his voice, though he was trying to mask it. It wasn't about the money, not really. I knew it was everything else—the stress, the unknowns, the constant moving pieces of our lives.

"Don't worry about it. I just wanted you to know I am bringing him more money to secure his alliance with us," I said, trying to sound reassuring.

The weight of everything started to settle back on me, a familiar heaviness. I needed to take a moment to breathe, to center myself, but there was no time.

"I've got a closing in the morning," I said, trying to lighten the mood a little. "And after that, I'll meet Bennett.

It's been dragging on for over a month, but tomorrow's finally the day for the closing."

Mark sounded genuinely happy for me, despite everything else. "That's great! I didn't know you had a closing coming up. I know you just wrote an offer on another house too. Seems like things are picking up for you."

His excitement for me, even in the midst of everything, reminded me of why I loved him. He could still make me feel like there was something to celebrate, even when it felt like the world was closing in.

"It's the one on Pinnacle Court. It's been a long road, but I'm excited it's finally closing tomorrow."

"That's amazing," Mark said, his voice warm and affectionate. "If I don't have any meetings, I'll let you know if I can make it with the private investigator. Love you, baby."

I could hear the tenderness in his words, and it grounded me just a little.

"I love you too," I replied softly, feeling the weight of the day slowly lift as I let myself imagine that moment when it would all fall into place.

The next morning, I couldn't shake the feeling of anticipation as I got ready. The thought of what Bennett was going to say weighed heavily on my mind. I had no idea what to expect, and that uncertainty gnawed at me.

Arriving at the closing, however, did lift my spirits a little. There's something about finality, the end of one chapter and the promise of a new one, that always brings relief. As I walked into the office, the air seemed a bit lighter, and though I was still wrestling with nerves, I could feel the tension in my shoulders easing. While I was in the middle of the closing, a message from Mark lit up my phone screen. He confirmed what I had suspected—he did, in fact, have a meeting that morning and wouldn't be able to make it to the meeting with Bennett. I sighed quietly, setting the phone back down on the table, already preparing myself to handle Bennett solo.

A couple of hours later, I walked out with a thick stack of paperwork tucked securely in my bag. The deal was done. I had closed it. I felt like I could breathe easily. No more hoops to jump through, no more dealing with the endless back-and-forth that's part of real estate deals. This was a win. My next stop was the bank to get some cash for Bennett.

After the bank, I headed toward the bar. The dry, cracked earth kicked up little clouds of dust as I rolled in. I cringed slightly at the sight—dust on my car wasn't ideal, but there was nothing I could do about it. I parked and paused before getting out. My hand instinctively reached over to the glove compartment, and I pulled out the white envelope I had just stuffed with cash. My fingers brushed the edges as I held it for a second, and a small rush of nerves stirred inside me.

I slipped in through the back door and found the quiet booth close to the door. I settled in, trying to blend in as much as possible, since the last thing I wanted was attention. The hum of the bar filled the air around me, the clink of glasses and soft laughter in the background, but all of it felt distant. I was already anticipating the conversation.

A few minutes later, Bennett walked in. I caught sight of

him right away. But I stayed still, making sure not to draw any attention. The less I was noticed, the better.

Bennett sat down across from me, his face unreadable. The air between us thickened with unspoken words, and I took a deep breath, bracing myself for whatever he was about to say.

"We need to talk, young lady," Bennett started, his voice low and serious.

Before I could respond, the waitress appeared at our table, cutting through the tension. We ordered drinks quickly, the motions automatic. Once she left, the silence returned.

"Please," I said, leaning in slightly. My voice was steady, but my heart raced with the need to know what he had to say. "Tell me what happened."

Bennett didn't hesitate. His gaze hardened as he began speaking again. "Typically, when I take on an investigation, it's for someone who suspects their spouse might be cheating, background checks, fraud, and other things like that. It's straightforward—nothing out of the ordinary. But with Ellie, well ... this is different. Even when she wasn't drinking, there was something raw, something primal in her. Over and over, she kept saying how much she hated her husband, Mark. It wasn't just anger, though. It was rage—a dangerous kind of rage. You could see it in her eyes, hear it in her voice. This wasn't just a fight between spouses. This was something much darker."

He folded his hands on the table and looked at me, as though he were trying to gauge my reaction. He was clearly concerned, maybe even worried for me. Whatever was happening with Ellie and Mark wasn't just messy—it was potentially dangerous.

I sat there, silent. My gaze drifted to the table, my fingers absentmindedly tracing the rim of my glass. I needed time to process all this, to truly absorb what I had just heard.

For a moment, I thought about how different this situation might be if Mark were here. If he could hear this, too. If he could feel the same urgency, the same sense of danger that Bennett seemed to think was looming over us. It might be easier to make him see reason, to confront the truth head-on, if he were present.

Bennett finally broke the silence, his voice steady but filled with a seriousness that sent a chill down my spine.

"Listen," he said, leaning forward slightly, his hands resting firmly on the table. "I'm not trying to tell you what to do. But if there's anything going on between you and 'the Mister'—" he paused, his words hanging in the air like a warning. "You might want to lie low for a while. This woman, Ellie, doesn't seem like someone you want to cross. If she finds out what's going on, she could do a lot of harm."

His eyes locked with mine, making it impossible to look away. There was no mistaking the intensity of his gaze, the seriousness in his tone. His instincts, it seemed, were telling him something far worse than I had initially imagined. Ellie —this woman I thought I knew—was capable of much more than I had ever given her credit for. The realization hit me hard. I had always known there was something off about her, but this ... this was darker than I had anticipated.

I felt my heart rate quicken, a mix of fear and disbelief thrumming in my chest. This wasn't the Ellie I knew. The Ellie I had spoken with, the one who laughed at my jokes and shared stories over drinks—she didn't seem like the type to harbor such destructive rage. But Bennett's words stuck with me, gnawing at me. There was something here I couldn't ignore, no matter how much I wanted to.

"So, what else?" I asked, my voice steadier than I felt. "What should I do—I mean other than lie low with Mark?"

I wanted answers, wanted to know what the next step was, and what I was supposed to do with this newfound knowledge.

CHAPTER THIRTY-TWO

"I have an idea. It's worked before," Bennett said with an air of confidence, but then he paused, his fingers drumming lightly on the table. "Well, I think it could work," he added, almost as if second-guessing himself, before finally leaning in a little closer. "First, let me fill you in on what Ellie and I talked about."

I sat back, waiting patiently, knowing that I would need to absorb every detail.

"She told me that she suspects her husband, Mark, of cheating on her," Bennett continued in a heavier voice. "She asked if I could help figure it out—get to the bottom of it, you know? She needed some answers. And I agreed. Of course." He let out a slight chuckle.

I nodded, my mind already starting to list the questions I would ask once he was finished.

Bennett's voice lowered just a bit, as if he were sharing something he knew to be important. "She gave me the rundown on where he works, where he golfs, and even the restaurant he frequents at the golf course. She said he spends most of his time between those few places, other than home. So, it seems like those are the key spots to watch."

I could already see the wheels turning in Bennett's head. He operated like a detective, methodical and precise.

"I told her I'd keep an eye on his office," Bennett went on, "watch for when he comes and goes, follow him if necessary—the usual routine for us." His eyes flicked toward me, and I could sense his focus sharpening. "I also told her she'll need to keep me posted on the days when he's playing golf or going out to dinner. Those are the details we'll need—the where, the when. I'm assuming that's the same golf club I met you at?"

"Yes, it is," I replied, trying to keep my expression neutral.

For a brief moment, I caught myself thinking about Mark's office, about the last time I'd walked in there. It was strange, knowing that Bennett could have been sitting outside in his car, waiting. I imagined myself walking into the back courtyard door, glancing toward the parking lot, and seeing Bennett's car parked there. I waved to him in my mind, but quickly shook the thought away.

"Do you have any questions for me?" Bennett asked, pulling me back into the conversation.

I exhaled slowly before asking, "Did she say why she thinks he's cheating on her?"

Bennett leaned back, resting his hands on the table. "She mentioned that he's been staying late at work a lot more recently. And, of course, she said she can't go to his work—it wouldn't be good if someone saw her there. Sounds like she never really goes there. Makes sense."

I nodded in agreement, understanding the implications. "Yeah, she's got a point there," I said, the pieces of the puzzle starting to fit together in my mind.

Bennett didn't seem to be done, though. He looked like he had more to say. "There's something else. I can tell from the way she talks and from her restless behavior that she's hiding something. There was a flicker in her eyes—sharp, defensive, almost haunted—and her voice crackled with a kind of anger that didn't feel entirely honest. It was the kind of tone that suggested she was swallowing something heavy, forcing it down so no one could see. But it was there, just beneath the surface. Whatever it was—whether it was her past or a decision she hadn't yet acted on—it was coiled tightly inside her. Maybe it was both. I am really puzzled as to why she even hired me if she is up to something more," he said before taking a long sip of his soda.

I watched him closely, knowing that his gut instincts were most likely right. "So, what's the next step?"

Bennett looked around for a second, as if ensuring no one else was listening in, then leaned in closer, lowering his voice. "Here's what I think we should do. I've got a partner I work with. A good-looking younger guy—probably just a little older than you two. We can ask him to get close to Ellie, maybe take her out for drinks, and see if he can get her talking. I've been doing this a long time, and let me tell you, there's definitely something going on with her. We just need to dig a little deeper."

I felt a knot form in my stomach. The idea of using someone to get close to Ellie felt ... unsettling. But I pushed the feeling aside for the moment and tried to look at the bigger picture.

"So, you're suggesting your partner seduces her under-cover?" I asked, a hint of frustration in my voice. "What if she hasn't actually done anything concerning? What if this whole night ends up being a bust, and we don't find anything at all?"

Bennett's eyes narrowed as he leaned even closer, his voice dropping to a conspiratorial whisper. "She told me that if her husband *is* cheating, she's going to get back at him. And she's been planning something for a long time anyway—something for all the crap he's put her through over the years."

I leaned back, the weight of his words settling in. Things from the past had been buried, and now they were surfacing. What had Mark done? What secrets were they both hiding? I felt my thoughts spiral. Maybe it would be better if Mark were here. He might have better questions. More questions.

"All right," I said, after a long pause. "Let me think this over and check with someone to see if this is a good idea. I'll get back to you soon—tomorrow, for sure."

Bennett raised an eyebrow, as if he already knew who that "someone" was, but he didn't say anything. He just nodded, the corners of his mouth twitching into a smile.

I reached into my purse and pulled out a white envelope, heavy with cash. "Here," I said, handing it to him. "This is for you."

Bennett took it without hesitation. "Thank you," he replied quietly, tucking the envelope into his jacket with a practiced motion.

As I watched him, I couldn't help but wonder just how messy this situation was going to get. I'd have to see it through, no matter where it led.

"I'll be waiting for your call," Bennett said, his voice calm yet firm as he stood up from the booth. He paused, his hand on the booth edge. "And don't worry," he added with a reassuring smile, his tone steady and confident. "When she sends me out to check on her husband's office or the golf course, I'll make sure to tell her that I've found nothing. We'll keep it clean."

I nodded, feeling reassured by his words, even though what he said about Ellie still didn't sit right with me. "Thank you," I said.

As he exited, I took a deep breath. I had planned to sit quietly for a moment longer, giving him time to leave the bar first.

Eventually, I stood up and stepped into the blinding midday sunlight; the heat hit me like a wall. The car was like an oven, the air inside thick with warmth. I just sat there for a second, my fingers lightly gripping the steering wheel. I needed to talk to Mark. The questions were working overtime in my mind—what his part was in all this, what he knew, and what he didn't know. But the timing had to be right, and the last thing I wanted was to push him into a corner.

I pulled my phone from my bag and typed out a quick, simple message to Mark: *Call me when you get a minute.*

CHAPTER THIRTY-THREE

Mark's call came through just as I pulled into the office parking lot. I hesitated for a split second, then answered the phone on my Bluetooth, backing out of the space I had just parked in. I glanced around at the busy parking lot. The last thing I wanted was to talk to him here, with people wandering past and possibly overhearing something.

"I'm going to head home and work from there," I said, scanning the road as I slowly maneuvered the car out of the parking lot. "It's quieter there, and we can talk without interruptions or eavesdroppers."

"So, how did your closing go? Actually, wait—how did the meeting go with the private investigator?" Mark asked, his voice warm but filled with that ever-present curiosity of someone who wanted to know everything.

I let out a soft exhale, finally feeling the weight lift from my shoulders. "The closing went well," I said. "It took a while, but I'm just glad it's finally over. We'll have time to celebrate later. After the closing, I went straight to see the private investigator."

I could feel the tension in the air as Mark's attention sharpened. "And? What did you guys talk about?" he asked, his voice tight with concern, as if bracing for what I was about to say.

I took a breath, trying to stay calm as I navigated through the traffic. "It was ... a lot. Honestly, there's a lot more going on than we thought. He's really worried about Ellie. He thinks she's going to do something to hurt you. And he also mentioned something about her being angry over something that happened years ago."

Mark's voice tightened, the shock in his tone unmistakable. "What? What happened years ago?" His words were laced with disbelief, as if the idea was preposterous.

"I don't know," I replied, my grip tightening on the steering wheel. "But that's what he said. He's concerned. He says she's holding onto some kind of anger, something worrisome."

I could hear Mark exhale on the other end, the tension easing slightly, but I could sense that he still had questions. "This is a lot to take in. What else did he say?"

I braced myself for the next part. "Well, he has an idea. He's got a partner—a guy who's a few years older than Ellie and me, someone who could try to get closer to her. He wants to use him to kind of ... seduce her, get her talking, and see if he can find out anything more from her. I told him I'd get back to him soon, that I would need to check with you to see if that's a good option."

Mark's voice softened, an edge of concern cutting through his usually calm demeanor. "Take a breath," he said. "This is a lot. I know. Let's just figure this out one step at a time."

"You're right," I said, trying to calm my racing thoughts. I took a deep breath in, letting it out slowly. "I just ... this whole situation seems like it's getting out of control."

Mark's voice was steady. "Yeah, I get that. Let's meet soon to talk more about it—figure out what the next step is. Just not at my office, okay?"

I couldn't help but chuckle, the tension in the air lifting just a little. "Right. Not at your office," I replied. "I've got an idea."

Mark was quiet for a beat before responding. "I trust you. What's your idea?"

I took a moment to gather my thoughts, trying to work through the logistics. "Can you be done with work around 5:30? I can swing by and pick you up—just drive around back so no one sees us. We'll head to my house. I can keep a low profile, and we can talk privately."

Mark didn't hesitate. "Yeah, let's do that. No one will suspect anything, and your back car windows are slightly tinted anyway, so we'll be fine."

I felt a mix of excitement and anxiety at the plan. It was sneaky, but it was the kind of discretion we needed. "All right," I said, checking the clock on the dashboard. "I'll see you in a while."

I stayed home and worked the rest of the day. Time seemed to crawl as I watched the hands of the clock move slowly toward the designated meeting time. At last, I got in my car and drove to the back of his office, where I parked next to his car at exactly half-past five. I didn't want to risk arriving too early and becoming a sitting duck in my car, trapped while employees filed out, catching sight of me and wondering why I was just parked there.

I could feel my pulse quicken as I waited for him. Then, just as we had planned, Mark slipped into the backseat of the car. "All right, let's go," he said with a low chuckle, his eyes darting around before he settled into the seat.

"This is so sneaky," I muttered, driving off quickly, my hands steady on the wheel as I focused on the road ahead.

Mark tugged off his suit jacket, tossing it onto the backseat. His cologne filled the car immediately, rich and intoxicating. I could feel my senses heighten, my emotions stirred by the familiar scent. "We've got to be careful, though," Mark added, glancing around as we drove. "It's still light out, and we don't want anyone noticing."

"Good point," I said, my eyes scanning the neighborhood as we neared the entrance. "I'm getting ready to turn in. Can you duck down, just for a minute?"

"I'm already crouching down," he said with a slight laugh, clearly amused by the situation.

I turned into my neighborhood, feeling the tension rise as I approached my house. "She's home," I said, noticing Ellie's car parked in her garage.

"I figured she would be," Mark whispered, a trace of worry in his voice.

I pulled into the driveway, quickly hitting the garage door opener. The door rose slowly. Once inside, I lowered the garage door.

We got out, and Jax immediately bounded over to Mark, jumping up to greet him. I smiled despite myself, knowing this would be a good distraction for a moment.

"We should stay toward the back of the house," I suggested, setting my purse on the counter. "Just in case someone sees us through the front window. It's still light out."

Mark followed me without hesitation from the kitchen to the family room in the back of the house, the atmosphere between us feeling ... different now. It wasn't supposed to be like this, not under these circumstances. And yet, I couldn't deny the pull between us.

As if on cue, his arms reached out to pull me close. His touch was gentle but firm. "I'm so sorry for all of this," he whispered, his voice low and soothing.

"It will be fine," I whispered, resting my head against his chest, the warmth of his body pulling me in as I closed my eyes for a brief moment, just savoring the comfort of being close to him. His heartbeat was steady and reassuring, and for those few seconds, I let myself forget about everything else. He felt so right, like a safe haven amid all the turmoil.

Mark gently pulled me closer, his arms around me providing a sense of security that I didn't realize I needed so badly. "Can we just sit down somewhere?" His voice was low and almost tentative, as though he needed that space just as much as I did.

I nodded, my hand gently squeezing his as I pulled away slightly to look up at him. "Yeah, that sounds perfect."

I led him toward the large, cozy couch that faced my large backyard. The view was peaceful—no houses, just the quiet expanse of greenery and trees. It was one of the few places where I felt completely hidden.

"Would you like something to drink? Maybe a glass of wine?" I asked, offering a small moment of normalcy.

"That would be great," Mark replied, sounding relieved at the suggestion, as if a drink would somehow help us both clear our minds, even for just a moment.

I got up to fetch the wine. The glass felt cool in my hand

as I handed it to Mark and took a seat beside him again. I positioned myself close, leaning slightly into his warmth.

"So, let's get the weird part out of the way," I said softly, trying to sound casual, but I knew it was far from a simple topic. I turned my face toward Mark, searching his eyes for some sign of how he was dealing with everything.

"The private investigator wants to use a partner of his to find out more about Ellie," I began, my voice dropping even lower as I spoke. "He thinks she's really up to something as I was mentioning—something really bad."

Mark frowned, his brow furrowing as he processed the information. "What? Did he say why? What exactly does he think she's planning?"

I took a deep breath. "He said so many different things. Something he said that stood out to me was that Ellie told him you're going to get 'what's coming to you.'"

Mark's face went pale, and he let out a sharp breath. "That's insane," he said, his voice tight with disbelief. "That doesn't even make sense. Why would she say that?" He paused, his frustration rising. "What did I do that she is after me? Okay, don't answer that. I just heard myself. I mean, I know she doesn't know about us. If she did, we would know she did. Just have him use the other person. At this point, I just want to know what she's up to. What else is she planning to do to me?"

His tone shifted, anger bubbling beneath the surface. "You know what?" He leaned back against the couch, his jaw tightening. "I don't care anymore. I don't even care if we get caught. I don't want to be with her, not after everything she's done."

I could feel the weight of his frustration and the ache of

betrayal. But then, without warning, he shifted his posture, a flicker of something else in his eyes.

"I have to show you something," he said, his voice growing softer, but with a raw intensity that made my stomach twist. "I used to be embarrassed, but not anymore. Look—look at my arms," he added, his voice trembling with barely contained emotion. Without giving me a chance to react, Mark stood and unbuttoned his shirt, his fingers moving in quick, sharp motions.

He turned slightly, and that's when I saw it. On one side of his upper arm were four long, fresh gashes. They were deep, angry marks, the skin still red and swollen from the force of whatever had caused them. It was clear that they had been inflicted recently.

I gasped, my hand flying to my mouth. Mark's anger was palpable, but there was something else in his eyes, something fragile that I hadn't expected.

"I didn't touch her," he said, his voice thick with emotion as he tried to hold back a mixture of anger and something far darker, something I knew he was struggling to suppress. "I didn't do anything to her. But she ... she gets in these rages. She—" He stopped, his voice breaking for a moment.

I could see the humiliation in his eyes, the way his entire body seemed to sag under the weight of the emotions he was carrying. It was more than just the physical pain of the cuts; it was the anguish of feeling trapped in a situation that seemed to have no way out, of being branded with something he didn't even understand.

"I'm sorry," I whispered, moving toward him instinctively, reaching out to touch his arm, as though somehow that could make things right. But nothing could. Nothing could erase the pain, the anger, the confusion.

"I don't know what's happening anymore, but it seems to be getting worse," Mark muttered, his voice shaking as he wiped a hand across his face, trying to regain some composure. "But I swear, I didn't do anything to her."

CHAPTER THIRTY-FOUR

"Wow … just, wow!" I gasped, my voice trembling in utter disbelief as I looked at his arms again. My eyes widened as I shook my head, trying to process his words. "The cuts … they're so deep," I said, my voice faltering. Each word he spoke seemed to dig deeper into my heart.

He sighed heavily, his gaze drifting away from me as if trying to escape the haunting memories. "It was mostly her nails," he murmured, his voice low and thick with sorrow. "She would claw at me, like she wanted to carve into me, to leave marks that would never fade. There was this one time —" He trailed off, his eyes clouding over with a distant, pained look. "She grabbed something from the kitchen. Some gadget with a sharp edge. She kept hitting my back with it, and all I could do was try to grab her, to stop her, but she didn't care. She just kept screaming at me. Yelling and telling me it was my fault."

I could feel a lump in my throat as I struggled to hold back the tears. How could anyone do that to another person? How could he have endured such torment? His words left a pit in my stomach.

For a moment, I considered asking Mark about all the gardening she had mentioned—the same gardening she blamed for the state of her nails. But the thought faded as quickly as it came. This wasn't the time for questions or small talk. Right now, he didn't need curiosity—he needed someone to listen to him.

"I've never left a mark on her," he said quietly, his voice barely above a whisper. "I've never hurt her, not once. I just ... I just wanted her to stop."

The tragedy of it all weighed on me, and I found myself unable to say anything that might ease his pain. All I could manage was a simple, heartfelt reply. "This is ... so sad," I whispered, my voice thick with emotion.

He remained silent for a moment, his eyes fixed on the window as though he was looking for something—anything—that could offer him solace.

I couldn't help but wonder why things had gone this far, why he had been so trapped. "The police," I began, taking a deep breath as I looked up at him, my expression full of compassion. "If it was this bad ... why didn't you ever call them? Why didn't you try to get help?"

He froze, his body tense, and then he sighed, slowly turning toward me. "I didn't want a police report out there because of my job. I couldn't—" He paused, his face reddening slightly as if admitting a weakness he'd long buried. "I just couldn't bring myself to do it. I thought ... maybe no one would care. I did tell her one time I was going to call them to get her to stop. She cried, begged, and pleaded with me not to ... she said she would change. Of course, she didn't change. This happened many more times after that. It's her rage ... when she starts, there's no stopping her."

My heart ached for him as I watched him struggle with the shame that wasn't even his to carry. It broke my heart to see him so vulnerable, but I knew at that moment that this was what he needed most—someone to understand.

"We'll get the investigator to bring in someone else, someone who can help us uncover more of what's really going on. We'll find the truth, no matter what," I said softly.

He nodded slowly, as if the idea of action gave him a small sense of relief. Then, he made his way back toward the couch, his movements sluggish with exhaustion. He collapsed onto the large cushions, letting out a long breath as if all the air had been sucked from his body. His eyes closed for a moment, his face marked by fatigue.

After a while, he sat up a little and looked over at me with a small, tired smile. "Let's just enjoy the rest of the time we have, yeah?" he said in a soft voice, as though searching for some peace, even if just for a few hours.

I gave him a warm smile in return. "Yes, that sounds really good," I replied, reaching for my wine glass from which I took a slow, calming sip. The smooth taste was like a small comfort, and I felt the tension in my body ease just slightly.

I stood up and walked over to the large back windows, pulling the blinds shut. The soft evening light was gently fading away. The stillness of the room felt comforting.

"I think I'll light a few candles," I said. "Just to help us relax, you know?"

His eyes lit up, the exhaustion in his face momentarily fading as a smile crept across his lips. "Ah, that sounds amazing," he said, his voice warmer, more sincere now. "Come sit back down next to me."

I returned to the couch, settling beside him. As I stretched my legs across his lap, his strong hands gently brushed against my skin. His touch was tender but firm, as if grounding me in the moment. Slowly, he rubbed my legs, his hands moving from my ankles to my knees, offering a comfort that seemed to seep deep into my muscles.

The feeling of his hands on my legs was soothing, but it also sent a subtle spark through me. His touch lingered for a moment longer than usual, his fingers trailing higher, moving under the fabric of my dress, and I felt a new energy between us.

Then, without saying a word, his hand moved to my face, his fingers gently cupping my chin as he leaned in to kiss me. We shifted, lying down on the couch, our bodies aligning as if we were meant to be in this moment together.

His leg gently straddled mine, the weight of his body pressing against me as I pulled off his dress shirt, my fingers gliding over the fabric before it slipped off his shoulders. Our lips met again, fiercely now, each kiss more passionate than the last.

Afterward, I found myself lying against his chest. Our bodies entwined under the plush warmth of the expensive couch fabric, our skin still glowing with the remnants of the moment.

After thirty minutes of heavy kissing, I slowly pulled back from him.

"What time is it?" I asked, my voice groggy.

Mark stretched slowly beside me, groaning as he tried to shake off the sleepiness. "It's 7:30. Yeah, we should go."

As if on cue, my phone dinged, alerting me to the

outside camera. I glanced at the screen, hoping it wasn't anything urgent, but my stomach dropped when I saw the notification.

"Oh no," I muttered, my fingers trembling as I opened the screen. "It's Ellie. She's at the front door. What would she want?" I felt the anxiety rising in my chest.

Mark watched me, still half-dazed, as I frantically glanced around the room. My eyes flicked to the front of the house, making sure there was no way she could see where we were in the house through the front windows near the door. The last thing I needed was for her to catch us like this.

"Just slide over," I said, my voice a little shaky as I gestured toward the far corner of the room. I knew it didn't matter—Ellie couldn't see us from where she was standing—but the situation still felt awkward.

"I mean, I know she can't see us back here, but this is just ... really weird," I muttered, my mind racing as I scrambled to pull on my clothes. I tossed his shirt over to him, trying to calm myself.

Mark nodded, a smirk tugging at the corner of his lips, but I could tell he was equally perplexed by the sudden appearance of Ellie at the door. "Yeah, this is definitely ... odd."

I quickly grabbed my phone, trying to think of a plausible excuse, something to stall her without making things too awkward.

A plan began to form in my head. I started typing quickly, sending the text before I could second-guess myself.

> Hi, I see you on the front camera. I'm in a video meeting with all the other realtors in our office. This was the only time we could all get together. Can I call you in a little bit?

Ellie's reply came almost immediately.

> Yes, that works. It was so nice out I thought I'd just walk over instead of texting. Do you want to go to Blue's later? I think that hot guy Gabe is working. Mark is working late, so I thought you might want to go.

I watched through the camera feed on my phone as she began to slowly wander off the porch, heading down the path that led to the street. I let out a breath of relief.

> Sounds great. I'll call you when I get done with this meeting.

Ellie seemed satisfied with the excuse. She continued down the path, her figure growing smaller as she left the frame of the camera. I sat back down on the couch. My shoulders relaxed as the tension of the moment eased.

"Crisis averted ... but what is it with all these trips to Blue's lately? Oh, never mind. She mentioned that Gabe guy," I said, glancing at Mark. I couldn't help but laugh a little at how ridiculous the situation had been.

Mark chuckled warmly as he ran a hand through his hair. "I can't believe she showed up here. But I'm glad you knew how to handle it so quickly," he said, his voice still relaxed.

CHAPTER THIRTY-FIVE

"We need to leave, but not yet," I suggested, my voice carrying a hint of uncertainty. "It'll be way too obvious if we leave now. Maybe in about twenty minutes? That should be okay."

"Yeah, sure," Mark replied, his tone strangely calm, almost too relaxed for the situation.

"You don't seem nearly as nervous as I feel," I said, hurriedly pulling my clothes back on. My hands were trembling as I buttoned my shirt.

"I guess I've just come to terms with it," he said with a shrug, pulling his pants on slowly, as though he had all the time in the world. "I've been wanting out of the marriage for a while now, so what does it really matter?"

I sighed, half in frustration and half in understanding. "I get it, but we still need to stay low-key. Lay low, you know? I just ... want to know more about what's going on with her." My mind was still racing. I couldn't shake the feeling that things were getting more complicated by the minute.

"Wow, you're even beautiful when you're anxious," he said, flashing a cheeky grin that momentarily lightened the tension in the room.

I couldn't help but giggle, though it was more nervous than anything. "Ha, ha, not the time for jokes, Mark," I replied with a wink, trying to hold it together. "When she texted me, she mentioned wanting to go to Blue's tonight, since Gabe is working," I continued, adjusting my clothes, my mind still running frantically.

"Huh," Mark responded with a dull indifference, as though her name didn't stir up any emotion in him anymore. It was like he had already checked out of that whole part of his life.

"I'm going to miss you," he said suddenly, walking over to me with an odd kind of finality in his steps. He reached out and pulled me close, almost ignoring what I had just mentioned about Gabe and Ellie.

I wrapped my arms around him, letting his presence offer me some comfort amidst all the chaos. The strange mixture of relief and anxiety was overwhelming, but in his arms, it felt a little more manageable.

We quickly made our way to my car, and Mark slouched down in the backseat, trying to make himself as inconspicuous as possible. I opened the garage door and checked the doorbell feed, just to be sure Ellie was nowhere in the front yard. She was still gone, thankfully. I backed out of the driveway swiftly, taking care to avoid anyone.

As I drove, I felt Mark's hand slip up my side. The touch was somehow comforting. I lowered my hand instinctively and found his, our fingers intertwining.

After some time, we arrived at the back lot of his workplace. By now, most of the employees were gone, with only a few stragglers left. I parked far off to the side, trying to stay as hidden as possible.

When I turned around, Mark was already leaning toward me, pulling me into a long, passionate kiss. It was the kind of kiss that said everything without words.

"I'll call you tomorrow," he murmured against my lips as he pulled away. "Let the private investigator do what he needs to do. Just keep me posted on how much you've paid him so far, and I'll pay you back."

"Okay," I said, still a little dazed from the kiss.

Mark got out of the car, moving quickly. As soon as I stepped back through the door at home, I grabbed my phone and texted Bennett.

> Let's move forward with the plan and bring in the other person.

It wasn't long before Bennett replied.

> Great. I'll keep you updated. I feel like she's on the verge of doing something dangerous.

> Okay. Keep me posted.

Maybe Ellie was just having a moment, something temporary. But Bennett was the expert, and I trusted his judgment. He knew what he was looking for.

CHAPTER THIRTY-SIX

I wandered over to the front living room with my phone. Jax made himself comfy on the couch next to me. I thought about how just an hour ago, Mark had been here in the house with me.

Bennett texted.

> When will you be at Blue's next with Ellie?

> I'm meeting her there tonight, but I'm not sure exactly what time yet.

Just as I sent this message, my phone pinged with a message from Ellie. I wrote to Bennett again.

> Actually, she just texted. We're meeting at 8:30.

A realization hit me—I needed to clean up, and fast. I couldn't let Mark's cologne cling to me. Not now. That strong, musky cologne of his was the last thing I wanted Ellie or anyone else to notice.

Bennett texted.

> Okay, let me check in with Stewart. He lives nearby. It just depends on whether he has anything else he is working on tonight.

> Perfect. Let me know.

I needed to focus—shower, get dressed, get my head straight. The smell of Mark still clung to me. I jumped into the shower with urgency, scrubbing away the residue of everything that had just transpired.

A quick glance at the clock told me I was running behind. I threw on my clothes, made sure my makeup was intact, and rushed out the door, hoping to reach Blue's on time.

Ten minutes later, Bennett sent a text that Stewart would be showing up at some point during the night. He reminded me to act like I didn't know him if I saw him. I reassured him right away with a simple message: *Will do!*

I wasn't sure how it would feel to play that part, but I wasn't going to let anything mess up the plan.

On my way to Blue's, I quickly dialed Bennett to give him the scoop on Ellie and Gabe. I asked him to have Stewart hold off until Ellie was about to leave, so he wouldn't be encountering her in front of Gabe—especially with Ellie and Gabe being romantically involved.

I arrived at Blue's just a few minutes after 8:30. The second I walked in, I immediately spotted Ellie at a high-top table near the bar. She was staring up at the bar. To no surprise, it was Gabe she was staring at. The actual bar was packed, which was not unusual because it was summer. Nearly every seat was taken.

I took a deep breath, trying to walk in with as much grace as I could muster.

"What a day," I said casually as I reached the table.

Ellie looked up with a concerned expression, her eyebrows knitting together, "What happened?"

I shrugged, slipping into the chair across from her. "Oh, nothing major. Just super busy." I put on a smile, but it didn't quite reach my eyes. "Just a busy day, a closing, and then a long meeting with everyone at work tonight." I let out a small, exhausted sigh, dropping my shoulders dramatically.

Ellie nodded, clearly sympathizing with me. "Sounds like you've had a full day."

I forced a smile, trying to mask the discomfort creeping up on me. "Yeah, it's been one of those days. Glad to finally be here, though."

We sipped our drinks and picked at plates of food as the conversation flowed, mostly gossip about the fresh faces who'd recently popped up at the country club. Gabe, true to form, was a blur of motion—far too swamped to swing by our table. We didn't take it personally; the place was buzzing. Ellie, who had spent the first part of the evening sneaking glances in his direction, eventually gave up. It was clear he had his hands full with the crowd.

Out of nowhere, Ellie leaned in close, her eyes sparkling with mischief.

"Don't look now," she murmured, barely containing her excitement, "but that guy across the room? He's been totally checking me out. And oh my God—he's *hot*."

I stifled a laugh, whispering back, "Okay, I *won't* look ... *right now*. Maybe I should 'accidentally' drop something... or take a totally unnecessary bathroom break?"

A couple of minutes passed before I rose from my seat with the casual grace of someone on a secret mission.

"All right ... showtime," I whispered, adjusting my stride just enough to make it believable.

As I turned, I cast a glance toward the mystery man's table—and instantly understood the fuss.

"Oh *wow*," I muttered under my breath as I turned back to Ellie. "You were not exaggerating. He's *actually* hot." He looked like he'd just stepped out of a GQ photoshoot—tall, dark, and effortlessly handsome, dressed down in crisp button-down slacks and a golf shirt that somehow made casual look couture.

By the time I made it back from the bathroom, Ellie had turned the casual glances into a full-on flirtation, smiling coyly at the man across the room. I gave her a knowing look, then subtly glanced toward Gabe—who was still completely unaware of our antics, busy charming customers with his usual grace.

Eventually, it was time to head out. We gathered our things, slung our purses over our shoulders, and as we made our way toward the door, Ellie paused just long enough to catch Gabe's eye and offer a smooth little nod goodbye—cool and casual, like nothing had happened at all.

CHAPTER THIRTY-SEVEN

"Excuse me, I don't think I caught your name," a smooth voice called out behind us as we were heading toward the door.

We both stopped and turned around in unison. There he was—the chiseled man Bennett had sent that Ellie had been flirting with. Judging by the fact that he seemed to be standing right behind us, he had clearly been watching us and waiting for the perfect moment to approach.

"Hi," Ellie said, a soft, almost mesmerized smile spreading across her face as she stared at him, clearly spellbound.

I stood there, unsure of whether I should join the conversation or gracefully bow out. My mind raced, and I had to decide fast.

"I'll leave you two to chat. I've got to get going," I said, keeping my tone light and casual. In truth, I knew I didn't really have to leave—I just didn't want to stick around and make things awkward. I could tell Bennett's collaborator was focused on doing his job.

Tonight, my drive home felt different. Everything I was involved in was pulling at me, a knot of nerves tightening in my stomach.

Right before I pulled into the neighborhood, my phone buzzed. It was Ellie.

"Hey, what's up?" I answered quickly, trying to sound casual, though my heart was racing. "How was your chiseled man?" I teased.

I had to admit, even though this guy was striking, I thought Mark was just as attractive—if not more so. But there was something about Ellie's pursuit of men that made me question her motives. It was like she used them, testing them for her own amusement.

Her voice was practically sparkling with excitement. "His name is Stewart. He asked me if I was single, and I said kind of," she giggled, her tone almost shy. I wasn't sure what to make of that answer. What did she mean by "kind of"?

I couldn't help but roll my eyes, a bit amused by her drama. "He asked you out? What, for a drink or something?" I asked, trying to sound as interested as possible.

"Oh my, yes!" she responded with unrestrained enthusiasm. "We're meeting for a drink tomorrow night. He's just so hot! And he's, like, our age—just perfect!"

"That's great! Where are you meeting?" I asked, keeping my voice upbeat and trying to sound supportive.

"We're meeting at Noble Cellar," she said, her voice almost dreamy.

"Wow, I've heard that place is really good. I can't wait to hear how it goes!" I said, smiling into the phone.

"I'll call you after and let you know how it went," she replied in a bubbly voice.

As the conversation ended, I realized that Ellie would be entirely consumed with this Stewart guy. She'd be distracted, and that worked in my favor.

I waited until around ten the next morning, knowing that Mark would be on his way to play golf. I had a feeling he would pick up the phone right away. And sure enough, he did.

"Hi, sweetheart," Mark answered, his voice making it nearly impossible to keep a straight face. That warm, smooth tone made me feel like melting right there.

I giggled softly, unable to stop myself. "Ugh, I miss you already," I said, my voice light but laced with affection.

"How's everything going?"

I let out a little sigh. "Everything's falling into place. She's meeting with Stewart tonight. We'll see what happens."

"Do you think it'll work out?" he asked, his voice tinged with genuine curiosity. I wasn't sure whether to interpret that as him being worried for Ellie or just curious to see if it all works out.

"I do," I said, trying to reassure him. "She seemed really into him. He definitely has her attention."

"Good. I hope it works," he said, his tone softening.

The rest of the day went by with Ellie texting and updating me about how excited she was for the night. I could tell she was focused on her latest crush.

Around three in the afternoon, I received another text from her that stood out:

> Ugh, my nails are horrible again. I need to get them done before tonight. Do you want to meet me at the nail place?

> I can't. I wish I could. I need to be in the office for a while and might have a showing. Waiting to hear back from the sellers. If anything changes, I'll let you know.

Okay. I can't wait to fill you in after tonight.

> Great. Have fun!

As the day wore on, I found myself increasingly thinking of Mark. I knew Ellie would be gone tonight, so I decided to take full advantage of the opportunity.

I sent Mark a text, knowing he was out on the course, lost in friendly competition and sunshine. Still, I hoped my message would remind him that I was thinking of him.

Hi, since she'll be gone tonight, want to meet?

I was eager for him to know I still wanted him—just as much, if not more, despite everything. I trusted the private investigator's judgment, and it gave me some reassurance.

A few minutes later, I received his reply, sending a thrill through me.

> Oh baby, let's spend the night at the St. Regis. I can request a private way up to the presidential suite. Dinner delivered, just the two of us.

His words sent a wave of excitement through me, and I couldn't help but smile. My heart raced just thinking about it.

> I would love to.

I texted back, swooning at the thought of the night ahead.

CHAPTER THIRTY-EIGHT

The day felt like a balancing act, where I tried to manage the clock and all the moving pieces of the jigsaw puzzle that was my life now. I couldn't afford to be distracted for long —I knew if Ellie called, I'd have to answer right away. I needed to be ready for whatever she might throw my way. Still, as much as I tried to keep myself grounded, the anticipation of the evening between Mark and me was steadily building.

Ten minutes later, Mark called back, his voice smooth and reassuring as always.

"I told her I have to be out of town overnight for business, even though it's a Saturday. I likely went way overboard explaining, rambling on about how it was a meeting with the president of a company we might acquire, and how—by pure coincidence—he just happened to be in our state for the weekend," he said, the words rolling off his tongue with practiced ease. "We're fine. Plus, she's so distracted with this other guy now anyway. I'll text you a few more specifics for the hotel soon. I have to get back to golf."

The knot of nervous energy in my stomach started to unravel, replaced by an exhilaration I hadn't felt in a while.

The hours passed, the steady rhythm of my day interrupted only by my thoughts of the evening. Around half-past four in the afternoon, Mark's text came through, and I couldn't help but smile as I read it.

> Pull around back to the private entrance garage door. Enter the code 1717. The door will open, and a security person will take you up to the suite. You can get there anytime. They will be expecting you. I'll be there around 7.

I texted back.

> I'll see you then.

The thought of the night ahead, the luxury of the suite, and the quiet privacy of it all made my pulse quicken. I knew Bennett was keeping things under control, so any calls with him could be dealt with at my leisure.

There was, however, one last thing to handle—Jax. I couldn't leave him alone in the house, especially since I was planning on staying out for the night. I called the kennel, and thankfully, they had an opening. It was one less thing to worry about.

Between phone calls with clients, I made multiple trips upstairs to pack; thankfully, my potential showing today was rescheduled. But as I stood staring at my wardrobe, I was suddenly caught in a whirlwind of indecision. What should I wear?

My fingers hovered over my lingerie drawer. I reached for a black lace slip dress—new, still with the tags on it.

I walked over and sat on the edge of my bed after skimming through my lingerie drawer. So many thoughts of Steven returned to assail me.

The ache of missing him was still fresh, even after all this time. I didn't know why I kept coming back to the things that reminded me of him. Maybe it was the closeness I felt, the way his absence still haunted me in moments like this. A tear rolled down my cheek. I looked at the bag I was packing, then at the empty space beside me on the bed. Mark wasn't Steven, but I felt a strange comfort in knowing Mark would be with me tonight. It wasn't the same, but maybe it could be enough.

I wiped the tear away and stood up, my heart heavy as I walked to Steven's side of the bed. I pulled open his nightstand drawer, the one that had been untouched since he passed. It had been a long time—more than I cared to admit. I wasn't sure why I had kept his things, but somehow, I couldn't bear to part with them. Doing so would have meant letting go of him completely.

The drawer was a strange assortment of items. A few business cards from people he'd met, about five or six pens —including a sleek black ballpoint with burgundy and gold stripes. I rolled it over in my hand to read the words *La Tourelle Hotel* etched on its side in a fancy font. A phone charger. A tube of ChapStick. It was such an odd collection, but it was his. It had meaning, even if I couldn't explain why.

Another tear ran down my cheek, and I could feel my chest tighten. This was the kind of grief you couldn't prepare for. It didn't go away, no matter how much time passed. I wasn't ready to move on, but I knew I had to. Mark was a step forward, even if he wasn't the same as Steven.

CHAPTER THIRTY-NINE

Just after six in the evening, I slid into the driver's seat of my car, feeling the familiar hum of anticipation as I backed out of the driveway with Jax sitting quietly in the passenger seat beside me. I'd given myself a little extra time to be on the safe side, wanting everything to go smoothly. After I dropped Jax off at the kennel, I pulled up my phone, typing in the address for the St. Regis.

When I arrived at the hotel, I followed the signs toward the rear entrance. Just as Mark texted me, I spotted the towering garage door, its bold sign reading *Private Entrance. You Must Have A Code To Enter.* Intrigued, I pulled closer, entered the code "1717" into the keypad, and watched as the massive door slowly creaked open. I wondered if this was where celebrities or high-profile figures came through.

As I eased my car through, I noticed two men standing near a small kiosk, both smiling and impeccably dressed in suits adorned with the hotel's emblem. I stopped just in front of them, unsure of the next move. I rolled down the window, feeling a slight flutter of excitement.

"Good evening, ma'am. May I ask your name?" the older man asked, his voice smooth and welcoming as he gave me a courteous nod.

"I'm Rachel. Rachel Sheffler," I replied. "I'm here to check in."

The man smiled warmly. "We'd be happy to take your car for you, ma'am. If you need assistance with your luggage, we'll be more than happy to carry it for you."

"Thank you," I said, stepping out of the car. I grabbed my bag from the backseat and handed it to the younger gentleman.

"I'm Joshua, and that's Phil," he said with a bright smile. "I'll show you to your suite while Phil parks your car." He gestured toward the elevator beyond a set of doors.

As we walked into a small, sleek hallway, I was immediately struck by the opulence around me. The elevator doors stood open, waiting, and I stepped inside, taking in the polished marble floors, gold-trimmed buttons, and the soft, ambient glow of golden lighting. Joshua pressed the button for the twenty-third floor, and we ascended in silence, the elevator music softly playing in the background.

When the doors opened, I was stunned. We hadn't reached a hallway that led to the suite; no, the elevator had opened directly into the heart of the room. I stepped inside and gasped, taking in the grandeur of it all.

"This is ... absolutely stunning," I murmured. The room was filled with lavish furniture, large and inviting. A gorgeous fireplace sat at one end, casting a warm glow across the room. The kitchen was fully equipped, with sleek countertops that reflected the soft lighting. In the dining area, a pale-colored table was surrounded by elegant chairs, and a plush rug covered the living space, topped with a coffee table stacked high with books. A striking feature of the room was one of the walls—covered in what looked like bamboo wood, its natural hues blending perfectly with the calming greys and whites. Rich velvet curtains framed the windows, adding an extra layer of luxury.

"Where would you like your bags, ma'am?" Joshua asked.

"Over near the chair, please," I replied, motioning to a nearby chair. I fished around in my purse and handed him a $20 bill for bringing my things up. He left, and I wandered further into the room, my fingers trailing over the smooth counters as I admired the tasteful decor. As a realtor, I couldn't help but be drawn to the quality of the design, especially the kitchen. It was perfect.

I was admiring the artwork on the walls when I heard the elevator doors open again. Mark stepped out, his presence lighting up the room as he quickly set his bag down and headed straight toward me. His eyes locked onto mine, and before I could say a word, he swept me up into his arms.

"Mmmm," he murmured in my ear, the sound of his voice sending a thrill down my spine. His lips met mine in an intense kiss that stole the breath from my lungs.

"I can't believe we get to share this amazing place all night," he said in a voice full of excitement.

"I know. It's incredible."

"Let me just put your bag here, Mr. Hoffman," Joshua said, gently reminding us of his presence.

Mark chuckled, the two of us having forgotten for a moment that anyone else was in the room. He walked over to Joshua, slipping him some cash, and the concierge reminded us of the dinner menu laid out on the table nearby. We could place our order through text, he explained, before the elevator doors closed behind him.

Mark walked over to the door and hit the lock button, ensuring no one would disturb us unless we allowed it. He took my hand and led me back into the living room, where we shared another long, passionate kiss.

"Let's look over the menu so we can order dinner," he suggested, his voice calm and content. I could tell how much he cherished these moments. There was a giddiness about him, but it wasn't over the top—just pure relaxation and happiness.

"What sounds good?" he asked, picking up the menu and scanning the options.

"I'll definitely be adding a bottle of wine," he added with a grin before handing the menu to me. "Take a look and let me know what you would like."

But before I could say anything, he exclaimed, "I have an idea! Let's go downstairs first and grab a drink at the bar inside the restaurant. The night is young, after all."

I gave him a quick smile and excused myself to freshen up in the bathroom.

There were two elevators in the suite—one marked "Private Parking" and the other simply labeled "Lobby." His hand gently slipped around my waist as the elevator began its descent to the lobby. His touch was subtle but intimate, resting between my waist and back.

We stepped out, and Mark guided me toward the restaurant. The atmosphere of the hotel was sophisticated and unhurried, like everything was designed to help us relax and enjoy the moment. The restaurant's entrance was just ahead, and as we walked inside, a friendly hostess greeted us.

"We'll be sitting at the bar," Mark said, offering her a polite smile. She nodded and led us in that direction while atmospheric music played in the background. Though it was only the early evening, the bar was already bathed in soft, dim light, casting a warm glow over the room. The effect was calming and intimate, perfect for a quiet evening with someone you wanted to be close to.

The bar itself was a long stretch of rich, polished wood, lined with ten or twelve high-backed chairs. We chose two seats near the middle and settled in. Mark took the seat beside me, close enough that our legs brushed lightly against each other.

"I'll have a glass of your pinot noir. One that you would recommend," I said to the bartender.

"Same for me," Mark added with a smile, his gaze lingering on mine.

As the bartender poured the wine, I took a moment to absorb the surroundings. The bar's soft lighting and the slow jazz that drifted through the space added to the intimate mood.

As the wine touched my lips, I felt myself relax even more. The first sip was smooth, warming, and rich, and for a moment, I was completely present in the here and now. Mark and I settled into an easy conversation, laughing about the small things that happened in our daily lives— the quirky little events, the amusing mishaps. It felt good to unwind, to share these ordinary moments that made up our lives. We made sure not to bring up Ellie's name.

But as I sipped my wine, my thoughts drifted, and I couldn't help wondering about her. Was she enjoying her time with Stewart somewhere, just as carefree? I tried not to let the thought bother me, but the comparison lingered in my mind. Her night was likely nothing like this, I reasoned—nothing as intimate or as romantic. But I quickly pushed the thought away, choosing instead to focus on the warmth of the moment with Mark.

The minutes slipped by unnoticed. It wasn't until I glanced at the clock that I realized it was almost nine and starting to get dark outside. A soft twilight had settled over the city, casting a peaceful stillness across the restaurant.

Mark stood up and casually paid the bartender. He offered me a hand, and I accepted it. Without a word, we walked back toward the elevator, our footsteps echoing softly in the quiet hallway.

In what felt like no time at all, we were back at our suite. The elevator doors slid open, and we stepped out.

"I'm going to place the dinner order. I'll order a couple of different dishes we can share," Mark said with a wink. There was something about him tonight—he seemed so confident, so at ease.

Mark moved across the room to light the fireplace. He paused for a moment, watching the flames dance. Then, with the same deliberate calm, he dimmed the lights until only a soft glow remained.

He had set the perfect tone for the evening—romantic, tranquil, and intimate.

He glanced over at me with a small, content smile as he connected his phone to the speaker to play some music. "There. Now it's perfect."

I returned his smile, feeling the warmth of the room— both literal and emotional.

CHAPTER FORTY

We nestled together on the couch, lips meeting in slow, lingering kisses. Soft whispers between us, fingertips tracing delicate patterns along each other's arms. A quiet fire smoldered beneath our restraint, the anticipation of dinner the only tether holding us back. Nearly thirty minutes had passed when the soft hum of the elevator filled the air. The doors opened— two waiters carefully maneuvering a large cart laden with exquisite dishes. Their movements were fluid, precise, as they wheeled the cart into the living room. The rich aroma of freshly prepared food wafted through the space.

The waiters didn't stop at just delivering the food. They reached for two elegant armchairs from the dining area, their smooth wood polished to a warm glow, and placed one at each end of the wheeled table. The chairs seemed perfectly suited to the evening's special moment. From beneath the table, they retrieved two tall, gleaming candlesticks, each holding a long tapering candle, and positioned them carefully between us.

"Would you like us to light the additional candles you requested, sir?" one of the waiters inquired with a polite, respectful tone.

Mark glanced up from his phone, which he was using to adjust the sound settings on the ceiling speakers, and nodded. "Yes, please," he said, his voice steady and sure.

One of the waiters nodded and, with practiced ease, retrieved five more candles from beneath the cart. He placed them strategically around the room, illuminating the space with soft, flickering light as he went.

"Is there anything else you require, sir?" the waiter asked, his voice low and professional.

Mark shook his head, his eyes meeting mine with a silent promise. "No, thank you," he said warmly, a soft smile tugging at the corners of his lips.

The waiters nodded respectfully and exited. Mark moved toward the elevator, locking it once again with a deliberate click, securing our privacy for the evening.

When he returned, his eyes met mine, filled with that familiar, loving intensity that always made my heart flutter. He reached for my chair, pulling it out with a flourish and a gentle smile.

"Let me pour us a glass of wine," he offered, his voice warm, as always.

The city lights twinkled in the distance, casting a soft glow against the darkened sky. "Wow, this view is amazing," I said, meeting his gaze. "But not nearly as amazing as the view I'll have across the table tonight."

Mark's expression softened, and for a moment, there was in his gaze a deep sincerity that made my heart swell.

I stood up, crossing the room to him. Without a word, I leaned in and pressed a soft, lingering kiss to his lips, a silent promise of my love. When I pulled away, his eyes held mine, and I returned to my seat without a sound. That kiss was my way of expressing everything I felt in that moment.

"Look at all of this," I murmured, my gaze sweeping across the table. "It's so beautiful."

Mark tilted his head, a soft smile playing at the corner of his mouth as he gazed at me, his eyes full of affection. "It's all for you," he said tenderly.

"The romantic dinner, the music, the candles ..." I continued. "Most of all, it's the time here with you that matters."

The music continued to play softly in the background as we savored our meal. Finally, Mark reached out a hand, his touch gentle but firm. "Let's dance," he suggested, his eyes shining with a mix of tenderness and mischief.

We stood next to the table, close enough to feel each other's warmth. The music was slow and soft as we moved together in perfect sync. The world seemed to fall away, leaving just the two of us, wrapped in the music and the soft light of the candles. I felt the warmth of his cheek against mine as we swayed together in harmony with the rhythm.

In those moments, it felt as though nothing else mattered but the love between us. Every so often, he kissed me—soft and slow at first, then deeper, more passionate, as if time itself held its breath. Mark always knew when to hold me closer and when to pull back just a bit.

My dress slipped from my shoulders, a whisper of fabric pooling at my feet in the dimly lit living room. I stood there in nothing but the black lace slip I had chosen so carefully for this moment. He watched me, his eyes dark with hunger, before reaching for his belt and unfastening it with one swift motion. His pants followed, falling in a heap as he loosened his tie. I stepped closer, fingers working the buttons of his shirt, savoring the feeling of his warm skin as each inch was revealed.

Hand in hand, we moved toward the bedroom, my bare feet soundless against the floor, his tie still draped carelessly and his shirt open. The air in the room felt charged as I settled onto the edge of the bed.

"I'll be right back," he murmured before dashing off to a corner.

Moments later, he returned, two candles in hand. He placed them carefully on the nightstand and dresser, striking a match to bring them to life.

The world outside faded into irrelevance as we moved together. We covered every inch of the bed, savoring the slow, deliberate unraveling of control, lost in the glow of candlelight and the softness of each other's touch.

I woke around three in the morning to a bedroom cloaked in silence. Mark's body was pressed up against my back, wrapping around me like a blanket. His arm was draped over my waist, holding me close even in sleep. The sensation was foreign—something I hadn't felt in so long. My body tensed slightly, startled by the intimacy, and that small movement was enough to wake him.

I didn't want to disturb him further, so I carefully slipped out from beneath his embrace. The cool air brushed against my skin as I reached for the plush robe hanging on the hook, wrapping it tightly around me before slipping away barefoot to the kitchen.

The refrigerator hummed softly as I opened it, reaching for a bottle of water. Just as I shut the door, I heard his voice, laced with sleep but still full of concern.

"Are you okay?"

I turned to find him standing near the kitchen, the dim light from the city outside casting long shadows across his face. His hair was tousled, and he wore another robe like mine.

"Yeah," I murmured, twisting the cap off the bottle. "I just woke up ... I guess I was thirsty."

Mark studied me for a moment, his expression unreadable. Then, he took a slow step closer. "I woke up to feeling you against me," he admitted. "I loved that." His voice was lower now, as if sharing something vulnerable.

I glanced down, almost embarrassed by the confession. "I loved it too," I whispered.

He gently reached for my hand. Without another word, he led me to the couch.

The faint glow from the surrounding buildings slipped through the cracks in the curtains.

Mark pulled me into his arms, holding me close without speaking, as if he knew I needed that more than anything else. His lips met mine in a slow, lingering kiss—one that deepened with each second, filling the room with soft sighs and quiet moans.

Before I knew it, my robe had loosened, slipping off my shoulders as I sat down on the couch and then leaned back. My legs dangled slightly over the edge as Mark knelt down between them, his own robe parting just enough for me to take in the strength of his chest. His hands traveled up my sides, his thumbs drawing slow, hypnotic circles over my stomach. The warmth of his skin against mine sent shivers through me, and when he pressed forward, I gasped softly, my fingers instinctively reaching for him.

There were no words this time—none were needed.

Earlier in the bedroom, it had been different. But this ... this was unhurried, deeper, almost reverent. The slow, intoxicating rhythm of our bodies left a sheen of sweat on our skin.

As the intensity ebbed into something softer, Mark leaned down, his lips brushing against mine in a kiss to seal the moment.

CHAPTER FORTY-ONE

I woke up the next morning to find the space beside me empty, the warmth of Mark's presence already faded from the sheets. I slipped out from beneath the covers, reaching for the robe I had let slip from my shoulders the night before. I caught the faint sound of typing from the other room.

Following the rhythmic clicks of the keyboard, I stepped out of the bedroom to find Mark sitting at the table, his laptop open before him. He was in the robe he had worn last night.

"Sorry, baby," he murmured without looking away from the screen, his fingers flying over the keys. "Just had to get a few things sent out for work."

I watched him for a moment before making my way over to the couch, my fingers absentmindedly tapping against my phone screen. Only work emails and a few messages stared back at me, nothing personal, nothing unexpected.

Mark closed his laptop with a quiet sigh. His gaze lifted

to meet mine, and for a second, a flicker of something tender passed between us as he got up from the table and walked toward me.

"This time with you has been nothing short of amazing," I said softly, leaning back on the couch.

His smile deepened. "We still have a little time this morning," he said, reaching out to brush his thumb alongside my cheek. "Then I have to head back to work."

He leaned in, pressing a soft kiss against my lips, and just as I was about to pull him closer, the distant chime of the elevator echoed through the room.

A young hotel attendant entered with a rolling cart, nodding politely before setting up our breakfast. "I'll leave this here, sir. Would you like me to take away last night's table?"

Mark gave him a small nod, and as the attendant wheeled away the remnants of our dinner. Moments later, I found myself absentmindedly picking at my eggs. My phone rested by my side, but something gnawed at the back of my mind. I hadn't received a single text or call from Ellie last night.

My gaze flickered up to Mark, but he seemed completely detached from the thought of her, as if she didn't exist in his world. Had he even wondered how things had gone? Did he care? If he did, he certainly didn't show it.

We ate in unhurried silence, but my mind remained restless. Mark's eyes locked onto mine as I took my last sip of orange juice.

Wordlessly, he stood up and reached for my hand, guiding me back toward the bedroom. As we neared the bathroom, he turned to face me, his fingers moving to untie my robe. His lips found mine, deep and lingering, and then I heard the familiar rush of the shower coming to life behind us.

There were two oversized rain shower heads from which water cascaded down in steady, rhythmic streams. We stepped in together, each under our own downpour, the heat wrapping around our bodies.

Mark raked his fingers through his damp hair, wiping the water from his face before his gaze darkened with something deeper. He moved toward me with deliberate slowness, his lips finding my neck, trailing fire in their wake.

I found myself facing the shower wall as my head tilted back, resting against his shoulder as his breath fanned against my ear.

A low, throaty moan escaped my lips, lost in the rush of water.

His hands explored me, pressing me firmly against him as we moved together beneath the streaming water. One hand lay possessively over my stomach, pulling me closer, while the other traced lazy circles across my skin, igniting every nerve.

"You feel incredible," he murmured, his lips brushing the shell of my ear.

The water pounded around us as we both came undone. Our movements slowed, and he turned me in his arms, his hands cupping my face as he captured my lips in a kiss that left me breathless.

As I wrapped my arms around him, my fingers traced the cuts and scars along his back—reminders of Ellie, of what still lingered in the corners of our reality.

CHAPTER FORTY-TWO

"I'll ride down with you," Mark said as we finished gathering our bags. Joshua had just arrived to take them down to our cars, making the moment of departure feel all too real.

"Okay," I murmured, stepping closer to him and pressing a lingering kiss to his lips. His warmth, his scent—it was intoxicating, and I didn't want to let go just yet.

As the elevator descended, I reached into my purse, my fingers grazing over my phone just as a soft chime sounded. A new message lit up my screen. It was from Bennett:

> Call me when you get a minute.

I tilted my phone toward Mark, watching as his expression shifted. He inhaled deeply, nodding once.

"Okay," he said, his voice measured. "Keep me posted."

I could hear the unspoken words behind his response—he knew, just as I did, that whatever Bennett had to say was going to shift everything.

I promised him I'd call him later to update him.

Once I had settled in my car, I pulled out onto the road behind Mark, my hands gripping the wheel a little tighter than usual. Using voice-to-text, I quickly responded to Bennett:

> I'll call you in about an hour.

The drive was uneventful—just a blur of roads, traffic lights, and thoughts running through my mind. I picked up Jax and returned to my home office. After putting my things away, I made myself a cup of tea and settled into my desk chair. I knew what had to come next.

I took a deep breath and dialed.

"Hey, I'm calling about your message," I said, my voice steady, though my pulse quickened with anticipation.

Bennett exhaled heavily on the other end. "Stewart met with Ellie," he started, his tone laced with hesitation. "And ...I don't really know how to tell you this."

I straightened in my chair, bracing myself. "Just tell me."

He took a beat before continuing. "Ellie had too much to drink. More than she should have. She and Stewart ended up at a hotel together ... and one thing led to another."

I squeezed my eyes shut, pressing my fingers to my temple. That alone was bad enough. But I had the distinct feeling there was more.

"Afterward, she passed out," Bennett went on. "And Stewart looked through her phone. There's a contact saved under the name 'Gabe.' From what he gathered, Ellie and this guy ... they're planning something. Against Mark. They are planning to get something significant from him, but the text didn't specify what."

My stomach clenched. "What do you mean, planning something?"

"They're conspiring," he clarified. "Stewart couldn't make sense of all the details, but there was repeated mention of 'the plan.' He said it felt deliberate. Calculated."

A chill ran down my spine as I stared out the window, my gaze locking onto Ellie's house. From my desk, I had the perfect view of her front door—something I had never thought much of before. But now, it hit me. You never really *know* the person living next to you, do you? And she could say the same about me and Mark.

Bennett sighed. "I know that's a lot to take in."

"It is," I said, still processing his words.

"I'll keep you updated," he added. "We'll talk later."

"Yeah," I murmured. "Thanks."

The call ended, but my mind was racing. I needed more information. I texted.

> Sooooo, how was last night?

A minute passed. Then another.
Finally, she responded:

> Wow. Let's meet. Blue's tonight? Not at the bar. Only a high top, okay? 6 p.m.?

> Can't wait to hear all about it. Seven works better for me.

I set my phone down, exhaling sharply. My next call was to Mark.

"Hey, I just talked to the private investigator," I began and told him everything—Bennett's call, Stewart's discovery, the cryptic messages about *the plan*.

Mark didn't react the way I had expected. No shock. No anger. Just a quiet acceptance. It was as if he had already made peace with whatever chaos Ellie had set in motion.

"I'm meeting her at seven," I said, shifting the conversation. "So maybe avoid Blue's tonight."

A small chuckle rumbled through the phone. "I will," he promised. "By the way, I haven't stopped thinking about every minute we spent together."

His voice and words sent a shiver down my spine despite the serious nature of our conversation.

"I'll see you soon," he added before we hung up.

The afternoon passed in a blur. At one, I had a meeting with new clients, so naturally, I took them to Blue's.

Inside, I spotted a large round table along the bar's edge —more intimate than a high-top, yet still casual enough for business. As I greeted the couple, I caught sight of Gabe behind the bar. I forced myself to ignore him, acting as if I hadn't noticed his presence.

The couple, empty nesters, were looking to downsize. Over lunch, I jotted down notes, narrowing down their preferences. By the end of the meal, I had three homes in mind and sent out showing requests in real time. Efficiency was key.

As we stepped out of Blue's, the evening air carried the faint scent of freshly watered flowers from the nearby gardens. I took a moment to comment on them, making small talk with the couple beside me. It was something I did intentionally—easing away from business for a bit, making interactions feel more personal.

As we continued toward our cars, I shifted the conversation. "So, what do you two enjoy doing in your spare time?" I asked, hoping to get a glimpse of who they were beyond the transaction.

They responded almost in unison, tossing out snippets of their interests—golf, pickleball, biking. Their voices blended into the background as something caught my eye over the wife's shoulder. A flicker of movement in the far end of the employee parking lot.

It was Gabe and Ellie. What was Ellie doing here in the employee parking lot?

I recognized them immediately, standing beside her car. Gabe handed Ellie a black duffel bag, and she quickly stashed it in the far back of her vehicle. My breath hitched. My mind scrambled for an explanation. What was that? Why was he giving her a bag? And why did it feel so … secretive?

"Do you enjoy golf?" The wife's voice cut through my thoughts.

I remained locked in a trance, eyes fixed on Gabe and Ellie, as if the world had narrowed to just the space between them.

"Do you?" she asked again, her voice slicing through the silence.

I blinked hard, forcing my gaze away from the parking lot. "Oh, yes. Yes, I do. I like it." The words tumbled from my mouth automatically, but the truth was, I had no idea what I had just agreed to. I had been so lost in the sight of Gabe and Ellie that I could have been responding to anything.

If she noticed my distraction, the woman was too polite to mention it. I, however, felt a sudden urge to wrap up the conversation. "Well, it was nice meeting you both," I said, flashing a quick smile. "I'll be sure to keep you posted on the showings."

I hoped I sounded composed, but inside, my pulse was thrumming in my ears. With a polite nod, I turned and made my way toward my car. My luck held—I moved my car to a few spots back, tucked behind other cars, making it easier to slip out of sight.

I ducked down inside, gripping the steering wheel, and let out a slow breath. What had I just witnessed? And more importantly, why did it feel like something I wasn't supposed to see?

CHAPTER FORTY-THREE

Easing into the driver's seat, I gripped my phone. My thoughts were running rampant at what I had just seen. Ellie was still in the parking lot, only a short distance away. I decided to text her; I wanted to see how she would respond. Would her words align with reality?

> I can't wait to hear your story. What are you up to this afternoon?

I hit send and looked up, my gaze flickering back to Ellie and Gabe. They stood by her car, still talking, their body language easy and comfortable. The way she tilted her head when she laughed, the way he leaned in just slightly as he spoke. My stomach churned.

Then, just before they parted, Gabe leaned in and kissed her.

My pulse pounded in my ears.

Ellie retreated back to the driver's seat of her car. Through the windshield and through the spaces between the cars, I watched her glance down at her phone. My phone buzzed a few seconds later with her message.

> I really can't wait to fill you in. I'm just over at my sister's house right now, trying to help her with a few things.

I stared at the lines, my jaw tightening.

Her sister's house? That was a lie.

I took a slow, steadying breath. I had to be careful.

> That's so nice of you. See you in a little bit.

I sent the message, my fingers tapping against the steering wheel as I thought hard. What were Ellie and Gabe up to? Why the secrecy? What was with the black bag? This must have something to do with what Bennett told me.

For a moment, I considered calling Mark. I wanted to tell him what I had just witnessed, to see if his gut reaction matched mine. But I hesitated; I didn't want to interrupt his workday.

Still, my mind wouldn't stop spinning. I replayed the scene in my head, dissecting every movement, every glance, and every small detail. Maybe the duffel bag was innocent. Maybe it just had gym clothes, and they were planning to meet for a workout later. Or was it something else entirely? Extra golf gear from the club for Ellie? She never really mentioned that she golfed, though.

Shaking off the unease, I forced my mind back to work. I had a showing coming up, and I needed to focus. This particular couple had been looking for weeks, and I had a feeling today's house might be the one. I had about a dozen clients at the moment, juggling showings, negotiations, and closings like a high-stakes balancing act. It was thrilling, exhausting, and unpredictable, but that was part of what I loved the most.

A while later, I met the couple at the property, giving them space to explore while answering their questions. They seemed engaged, nodding along as they moved through the rooms. Every so often, as I guided my clients through the house, my mind would drift back to that black duffel bag. No matter how much I tried to push it aside, it lingered in the back of my thoughts like an unsolved puzzle. I'd shake my head, forcing myself to refocus. This was an important showing. By the time we stepped outside, the couple drifted toward the backyard to look over it one more time.

I didn't mind. I knew they were debating making an offer, or they were crossing the house off their list. Either way, I would have my answer soon.

While they deliberated, I pulled out my phone, a thought creeping into my mind. If Ellie was hiding something, maybe there was a way to push her a little, see if her actions matched her words.

> Do you mind picking me up when we go to Blue's? My car isn't running well.
> Otherwise, I'll have to postpone.

I sent the message and waited, watching the three little dots appear almost instantly.

> I'll pick you up at your house at 6:50.

> Great. Thank you!

I set my phone down, a smile forming on my lips. If Ellie and Gabe were up to something, I needed to find out.

CHAPTER FORTY-FOUR

At a quarter past six, I stood in my foyer, staring at my reflection in the mirror, smoothing out the fabric of my blouse with slightly trembling hands. There was nothing out of the ordinary about my outfit—just a simple, well-crafted look. My mind was racing ahead of me, trying to piece together the things Ellie might and might not say.

I picked up my phone and typed out a quick message to Mark.

Love you. Don't text—I'm heading to Blue's with Ellie.

His response came almost instantly.

Ok. I love you too.

Simple. Steady. Uncomplicated.

A few minutes later, Ellie pulled into my driveway. I grabbed my purse and walked out, sliding into the passenger seat as soon as she stopped.

"Wow, sooo ..." I said, barely giving myself time to fasten my seatbelt. "Tell me everything." My voice was light, but my anticipation was anything but.

Ellie giggled, flashing me a knowing smile. "I will," she promised. "But let's wait until we sit down."

Ellie looked slightly overdressed, wrapped in a sleek black cocktail dress that shimmered just a little too boldly for the setting. Her hair was freshly sculpted, every strand in perfect place, like she'd stepped straight out of a salon chair—sharp new cut, flawless finish, and all. Was this all for Gabe? What about her new man?

I exhaled dramatically. "Fine," I said, playing along, though my curiosity was practically burning a hole through me. I shifted in my seat, fidgeting with the strap of my purse. "Anyway, how was your sister's?" I asked in a casual voice while sharply watching her out of the corner of my eye.

"My sister's?" She looked confused before saying, "Oh, that's right. Good. I was there most of the day. Just helping her with some things around her house. You know how she is—she has a lot of issues right now."

My question had hit like an unexpected gust of wind, leaving her momentarily off balance. The slight hitch in her voice—it was all the confirmation I needed.

I nodded along, but my mind went somewhere else entirely. I had mostly ever heard about Ellie's past and family through Mark.

We continued making polite conversation about her sister's house, but mentally, I was already turning over everything I knew—or thought I knew—about Ellie.

I led the way as we walked in, and just as we were settling in, a voice rang out over the hum of the restaurant.

"Hey, ladies! I have some seats at the bar," Gabe called out before I had even turned to look.

Ellie's entire body tensed for the briefest second before she composed herself.

"Oh, we're going to stay here at the high-top," she said smoothly, flashing him a quick smile. "I think we have a few more girls meeting us, so this will be easier."

I raised an eyebrow as I leaned in closer, lowering my voice just enough so only she could hear. "You don't have anyone else coming, do you?" A smirk played at the corner of my lips.

Ellie rolled her eyes, shaking her head. "No," she admitted. "I just had to say that so we could stay put." She let out a small, breathy laugh. "Honestly, I don't even know why I picked this place. I guess I'm just so used to it."

"It's fine," I reassured her, taking a slow sip of my water that the waitress had just filled. "We're tucked away over here. No one can hear us." I set my glass down and leaned in slightly. "So ... tell me everything."

Ellie's face lit up with excitement, her cheeks looking slightly flushed as she exhaled like a giddy teenager about to spill a well-guarded secret.

The waitress reappeared, and without missing a beat, we ordered two glasses of house wine. Then, we slipped right back into our conversation.

"Well," she started, lowering her voice just a little, "we met at the wine cellar place. He was just as dreamy as he was the other day." She bit her lip, eyes flickering with amusement. "We sat for hours—had drinks, some food ... and the more drinks I had, the more I kept touching his arms, his chest, you know ..."

I raised an eyebrow but said nothing, just waiting for her to continue.

"And then," she went on, her voice brimming with

excitement, "he did the same ... touching my arms, legs, and back continuously. Before I knew it, we were walking across the street to the hotel. He got a room, and ..." She trailed off, shrugging, as if that explained it all.

"And then you ...?"

"Exactly."

She flashed a playful grin. Our conversation briefly paused as we ordered our food.

I reached for my wine glass, watching her carefully. "So ... are you going to see him again?"

Ellie hesitated for only a second before nodding. "Yeah, I think so," she said, her voice filled with that same giddy excitement. "I mean, he wants to get together tomorrow night. He said he can't tonight." She flicked her eyes up to meet mine, something mischievous in her expression. "But I'll have to come up with something to tell Mark."

My stomach tightened, but I kept my face neutral.

She leaned back in her chair with a playful smirk. "I'll just tell him I'm going to my sister's."

I forced a small smile, but inside, something twisted.

Ellie thought this was a game.

And I wasn't sure yet if I was playing along ... or if I had just become a piece in it. And yet, with everything unfolding between Mark and me, I wasn't exactly in a position to point fingers. At this point, I was more concerned for Mark's safety.

"Wow, I can't wait to hear how it goes again," I said, my excitement mirroring Ellie's. She practically glowed.

I let her bask in it for a moment before nodding subtly toward the bar. "And Gabe? What about him?" I asked, keeping my voice low. I cast a quick glance in his direction, careful not to let my gaze linger too long. He was on the other side of the bar, focused on filling a waitress's drink order.

She ignored my question. She was too enthralled with Stewart now.

Ellie's eyes sparkled with an energy that felt different from her usual excitement. This wasn't just a casual fling for her. She was already invested, maybe more than she realized.

Our food arrived, but Ellie barely acknowledged it. She went on and on about how *hot* he was, how *incredible* he looked, how his arms were *so* toned, and how his smile was perfect. But that was all.

She never mentioned whether he was kind. Or polite. Or thoughtful.

She never said if he made her laugh, or if he opened doors for her, or if he made her feel special in any way other than through sheer physical attraction.

I took a bite of my food, nodding along, but my mind was already working through the implications. Ellie had always been drawn to good looks, but this felt ... different. Almost obsessive.

I was about to ask more when I spotted movement out of the corner of my eye.

"Gabe's coming over right now," I muttered.

Ellie's expression shifted instantly.

"Gabe. I see him walking over. *Change the subject,*" I repeated, my voice barely above a whisper.

Ellie straightened in her seat just as he arrived.

"So, how are you two ladies? How's the food?" Gabe asked smoothly, his voice warm but calculated.

"Good!" Ellie and I answered in unison.

He leaned across the table, settling in. Not in a "just

checking in" kind of way, but in a "making himself comfort-able" kind of way.

As Ellie began texting on her phone, I turned to Gabe, steering the conversation toward the standout appetizers I'd tried recently. He nodded in agreement, remarking on how the restaurant had truly stepped up its game with an impressive upgrade to its menu.

I rubbed my lips together, shifting slightly in my seat. "Ugh. My lips are so dry," I murmured, mostly to myself. Then, as if struck by sudden realization, I reached for my purse and started rummaging through it.

"Oh, shoot," I sighed, my frustration feigned just enough to sound natural. "I think my ChapStick and lipstick slid out on the way here."

I looked at Ellie expectantly. "Can I grab your car keys? I might've dropped them in your car when I got in."

Ellie barely hesitated before fishing her key fob out of her bag and handing it over. "Yeah, sure, here."

The bag ... the black duffel bag from earlier. I needed to get to it to see what was in it.

I took the keys, standing quickly, but not too quickly —just enough to appear inconvenienced, not hurried. I walked toward the entrance at a natural pace, but as soon as I stepped outside, I quickened my stride. I thought it was a perfect time: they both had each other for company.

Ellie's car wasn't parked far from the door, which worked in my favor. I reached it in seconds, my heartbeat quickening as I unlocked the passenger side and pulled the door open.

I ducked down, pretending to check under the front passenger seat, moving my hands around just enough to make it look like I was searching. Then, I lifted my head and let my gaze drift toward the back seat.

And there it was.

The black duffel bag.

My stomach tightened.

I glanced around the lot. No one was looking.

Moving quickly but carefully, I slipped around the door to the back seat, my heart hammering as I crouched down and reached for the bag. It wasn't zipped all the way, the gap just wide enough to hint at its contents. I tugged the zipper open a little more, just enough to see—

Black fabric. A long wire.

For what?

I moved to open it further, my fingers grazing the material when—

"Rachel! Rachel!"

I yanked my hand back and, without hesitation, shoved the bag into the exact position it had been in before. Then, forcing myself to stay composed, I crouched down, pretending to inspect the floor of the car.

Footsteps pounded against the pavement—*fast*. Not a casual walk. A sprint.

Gabe.

I felt the pull of the car door fling open further, and there he was, slightly out of breath but trying to mask it with an easy smile.

"Wait, do you need help?" he asked, his voice smooth but marked with something else. Something *off*.

I blinked up at him, feigning confusion. "What? I was just looking for my ChapStick and lipstick."

He exhaled, rubbing the back of his neck like he was

trying to play off his rushed arrival. "I know, but ... it's starting to get dark out," he said, his breath still uneven.

I frowned slightly. "Okay ...?"

"I just didn't want you out here alone," he added, shifting his weight like he was trying to make the reasoning sound natural. "You know, with it getting dark and all."

A chill ran down my spine, but I kept my face neutral.

This was a country club. A safe, well-lit place.

No one had ever been attacked or approached here.

He wasn't concerned for my safety.

He was concerned I might come across the bag.

CHAPTER FORTY-FIVE

When I stepped back inside, I forced myself to sit down calmly, though my heart was still racing. I shifted in my chair, my eyes drifting to Ellie, studying her every move. She was fidgety, her fingers tapping lightly on the edge of the table, her gaze darting toward the door as if expecting someone—Gabe.

Sure enough, a moment later, he walked in behind me, his expression unreadable, but I could sense the tension rolling off him. I reached for my cloth napkin and placed it in my lap, wrapping it tightly around my finger under the table. With each twist, I channeled my frustration into the fabric, pulling it tight. They couldn't see my irritation, but I was gripping that napkin fiercely.

Gabe stood over the seat beside Ellie, his arm draped casually over the back of her chair, but I wasn't fooled by the relaxed posture. He was just as jittery as she was. Something was going on between them. I could feel it. Something more than just the physical aspect.

Breathe. Stay cool.

I picked up my fork and absentmindedly poked at my steak salad, though my appetite had completely vanished. My thoughts were racing, colliding into one another like an out-of-control train.

Ellie leaned forward slightly, her eyes sharp and questioning.

"Did you find it?" she asked.

When I didn't respond immediately, Ellie tilted her head, studying me, as if trying to catch a crack in my expression. "Did you find what you left in my car?" she repeated, this time more pointedly.

I forced a small, easy laugh and shook my head. "Oh, no, no, I didn't. I must've left it in my own car or at home. I could've sworn it slid out in yours, though. My purse was open, and it was tilted on my lap, so I thought—" I let my voice soften, keeping it casual, reassuring "—but I guess I was wrong."

Ellie's shoulders seemed to relax slightly, though I wasn't sure if she truly believed me or if she was just pretending to let it go. "Oh, okay," she said finally, nodding as if satisfied.

Gabe, however, remained still. His hand rested on the back of Ellie's chair, I assume, rubbing her back. I couldn't see if he was, but I could feel the silent communication passing between them. They were working together. That much was clear.

But what else was in that black duffel bag? The image flashed through my mind again—a long wire, some fabric in black. I could only make out pieces, but those pieces weren't adding up.

I absentmindedly stabbed a piece of steak with my fork, turning it over rather than eating it. My gut told me I had missed my chance. I should not have gone to Ellie's car when Gabe was still at the table. Instead, I had let my nerves get the best of me. Gabe had come running after me like a man with something to hide.

I glanced up at him with a small, amused smile, playing my role perfectly. "Now, Gabe, what on earth made you come running after me like that?" I asked, letting out a light giggle, as though the whole thing was just a silly misunderstanding.

He hesitated, just for a beat, before forcing a chuckle of his own. "Oh, ya know. It's getting dark, and I just don't think it's safe for a woman to be walking to her car alone. Ever."

He smiled, but his voice betrayed him—just a little. It was nervous. I smiled back.

As if wanting to put the whole conversation to rest, he flashed a quick smile and said, "Let me get you ladies more water," before walking off, his pace just a little too quick.

I watched him disappear toward the other side of the bar, then turned back to Ellie with a bright, carefree expression. "Awww, he's just so cute," I gushed, forcing out a lighthearted giggle, hoping to reassure her that I didn't suspect a thing.

Ellie gave me a small smile, but I could see her studying me, as if trying to gauge whether I really meant it. "Anyway, your new mystery guy, Stewart—you have to tell me if you see him again soon. I mean, once you find out," I said with a grin, as if that was all I cared about.

She relaxed at that, the shift in topic allowing her to drop her guard.

Later, as we made our way toward the exit, I stopped at the front restroom while Ellie waited outside. When I came back out, I spotted her standing by the outside entrance, phone in hand, a huge smile spreading across her face. Her fingers flew over the screen, texting quickly, her body practically buzzing with excitement.

I raised a curious eyebrow as I approached. "Well, you won't believe it," she said, eyes still glued to her phone, her voice filled with barely contained giddiness.

"What's up?" I asked, mirroring her smile as I stepped beside her.

She let out a tiny squeal, practically bouncing on her toes. "He texted. He wants to see me again tonight. Already." She looked up at me, her face glowing with excitement. "Oh my God, he's so hot."

I let out an exaggerated gasp. "Wow, that was fast! I can't wait to hear how this one goes again." I nudged her playfully. "I can tell how excited you are."

Ellie nodded eagerly. "Yes! Let's go," she said, suddenly moving toward the door with a renewed sense of urgency, as if she had somewhere to be—somewhere other than home.

I slipped into the passenger seat of her car as she got behind the wheel. Little did she know that an idea was already forming in my mind.

As she focused on driving, her hands gripping the wheel just a little tighter than usual, I took the opportunity to tilt my phone away from her and quickly type out a message. My fingers moved swiftly, ensuring she couldn't see what I was doing.

To cover myself, I let out a small, frustrated sigh. "Ugh, I'm just trying to find a good recipe for a couple of the dinners I had in Blue's lately. Sometimes I can recreate them pretty well." I spoke in a casual, distracted tone, my eyes still on my phone as if I were really scrolling through recipes.

Ellie didn't even glance my way, too absorbed in everything going on with Stewart.

> I'll call you in 20 minutes. I need to talk to you. Don't call or text me back.

After typing my message and hitting send, I locked my screen and slipped the phone back into my lap, staring out of the window as if nothing had happened. I cast a slow, subtle glance over my shoulder, toward the direction of the black duffel bag. It sat there in the far back of Ellie's car, unassuming yet heavy with possibility. Could it be holding the answers? Or was I just overreacting?

CHAPTER FORTY-SIX

As Ellie pulled into my driveway, the headlights cast long shadows across the pavement. I turned toward her with a bright smile, keeping up the act.

"So, remember—call me later tonight or tomorrow. I can't wait to hear about it again," I said, my voice light and enthusiastic.

She gripped the steering wheel tightly with both hands, her knuckles whitening as if she were holding back an explosion of excitement.

"Oh, I will. You *know* I will," she said, her grin practically stretching from ear to ear. At that moment, it was as if the entire situation from earlier—the tension, Gabe running after me, my little detour to her car—had completely vanished from her memory. The distraction of her new man had done its job. It worked out perfectly for me.

I had my own distraction now—someone I needed to call.

Just as I reached for the handle, Ellie gave me a warm

look. "I always have a great time with you," she said, her eyes gleaming under the glow of the dashboard lights.

"Same here," I replied, flashing her one last smile before stepping out.

Once I was through the door, I hit the garage button, watching as the heavy door lowered back down, sealing me inside. The house felt quiet, still. But my mind was anything but.

Jax trotted over, tail wagging. "Hey, buddy," I murmured, scratching behind his ear as I walked past him toward my office.

The moment I sank into my chair, I exhaled slowly. I slipped off my shoes, setting them neatly beside my chair, then reached into my purse, fishing out my phone. My fingers hovered over the screen for a moment before I tapped the name I needed. The line rang twice before he picked up.

"Hi, I have some new information," I said, keeping my voice steady.

"I do as well," Bennett replied, his tone calm but edged with something unreadable.

I leaned forward slightly, lowering my voice as if someone could be listening. "Well, I was with Ellie tonight. She's seeing Stewart again. She really likes him."

Bennett let out a quiet chuckle. "I really hope she's not getting *too* attached," he mused.

I shook my head. "She won't. She seems to go through men pretty fast these days."

"Good." His voice was firm. "She's in for a rude awakening if she thinks otherwise."

I sighed, my fingers tapping lightly against my desk. "She just uses guys anyway, so I doubt she'll even care when it's over. But listen—earlier today, I saw something strange. She was flirting with Gabe from the golf course, the one who works there. And then, right before she left, he handed her a black duffel bag. Gabe is the guy whose texts Stewart saw on Ellie's phone."

Bennett was silent for a beat. "Go on."

"She put the bag in the back of her car. I went out to her car tonight when I was with her, pretending I forgot something, and then ..." I hesitated.

"Let me guess," Bennett interrupted, his tone dry. "She knew you were on to something?"

I smirked. "No. Not her." I let the words hang for a second before adding, "*Him.* Gabe. He came after me."

Bennett exhaled sharply. "Of course he did."

I frowned. "How did you know?"

"They don't want anything exposed," he said simply. "And if they are planning something, it means they already suspect you're onto them, or worried you might find something out."

I shook my head, even though he couldn't see me. "I don't think they actually *believe* that. Everything seemed fine later. At first, they looked nervous—like I had found something—but then Ellie completely forgot about it."

"She's distracted by Stewart now," Bennett mused. "That works in your favor."

"I know." I hesitated, then stood up, pacing my office. "I was hoping Stewart could check out what's inside that black duffel bag." My voice lowered instinctively. "It's been sitting in her car since this afternoon. If there's something in there we need to know about—"

"I'll see what we can do, but I can't promise anything," he said, trying to sound confident.

I nodded, even though he couldn't see me. "Good."

Bennett let out a small chuckle. "You know, I was going to call you with an update, but it seems you already know."

I smiled faintly. "You were going to tell me they're meeting again tonight."

"Exactly."

"Well, now we both know," I said, laughing.

"Seems that way."

A brief silence stretched between us before I exhaled. "All right. We'll be in touch."

I lowered my phone slowly, staring at the darkened screen as my mind raced.

Ellie had no idea what she had gotten herself into.

I wandered over to my front window, the sheer curtains barely swaying as I peered across at Ellie's house. Her garage door stood wide open, Mark's car nowhere in sight.

Without thinking, I reached for my phone and dialed. It rang twice before he answered.

"Hi, how are you?" I asked, keeping my voice casual, though my fingers tightened around the phone.

Mark exhaled softly. "I'm at the driving range at the golf course. How was your day?" His tone was relaxed.

Then, without giving me a chance to answer, his voice shifted, dropping into that low, intimate register that never failed to make my stomach tighten. "Do you wanna meet me at work?"

Ellie had just dropped me off, and yet—"I can," I murmured, already trying to work through the logistics in my mind.

"I would really like going right back to the St. Regis with you, even though we just left there," Mark said, drawing out each syllable in that same sultry tone.

A slow, satisfied hum escaped me. "Ugh, that would be amazing."

In a quieter voice, he added, "I'm leaving in a few minutes to head there. I'll leave the door unlocked."

I glanced down at myself, smoothing my hands over my clothes. Then, with a decisive breath, I slipped into my master bathroom, brushing through my long hair, touching up my lipstick, changing into a fresh skirt, and a long-sleeved airy blouse, and making sure I looked effortlessly put together.

By the time I stepped outside, the sky had deepened into the night, the last remnants of daylight barely clinging to the horizon. It was late summer, the kind of warm night that made the air feel thick.

I rushed through the lush green path that wound toward his office, my sandals whispering over the stone pathway. As I reached the door, I hesitated for just a second before pushing it open.

Darkness.

The entire office was dimmed with only shadows inside, all the blinds drawn tight. Only a faint, flickering glow from the courtyard's lamppost sliced through a small open area in a blind that was closed completely, casting a long, ghostly shadow.

And then, I saw him.

Mark stood partially obscured in the shifting light. As I stepped further inside, he moved toward me, his presence overwhelming, pulling me into his orbit. He took my purse from my hand, setting it on his chair with a deliberate slowness.

I barely had time to react before he backed me against the nearest wall, his body pressing into mine.

His lips ensnared mine, hot, urgent, searching. His hands knew exactly what they were doing, sliding down my waist, gripping the hem of my skirt, lifting it ever so slightly as his fingers skimmed along my leg. A shiver rippled through me at the feather-light touch of his thumb tracing circles on my inner thigh.

He kissed down the curve of my neck, his breath hot against my skin, and in the next instant, he led me to the couch.

"Wait," he murmured suddenly, pulling away for a fraction of a second.

I blinked, dazed, watching as he reached for the decorative throw draped over the back of the couch. With a slow, almost reverent motion, he spread it out over the expensive leather.

"I just don't want the leather to be too cold for you," he said softly. The tenderness of the gesture sent a flutter through my chest.

As his hands found me again, as he whispered things against my skin that made my pulse race, time became irrelevant.

"I love you," he murmured between kisses, the words threading into my thoughts, sinking deep, branding themselves against my heart.

Later, when the air between us had settled into something quieter, more reflective, I sat up, reaching for my scattered blouse and skirt. Mark, still lounging on the couch, watched me with an unreadable expression.

"There's something I've been wanting to talk to you about," he said suddenly, his voice different now. He wasn't teasing anymore.

Something in his tone made me pause. I turned to him fully. "What is it?"

He ran a hand through his hair, exhaling like he was trying to gather the right words. Then, with a small, self-deprecating chuckle, he gestured to himself.

He moved to sit up at the edge of the couch. Then his eyes locked onto mine, serious, unwavering. "I need to say this. I just want to be with you."

I stilled, the air between us shifting, crackling with something heavy.

Mark leaned forward, elbows resting on his knees. "I'm going to tell Ellie I want a divorce."

The words hung in the dimly lit room, altering everything.

As I searched his face for a trace of sincerity, the gravity of his confession stirred something deep inside me, emotions rising like a storm. And deep down, I already knew this was coming from how much he had fallen for me lately.

CHAPTER FORTY-SEVEN

"No, you can't," I said quickly, my voice sharper than I intended. Then, realizing how that might sound, I softened. "I mean—yes, yes, I want you to. I want you to be free of this. But Mark—" I took a step toward him, searching his face. "I really feel like she's up to something. Something bad. Don't you think we should figure out exactly what that is first? To know if we would be in even worse danger after telling her you want a divorce?"

Mark sighed heavily, the words weighing down on him.

"There's so much more I need to tell you," I pressed, my pulse quickening. "I found out something else—"

But he shook his head, cutting me off.

"I don't want you to take this the wrong way, but I don't care," he said, his voice low but firm. His eyes met mine, dark and unwavering. "I just want to be with you."

A lump formed in my throat.

"I know, baby," I murmured, walking toward him, my hands instinctively reaching for comfort—for him. "And I want to be with you too."

He stood there, his golf shirt crumpled in his hands. That's when I noticed—

"Oh my God." My voice wavered as I reached out, touching his lower side just above his waist, as if making contact with it would confirm what I already suspected. "Did she do this again last night?"

Mark hesitated, his jaw tightening. Then, reluctantly, he nodded. "Yes."

A sickening wave of anger rolled through me as I got closer to look at him, my stomach twisting at what I saw—new cuts and scratches. Some dried, some fresher.

"Look at this," I whispered, my hands trembling as I gently touched his waist.

Mark swallowed hard. "And she did some this morning," he admitted, his voice barely audible. "The way she spirals into rage," he muttered, eyes dropping to the floor, as if ashamed to even give the words air.

I sucked in a breath, my mind replaying how dark his office had been when I arrived tonight. The drawn blinds, the shadows. He had been hiding. He must have felt so embarrassed, so drained, so trapped.

I pressed his golf shirt to my face, the scent of him still clinging to the fabric, as a wave of fury surged through me —fury at what she had done to him, at the damage she left behind.

"Come here," he murmured, stepping forward, his arms circling me, his hand moving gently along my back.

"I should be the one comforting you," I said, my fingertips still gripping his shirt.

Mark exhaled, his hand tightening around my waist as if he needed to steady himself.

"Give me a few more days," I said, pulling back just enough to look into his eyes. "Let me see what I can find out. Then you break the news to her. What do you think?"

He studied me for a long moment before nodding.

"I'm so sorry," I murmured, my voice thick with emotion. "For everything you're going through."

I leaned my head against his shoulder, exhaling shakily. "I really am so sorry."

"I know," he said softly. "I love you." He hesitated, then sighed. "I know what we're doing isn't right ... But I can't stay with her anymore. I just can't."

I nodded against him, feeling the tension in his body, the exhaustion of fighting a battle no one else could see.

And then, something caught my eye.

"Your shirt—oh no."

Mark barely reacted, his thoughts clearly elsewhere. "What?"

I turned the fabric under the light. "I got lipstick on it when I buried my face in it. In a few places." My voice was small, almost guilty. "This isn't good."

Mark let out a quiet chuckle, shaking his head. "It's fine. Don't worry about it."

"No, really, Mark—" I studied the stains, my mind already racing. "I'll take it to the dry cleaners. Just so she doesn't find it."

He shrugged. "If you want to. Otherwise, I can just throw it out. I have a few extra golf polos I keep at work here. Plus, she is preoccupied. Would she even notice?"

"No, no." I shook my head. "I need to make sure it's accounted for. No remnants of lipstick, no evidence. Right now, it's probably not good if you have a shirt that's not accounted for either."

I reached up, gently cupping his cheek, guiding his eyes back to mine.

His gaze softened. "I wanna see you tomorrow."

His lips brushed my forehead, lingering just long enough to send warmth through me.

I smiled. "I'll be here tomorrow."

But he shook his head. "Not here. Let's go somewhere else. I'll let you know where."

I considered the proposition. Then, I smiled again, slow and knowing, letting him see my agreement in the way my eyes met his.

Mark exhaled and then started slipping into a new golf polo he pulled from his office closet.

"These come in handy when I'm heading to the golf course right from work," he said, "or when a certain special someone gets lipstick on my shirt."

He gave me a wink.

I laughed, shaking my head. "Ha, well, I'll get this one cleaned up."

CHAPTER FORTY-EIGHT

I stepped through the door of my house, the stillness wrapping around me like a heavy blanket. The only sound was the faint click of the lock as I turned it. Mark's shirt was clutched in my hand, a reminder of everything that had just happened. Without thinking, I made my way straight to my bedroom, my feet moving on autopilot as Jax arose from the couch and followed me upstairs.

Once inside, I tossed the shirt onto the floor near the wall, watching as it crumpled into a careless heap. For a second, I just stood there, staring at it.

Why did I even bring it inside?

I had to take it to the dry cleaner tomorrow—I should have left it in my car. But my mind had been spinning the entire drive home, and now, as I stood in the dim light of my bedroom, exhaustion crept in.

Jax followed me to the bathroom, his golden eyes watching as I reached for the faucet, twisting it until steaming water poured into the tub.

I needed to escape. Just for a few minutes.

Leaving the bath to fill, I made my way downstairs, my body moving as if on instinct. The house was eerily quiet–I grabbed a bottle of wine from the kitchen, poured myself a generous glass, and took a slow sip. The warmth slid down my throat, but it did nothing to steady the racing thoughts in my head.

I closed all the blinds, one by one, my fingers lingering on the cords. A deep unease settled in my chest as I double-checked the locks and set the house alarm. Then, I climbed the stairs again, my feet feeling heavier with each step.

Once inside my room, I moved to the windows, drawing the blinds and curtains shut completely. No one could look in now.

A single candle sat on the nightstand—Steven's night-stand. I hesitated for a moment before striking a match, watching as the flame flickered to life. It cast a soft, golden glow across the room, illuminating the space with a warmth that felt almost deceptive.

Then, I stripped off my clothes. The fabric slid from my skin, pooling at my feet, leaving me bare in the dim candlelight.

So many things raced through my mind. The duffel bag. Gabe. Mark wanting a divorce. Bennett. I didn't even tell Mark about the bag yet.

A few months ago, it had been just Mark and me. Now, it felt like I was tangled in a web of complications, each thread pulling me in a different direction.

I exhaled slowly, shaking the thoughts away as I reached for my wine glass and phone, placing them on the ledge by the tub. The water was steaming now, the scent of lavender and vanilla curling into the air.

I stepped in, my legs sinking beneath the surface first,

then the rest of me. The warmth enveloped my body, and I let out a slow, contented sigh as I melted into the heat.

The tension in my muscles, the endless swirl of thoughts—gone, if only for a moment.

I leaned my head back against the cool porcelain, my arms draping over the edge of the tub as I let my mind drift into the quiet.

Just as I began to lose myself in the coziness of it all, my phone buzzed. I hesitated for a second, my fingers hovering over the edge of the tub, reluctant to disrupt the moment. But curiosity got the best of me.

I wiped the condensation from the screen and saw Ellie's name flash across it.

> What's up, friend? Drinks tomorrow with Chloe and me? At home this time?

I exhaled softly at the message. Mark had already hinted at wanting to see me again tomorrow. I needed to determine if he preferred meeting earlier or later before making a decision.

> Yes. Sounds good. How's your date with Stewart going? Let's have drinks at your house?

The response came almost instantly, as if she had been waiting for me to reply.

> No, Mark will be at home working. He won't want us around. Can we have drinks at your house?

I frowned. *Mark will be at home working?* I knew for a

fact he wouldn't be there, because we were planning on seeing each other.

Before I could process it, another message popped up.

> I just left the bar with Stewart. We decided to go to a different hotel this time. I drove separately and got here before him, so I thought I'd text you while I wait. I'll fill you and Chloe in tomorrow night over drinks. I'm sure it'll be good :)

I stared at her words, my mind spinning before I typed out a response:

> OK. My house it is. Can't wait to hear how it goes :)

A few seconds passed before her final message arrived.

> He just got here. Talk to you later.

I watched the screen until it dimmed, then set the phone back down on the ledge beside my wine glass. The uneasy feeling in my stomach deepened.

I let out a slow breath and slid down further into the water, letting it rise over my collarbones. A thin veil of steam hovered just above the surface, curling upward in ghostly ribbons. I watched it for a moment, trying to push away the thoughts racing through my mind.

The candle on my nightstand flickered. Beyond it, I spotted Jax curled up on my bed, his chest rising and falling steadily. At least *he* was unbothered.

I closed my eyes, forcing myself to savor the quiet, but my mind wouldn't settle. Mark. The duffel bag. Ellie's lies.

Everything was tangled together, an ever-growing knot I couldn't seem to loosen.

Fifteen minutes passed before I finally dragged myself out of the tub, my skin warm and flushed from the heat. I wrapped a towel around my body, glancing at my reflection in the mirror. My damp hair was up in a clip with a few loose wet strands that clung to my shoulders.

I slowly walked into my bedroom, throwing on some comfortable pajamas before heading downstairs. The house was silent, the kind of stillness that usually brought comfort but now felt suffocating. I curled up on the couch, tucking my legs beneath me as I wanted to fall asleep. At some point, exhaustion took over.

I drifted off into a restless sleep, only to jolt awake at three in the morning, my neck aching from the awkward position I had collapsed into. Jax was curled up in a ball at my feet on the couch.

But my thoughts were just as chaotic as before. I had no advice to give myself. If I told myself to *focus*, *what* would I focus on?

I sat there, staring into the darkness, knowing deep down that things were about to unravel. And when they did, I wasn't sure I'd be ready. Clutching my phone like a lifeline, I tiptoed upstairs, drawn to the quiet promise of my bed—hoping that sleep, elusive and gentle, might finally find me there. I heard the faint sound of Jax following softly behind me.

CHAPTER FORTY-NINE

I woke up the next morning feeling like I hadn't slept at all. It was the kind of beginning that made the whole work week feel doomed before it even started. My body ached with exhaustion, and my mind felt foggy as I fumbled for my phone on the nightstand. The screen lit up, and I squinted against the brightness, scrolling through my schedule for the day. A morning house showing and two back-to-back closings in the afternoon. My brain was already strategizing when I could squeeze in a brief nap before the evening.

I let out a long, weary sigh as I dragged myself upright, the sheets cool against my skin. The weight of the day ahead pressed against my shoulders. I needed to get through my work quickly and somehow look refreshed for Mark. Then Ellie and Chloe were coming over tonight, which meant even more energy spent. So much is happening at once.

And then there was *Bennett*.

What new information would he have for me from last night?

Pushing that thought aside for now, I forced myself out of bed and turned on the shower, making it colder than usual in an attempt to wake up. As the water ran, I grabbed my phone again and sent a quick text to Mark. He'd be at work already—he always went in early.

> Morning. What time should we meet later today?

I sat back down on the bed while I waited for his reply. The response came almost instantly.

> Morning. How about 5:30? I need to get home afterward for some work.

Ellie was right. He would be there doing work, although she probably didn't even really know that for sure at the time she had texted me; it was most likely just an excuse.

> Sounds great :) I can't wait to see you.

> I can't wait to see you. Love you :)

I stared at the words for a second longer than necessary before setting my phone down.

Stepping into the shower, the sharp chill of the water jolted me fully awake. It was a temporary fix, but it worked. By the time I was dressed, I felt more prepared for the day.

I headed downstairs, opening all the blinds and curtains one by one. Sunlight streamed in, casting long, golden rays across the floors. I paused at the large front window, my eyes lingering on the lush green trees lining the street. The neighborhood was peaceful, calm.

I shook my head, forcing myself to refocus. Today had a strict timeline of work appointments, and I needed to stay ahead of it. Before Ellie had the chance to take control of the evening's plans, I quickly set the time with her and Chloe.

> Hi ladies! Sounds like we're having a get-together tonight. Does 7:30 work? I have a showing right before then.

Chloe replied first.

> Sounds great! Can't wait to see you both.

Then Ellie texted.

> Yes! Can't wait!

> Great. See you both then.

With that settled, I felt a small sense of accomplishment. At least one thing was under control.

Grabbing my work bag, I headed out to my car, sliding into the driver's seat. Just as I was about to back out of the driveway, I froze. *Mark's shirt.* I had left it inside.

Letting out a frustrated sigh, I pulled back up, ran upstairs, and grabbed the shirt off the floor. Tossing it into the backseat, I finally got on my way. Fifteen minutes to nine and a temperature of 76 degrees—my dashboard said. The warmth, paired with the bright green trees outside, gave me a sense of peace. I needed this. Even if it was temporary.

Before my workday started, I stopped by the office to get settled. I was surrounded by colleagues—people I considered friends—but none of them had any idea what was really happening in my life. They had no clue about the mess I was balancing, the secrets, the stress. I sat at my desk, trying to drown out the noise around me, focusing on preparing for my workday.

It went well. *Really* well. The house checked every box for my clients—the sleek white kitchen they had dreamed of, a master suite with both a soaking tub and a separate shower, a spacious bonus room for their kids, and a garage big enough for all of his weekend projects. As usual, I encouraged them to walk the property one last time, knowing it helped solidify their decision.

While they explored, I took the opportunity to check my messages.

A new text from Mark:

Baby, I can't wait to see you later.

My stomach did a slow flip. He had me melting, every single time.

I can't wait to see you too :)

Meet me at the Pier Hotel, he wrote. I already have Room 241 reserved. Just go straight there. I'll be there at 5:30—I'm leaving work early.

I'll see you then. I love you :)

I felt a rush of anticipation as I set my phone down.

After wrapping up my two afternoon closings in the late afternoon, I decided to go home. On my way, I spotted a dry cleaner just on the outskirts of town and decided to pull in. I could finally drop off Mark's shirt.

Grabbing it from the backseat, I stepped inside. The place had the same upscale, polished feel as most businesses in the area—brick exterior, pristine interior. Behind the counter stood a woman in her mid-forties, her smile polite as she greeted me.

"Hi, I just need to drop off this shirt, please," I said, setting it on the counter.

She nodded, pulling up the system. "What's your name?"

"Rachel. Rachel Scheffler."

She frowned slightly, typing into the computer. "I don't have you in the system. Are you new here?"

"Yes, first time," I replied, shrugging.

"All right, let's get your information." She asked for my address and email, and I rattled it off without thinking.

Then she hesitated. "Hmmm ... I already have someone in the system at that address." Her brows furrowed. "A Steven ?"

My breath hitched.

"Are you related to him?" she asked casually.

I swallowed hard, my voice feeling distant. "Yes. He was my late husband."

The woman's expression softened with recognition. "Oh! Yes, I remember him. He came in here a couple of times with his dress shirts. Such a nice fella, though."

My stomach twisted. What was Steven doing at a dry cleaner on this side of town? It was miles from his office and nowhere near our house—completely out of the way.

I forced myself to keep a neutral expression. "When can I pick up the shirt?" I asked, steering her back to the task at hand.

"In a few days," she said, nodding. "You'll get an email when it's ready."

"Great. Thank you." I turned and walked out the door, completely numb.

Sliding into my car, I gripped the steering wheel. Some strange, ominous feeling was curling in my gut.

CHAPTER FIFTY

I shook off my wandering thoughts and tried to refocus on Mark. I decided to text him, but the bag loomed in my mind, gnawing at my conscience. I had to tell him. It refused to be ignored.

I wrote to him:

> I just can't wait to see you. Today has felt impossibly long already. Every minute is dragging, and all I want is to be with you.

He responded:

> Same here. Just hold on a little longer. We're going to have such a nice night tonight.

> I can't wait. I know I don't have much time since Ellie and Chloe are coming over later, but that doesn't change how much I need this—how much I need you.

> I love you. I'll see you soon.

A wave of warmth rushed through me. Just thinking about Mark, about being near him, melted away some of the weight I had been carrying all day.

When I got home, I felt the tension from the day rising up in me again, making me crave the soothing warmth of a bath again, but time was already slipping away. Instead, I opted for a quick shower, letting the steaming water wash over me, rinsing away the stress, and leaving behind only anticipation.

Afterward, I wrapped myself in a plush towel and sat on the edge of my bed, allowing myself a brief moment to breathe. My eyes wandered absently around the room, finally settling on Steven's nightstand drawer again. Curiosity tugged at me, tempting me to go through it, but I pushed the thought aside. Not now.

Glancing at my phone, I realized time was running short. I needed to get dressed.

I walked to my closet and pulled out a pair of fitted jeans and a silk blouse that buttoned all the way down— one of my reliable go-to outfits, yet easily transformed into something special with the right accessories. I chose a pair of gold dangling earrings that caught the light just enough, slipped on nude heels, and grabbed a sleek brown handbag that perfectly complemented my ensemble.

For my hair, I twisted it up into a clip, knowing that when I let it down later, it would fall off my shoulders and down my back. A touch of light pink gloss completed my look, subtle and natural, since I knew it wouldn't last long anyway.

Before I knew it, I was pulling up to the Pier Hotel, a luxurious boutique hotel nestled downtown. The soft glow of lights illuminated the entrance, casting a warm, golden hue against the evening sky.

As I stepped out of my car, the warm night air kissed my skin.

"Good evening, ma'am. Do you have any bags to check?" A valet greeted me with a polite nod. He was an older gentleman, probably in his late sixties, doing this job more out of habit than necessity, a way to keep himself busy in retirement.

"No, thank you." I handed him my keys and quickly made my way inside.

The sleek, modern interior of the hotel was a stunning contrast to the old-world charm of the exterior. I walked discreetly through the lobby, avoiding unnecessary small talk, and located the elevators.

A well-dressed couple emerged from it, their polished looks and easy smiles suggesting they were off to dinner. I slipped inside before the doors could fully close, pressing the button for the second floor.

A few moments later, I was standing in front of room 241. I knocked gently, and within seconds, the door swung open, revealing Mark.

He looked effortlessly attractive in his work pants and a fitted white undershirt. The way the fabric stretched across his chest and shoulders made me flutter with excitement. Even with the lingering marks on his arms—Ellie's doing— he didn't seem the least bit self-conscious with me now. He trusted me.

"How was your day? How'd the showings go?" He leaned in, pressing a lingering kiss to my cheek.

"Good," I replied breathily, stepping further into the

room. My heels slipped off at the foot of the bed, and I let out a soft sigh of relief.

Mark's eyes glimmered with something playful. "I have an idea for something different tonight."

I tilted my head, intrigued. "Oh? And what's that?"

"What's your favorite thing on TV?" he asked, a smirk playing on his lips.

I laughed, caught off guard. "Uh ... I don't know?"

He chuckled. "I know what you're thinking—you didn't come all the way here just to watch TV." He grabbed the remote, flipping through the channels.

Before I could respond, he settled on an old rerun and casually tossed the remote aside. Then, without hesitation, he gathered all four pillows from the king-sized bed and stacked them against the headboard before reclining against them.

"Come here," he said, his voice deep, inviting. He patted the space between his legs.

A slow smile spread across my lips. I slid my heels off, and then I reached up, unclipping my hair before climbing onto the bed. I nestled into him, my back resting against his chest, his arms wrapping around me in a way that felt both protective and effortless.

He pressed a gentle kiss to my temple, his lips lingering just long enough to send a shiver down my spine.

"This," he whispered, his breath warm against my skin. "This just sounded so good with you."

I sighed, my fingers tracing lazy patterns over his arm as we watched the screen. The world outside faded, the noise, the chaos, the worries—none of it mattered in this moment.

Because here, in his arms, I felt it. I knew it. We were both in love with each other.

CHAPTER FIFTY-ONE

Soon, we had both drifted off in the soft glow of the television, and it sounded like nothing more than a murmur in the background. The warmth of Mark's body against mine had lulled me into peaceful slumber. When we finally stirred about forty minutes later, it was as if we had never moved—our hands were still intertwined, our bodies entangled.

We began to slide down onto the bed more. I turned around, and we found ourselves lying on our sides and facing each other.

"I should get going soon," he murmured, though his voice carried no urgency.

I nodded, but neither of us moved. His fingers traced slow, soothing circles along my arms, his touch absent-minded yet deeply intimate.

"I know you have to meet the others," he said softly.

We continued like that for a while, our touches lingering, growing more deliberate. It wasn't rushed. It was just us, lost in the quiet moment.

Without a word, Mark gently rolled me over so that my back was against his chest. His arms tightened around me, his warmth completely surrounding me. Then, I felt it —the slow press of his body against mine, the shift of his breathing. Slowly, we peeled away our own clothes. A slow thrill ran through me as I realized what was happening, the unexpected nature of it making it all the more intense.

His lips found my neck, pressing soft, lingering kisses along my skin, moving to my ear, my cheek. Every breath, every whispered "I love you," sent a shiver down my spine, making me squeeze my eyes shut, wanting to savor every second, to capture the feeling and hold onto it forever.

Afterward, as reality crept back in, I sighed, knowing what was coming next.

"I don't like this," Mark admitted, his voice quiet but firm. He exhaled heavily against my shoulder before continuing. "I mean, I do ... but I hate that you always have to leave right after. The night at the hotel in the suite was my favorite."

I slowly started to shift, sitting up, reaching for my jeans at the edge of the bed. Mark remained lying there, watching me, his expression unreadable.

As I started to slide my jeans back on, he suddenly grinned mischievously. "Let's just stay longer," he said in a light, teasing voice.

Before I could answer, he reached for my hand and pulled me back down. I let out a surprised laugh as I lost my balance, landing against him. Within seconds, he had rolled me onto my back, his body hovering over mine.

"Mark—"

"I'm serious," he cut in, his eyes locking onto mine. He

brushed a stray strand of hair from my face, his touch gentle. "I want to be with you. And only you."

My breath caught. The intensity in his gaze, the certainty in his voice—it sent a rush of emotions through me.

"I know," I whispered, my hand resting against his cheek. "And I want to be with you, too."

He rolled onto his back beside me, watching me with a faint smirk as I once again attempted to stand up and put my jeans on.

"We should just let all of this go with Ellie," he said suddenly, his tone more serious now. "I'm over her. I'm over all this—what she does, the way she makes me feel, the control she tries to have over me." He shook his head, his frustration evident.

"Hey," I said softly, turning to him. "I know. I know you're done."

He nodded, but there was still something heavy in his eyes.

"I'm seeing them tonight," I reminded him. "I'll call you first thing in the morning."

Mark sighed, pushing himself up and reaching for his shirt. He dressed in silence, then glanced at me as I slid on my shoes.

"Wait for me," he said suddenly. "We can walk out together."

I hesitated. "Do you really think that's a good idea?"

Mark held my gaze. "Like I said," he repeated, his voice steady, sure, "I'm done with my marriage to her."

And as we walked toward the door together, side by side, something in my gut told me everything was about to change.

CHAPTER FIFTY-TWO

Pulling out of the hotel parking lot, I reached for my phone and dialed Ellie's number. It barely rang twice before she picked up.

"Hey! What should I grab at the store for snacks tonight?" I asked, keeping my tone casual.

"Oh, I don't know," she said lightly. "Just some drinks, maybe some meat and crackers. I'm bringing a few drinks too—and some dips."

An idea flickered in my mind. Maybe—just maybe—I should grab something stronger. If Ellie got tipsy enough, would she finally spill more details about whatever was going on with Gabe? I wasn't naïve. I knew she wouldn't just outright admit it, no matter how much she drank. But I figured it wouldn't hurt to try.

I grabbed a cart, steering it directly toward the liquor aisle, all while chatting with Ellie, who was peppering me with questions about my day.

My fingers trailed over the bottles, hesitating only for a moment before grabbing a bottle of tequila and another of vodka—both strong enough to loosen lips. Next, I reached for some mixers, something sweet and inviting that wouldn't make the drinks taste too harsh. Satisfied, I turned down the snack aisle and grabbed the usual—crackers, cheese, meat. I wasn't even sure how much of it we'd eat.

"I'm just checking out now. I'll be home in twenty minutes," I said, wheeling my cart toward the self-checkout.

"Twenty minutes?" Ellie asked, sounding surprised. "What grocery store did you go to? Ours is like three minutes away."

I hadn't thought about that. My mind scrambled for an excuse, something simple but convincing.

"Oh, I had a showing on the other end of town," I said, forcing an easy, casual tone. "I just stopped at the closest store afterward."

There was a pause, but then Ellie replied, "Ah, gotcha. Well, if you're gonna be home in twenty, we will come right when you get there. No point in waiting."

My stomach twisted. Why did I have to say exactly when I'd be home? I needed time. I needed to shower—again. Mark's scent still clung to me, his unique cologne that Ellie would pick up on in a heartbeat.

I thought fast. "Actually, let's make it forty-five minutes," I said, shifting my bags into my cart. "I forgot—I need to stop at a client's house on the way and drop something off."

Ellie didn't question it. "Oh, okay. Forty-five then."

I let out a slow breath of relief as we ended the call.

What would I even be dropping off? Luckily, she hadn't asked for details.

When I pulled into my driveway twenty minutes later —right on schedule—I felt a twinge of anxiety. If Ellie happened to see me arrive, I had my excuse ready: The client wasn't home.

I hauled the grocery bags inside, setting them on the counter before practically sprinting up the stairs. I still had time, but not much.

Jax wagged his tail impatiently as he followed me upstairs, waiting to be let out. "Give me a few minutes, buddy," I muttered, rushing past him.

In my bedroom, I hesitated. Do I shower? Or can I get away with just wiping a wet washcloth over me to remove any lingering smells?

No. I had to shower. Fast.

I clipped my hair up, turned the water on—even though it hadn't warmed up yet—and stepped in. The chill made me shiver, but I didn't care. I scrubbed quickly—my neck, my chest, my arms—washing away every last trace of Mark's scent. Stepping out, I grabbed a towel as goosebumps pricked my skin.

Moving quickly, I threw on a lightweight sweater, linen pants, and some sandals. With a light misting of my signature perfume, I gave myself a subtle armor to make sure it was the only scent anyone would catch on me.

Before heading downstairs, I scanned my room, making sure I hadn't left anything out of place. Then, at the last second, I turned back and grabbed the clothes I'd been wearing earlier, stuffing them into my laundry hamper.

Down in the kitchen, I arranged the snacks on a serving platter, opened a bag of chips, and poured some of the mixers into glasses so it looked like I'd been prepping the whole time.

And just as I placed the last item on the counter, the doorbell rang.

I let out a slow breath, plastered on a smile, and walked to the door.

Ellie and Chloe stood there, looking effortlessly casual. "Hi, ladies, come on in," I said, waving them inside with a welcoming hand.

As Chloe stepped in, she kicked off her shoes, already making herself at home. "We actually started with a drink over at my house before coming here since you were running late," she said, grinning. Then, in an offhand comment that sent my stomach plummeting, she added, "I saw you get home a little while ago."

My breath hitched for the briefest second before I forced out a light laugh. "Oh yeah," I said smoothly. "My client wasn't available, so I just came straight home."

Chloe didn't say anything—just nodded, walking toward the kitchen.

Ellie followed her, looking like she had not given it a second thought.

But as I closed the door behind them, my heart was still racing. I had barely covered my tracks in time.

And something told me I needed to be extra careful tonight.

I forced a bright smile, hoping to steer the conversation to safer pastures. "Well, I got a ton of snacks," I said, gesturing toward the kitchen island where I had set everything up. "Seriously, look at this spread."

Ellie and Chloe leaned in, glancing over the assortment of food and the bottles of liquor I had carefully selected.

"Wow," Chloe said, her eyes lighting up as she spotted one particular bottle. "Look what you have. Tequila. Yum." She set down the bag she had brought and turned to me with an expectant grin. "Yeah, I'll take something with tequila."

"And for you, Ellie?" I asked, already reaching for the glasses I had lined up earlier.

Ellie hesitated for a second. "Hmm, I was going to have tequila too, but actually, make mine something with vodka. Maybe a martini," she said, eyeing the bottles as if mentally running through her options.

"Got it," I said.

As I started mixing their drinks, Ellie and Chloe busied themselves with unpacking the snacks they had brought, setting them out on the extra plates I had laid out for them. I carefully measured the tequila for Chloe's drink, poured vodka for Ellie's martini, and then—subtly—made my own drink significantly weaker. I needed my head to stay clear tonight.

I handed them their drinks with a big smile. "Here you go, ladies."

They settled onto the barstools along the kitchen island, sipping their drinks with appreciative hums. I took the seat at the end, cradling my own glass.

"Ugh, this is so nice," I sighed, swishing my drink before taking a small sip. "What a perfect way to end the day."

Ellie leaned her elbow on the counter, looking relaxed. Chloe, however, had a glint in her eye—she was ready for gossip.

"So, what's new with that guy from your country club you were telling me about?" she asked, tilting her head curiously. "Do tell."

Ellie smirked, her cheeks flushing slightly. "Oh, I don't know. But," she paused, giggling as she twirled her glass between her fingers, "there's actually someone else I met a few days ago."

Chloe gasped, grinning. "Okay, now I *really* need details."

Ellie glanced between us, her expression suddenly serious. She set her glass down and placed her hand gently on the counter as if sealing a pact. "All of this stays *right* here, okay?"

I nodded immediately. "Yes, for sure."

"Of course," Chloe added without hesitation.

Ellie exhaled, reassured. "Okay, good."

She leaned in slightly, lowering her voice. "So, I met this *really* cute guy the other night when I was leaving the club. Okay, don't judge me," she said, already giggling.

Chloe rolled her eyes playfully. "And? Come *on*."

I stayed quiet, pretending to be just as intrigued as Chloe. In reality, I already knew this part.

Ellie grinned. "We went out for drinks. And, well ... you know how it goes. One thing led to another."

Chloe gasped, dramatically clutching her chest. "Ellie!" she shrieked, before bursting into laughter.

I joined them, forcing a giggle, though my mind was elsewhere. Ellie had no idea I already knew this was all part of Bennett's plan.

The conversation continued, Ellie diving into the details of her night with Stewart. I half-listened, nodding at the right moments and sipping my drink slowly as I let them chatter.

After a while, Ellie tilted her empty glass in the air. "Another drink for me, please."

"Same here," Chloe said, standing up. "Also, I need to use your bathroom."

As she walked past Jax, she paused to scratch behind his ears. "Aww, your dog is just *so* cute."

I smiled. "He knows it, too."

As Chloe disappeared into the hallway, Ellie wandered toward the breakfast area across from me, picking up a framed photo from one of the shelves. I stayed behind the counter, preparing their drinks.

Then, Chloe returned, and her voice broke through my thoughts.

"Is this your late husband?" she asked, looking over Ellie's shoulders at the picture she was holding.

I turned just as she had taken the picture frame from Ellie's hand and held it up to show me.

"Ellie told me he passed away a while ago," Chloe added.

"Yes," I said, my voice even as I wiped condensation from the cocktail shaker. I stepped closer to see which photo she had picked up. It was one of the last pictures of us together—taken at a secluded beach in upstate New York. The sunlight had been golden that evening; it was a great day we had spent together. But the seams of our marriage had been starting to fray at that point.

Chloe studied the picture, tilting it slightly. "He was really handsome. You two looked amazing together."

"Thank you," I murmured.

Then, Chloe's expression shifted. She squinted at the image, bringing it closer.

"What happened to him?" she asked suddenly.

"With what?" I frowned, pouring the last of Ellie's drink into her glass.

"His arms," Chloe said, her voice quieter now. "Both of them. They're all scratched up. Badly too, look—from the elbows down."

She leaned in, studying the picture more closely.

My breath caught in my throat.

Smash.

The martini glass had slipped from my fingers, shattering against the kitchen floor.

A sharp silence fell over the room.

CHAPTER FIFTY-THREE

I forced a shaky laugh, my pulse pounding in my ears. "Ugh—slipped right out of my hand," I said, quickly bending down to pick up the shards.

But my hands trembled as I gathered the broken glass. Because now I knew exactly what she was talking about.

But Chloe didn't know.

And I needed to keep it that way.

"Are you okay?" Chloe's voice shot across the room, sharp with concern. She hurriedly set down the picture frame and rushed toward the kitchen. Ellie was right behind her, both of them moving quickly, their eyes darting from me to the shattered glass on the floor.

"What happened?" Chloe asked, her gaze flicking between me and the mess at my feet.

Think. *Think.* My mind raced for a believable excuse.

I forced a breathless laugh, shaking my head as I reached for a dish towel. "Jax. Jax jumped up on me." I glanced down at Jax, who sat obediently at my feet, his head tilted innocently. "I turned around too fast, and he got excited."

Ellie and Chloe's eyes dropped to Jax, who was wagging his tail slowly, blissfully unaware that he had just been blamed for something he hadn't done.

"He's never done that while I was holding a glass before," I continued, forcing a sheepish chuckle. "Guess he still thinks he's a puppy."

Chloe exhaled, her shoulders relaxing. "Oh gosh, that scared me."

"Me too," Ellie added.

"We'll help you clean up," Chloe offered, already reaching for the larger shards.

"Yeah, where's your broom and dustpan?" Ellie asked, looking around.

I swallowed, relieved they weren't pressing the issue. They had completely accepted my explanation. Neither of them had been facing me when it happened, which meant they hadn't seen my hand simply let go of the glass.

"Oh, no, don't worry about it," I said quickly, waving them off. "I'll take care of it. You two relax."

"No, we are helping. Where are the cleaning supplies?" Chloe brushed past me, already searching for the cleaning supplies.

I hesitated, but nodded toward the pantry. "They're in there."

As they busied themselves sweeping up the glass, I focused on my next problem—the photo. I needed to get over to it. I *had* to see it again.

After they helped to clean things up, I took a slow breath, masking my urgency. "Here's a fresh martini and tequila sunrise," I said, handing Ellie and Chloe the drinks I had just remade for them.

They took the glasses with grateful smiles. I began to wander toward the front living room. "Let's move in there," I suggested. "It's more comfortable."

They nodded, and we made our way to the oversized couch and plush armchairs. The high ceilings and grand fireplace made the space feel warm and inviting—something I had always loved about this house.

As Ellie and Chloe settled in, I forced myself to stay casual. "Oh, I left my phone in the kitchen. Be right back."

They were too absorbed in their conversation to pay any attention as I slipped back into the dining area. My heart pounded as I approached the cabinet where they had been looking at the picture earlier.

I picked it up with slightly trembling fingers.

The moment my eyes landed on the image, my stomach clenched.

The scratches on Steven's arms were unmistakable. They ran up and down his forearms. Just as they had ... on *Mark's* arms now.

My breath caught in my throat.

They were the *same.*

Same placement. Same jagged marks.

I squeezed my eyes shut for a moment, trying to steady my thoughts.

What did this mean?

Had Ellie done that to him? *How? Why? When?*

My pulse thundered in my ears.

I suddenly felt trapped between two choices—keep them here, pour more drinks, and see if I could draw more information out of Ellie ... or find a way to get them to leave so I could start digging into this mystery *now*.

I glanced back toward the living room, where the two women were laughing, completely oblivious to the storm raging inside me.

CHAPTER FIFTY-FOUR

For the next few hours, I tried my best to stay present—laughing when they laughed, chiming in where I needed to—but my mind kept drifting back to that picture. We passed the time swapping stories about nosy neighbors, husbands, the chaos of family life—and, of course, topping off our glasses. No matter how much I tried to push it away, the image of Steven's scratched-up arms kept gnawing at me like an itch I couldn't reach. I remembered Steven insisting for weeks that he must have brushed up against poison ivy—that was his explanation for the angry red marks along his arms.

I forced myself to focus on the conversation. Chloe was talking about her move to the area and how she loved the neighborhood. But as the night stretched on, and the clock crept closer to eleven, I found myself secretly hoping that Ellie would be the first to call it a night. And then, finally, she yawned.

Yes. *Finally.*

"It's been fun, ladies," Chloe said, stretching her arms as she stood up.

She turned to Ellie with a knowing look. "I'm going to head out."

Ellie blinked, then nodded, rubbing her eyes. "Yeah, I should get going too."

I feigned surprise, glancing at the clock even though I'd been watching the time all night. "Oh wow, it's almost eleven? That went by fast."

I stood up as well, grabbing my empty glass and following them into the kitchen. As we gathered up the snacks they had brought, I carefully packed them into bags, all while keeping one eye on the dining area where the picture frame sat.

As we made our way to the front door, Ellie's arms finally gave in to the balancing act—her purse slipped from her shoulder and everything came tumbling down. Between the bags of snacks and her oversized handbag, her hands never stood a chance. The foyer became a scatterplot of her belongings: her wallet slid one way, lipstick and loose change rolled across the floor, pens clattered in all directions, a couple of pill bottles spun on their sides, and a portable phone charger landed with a thud.

We all dropped to our knees to help, reaching and gathering her things in a quiet flurry. I scooped up her wallet, then started collecting pens, my hands quickly filling with them. As I glanced down, one pen caught my eye—it looked strangely familiar. I paused for half a second, turning it slightly in my fingers. *Where have I seen this before?* The question flickered, then faded. I shrugged it off and kept collecting.

After all the goods were gathered back in Ellie's purse,

they both stepped onto the porch. Chloe turned back with a bright smile. "We need to do this again soon."

"Absolutely," I agreed. Then, without missing a beat, I turned to Ellie. "Should we do it at your place next time? Maybe next week?"

I had a feeling she was going to say no, but I wanted to see her reaction.

Ellie hesitated, then quickly shook her head. "Oh, I think Mark is working from home most of next week ... I don't know if that'll work, but I'll let you know."

I gave her a casual nod, masking any hint of expectation. "No big deal. Door's always open if you feel like dropping by again."

We exchanged quick hugs before I closed the door behind them and then locked it. But I didn't move away just yet. Instead, I lingered near the front window, pulling back the curtain ever so slightly to watch as they walked down the driveway, their figures disappearing into the night.

The second they escaped from my view, I turned and hurried back to the dining room. My fingers trembled as I picked up the picture again, holding it closer to my face, studying every inch of it under the warm glow of the chandelier.

Chills ran down my spine.

I needed answers.

Setting the frame down with more care this time, I turned and walked briskly toward my office. I pulled open the bottom desk drawer—the one where I stored important but rarely accessed documents. It was a mess of tax papers, property records, and old legal files, but I knew exactly what I was looking for.

Midway through the stack, I found it.

A manila folder labeled STEVEN SCHEFFLER in black marker.

I hesitated, my fingers hovering over the folder's edge. I hadn't touched it since the day I had received it. When the investigator handed it to me, he told me to call if I ever needed anything. At the time, I had been too broken, too overwhelmed to do anything but accept it.

But now ...

I needed to know.

I flipped open the folder, my eyes immediately landing on the top page. It contained all the official details of his death—his name, the date, and then, in bold capital letters:

CAUSE OF DEATH: STRANGULATION.

I swallowed hard, my stomach twisting.

The investigator had once told me that Steven may have gotten mixed up with the wrong people through work. "Bad deals. Dangerous connections. Someone could have been out to get him," I remembered him saying.

But this ...

I had accepted that narrative back then, but suddenly, with the scratches on his arms staring back at me, I wasn't so sure.

I flipped through the folder, searching for the full autopsy report.

But it wasn't there.

My breath caught in my throat.

Where was it?

I sifted through every page, my fingers moving faster, more frantic.

Nothing.

Had it never been included?

I clenched my jaw. I needed to call the investigator.

I glanced at the clock—it was just after eleven. *Too late to call now.* I would have to wait until morning.

Frustrated, I closed the folder, poured myself another drink, and moved to the living room. I sank onto the couch, my mind racing in every possible direction, trying to make sense of it all.

Something didn't add up.

Eventually, I drifted upstairs to my bedroom, hoping to get some sleep.

But I barely slept, staring at the ceiling all night, my thoughts refusing to settle.

———

By the time my alarm went off at six the next morning, I was already wide awake. I got up, showered, and made coffee, pacing as I waited for 8 a.m. to roll around.

At exactly 7:47 a.m., I sat down at my desk, coffee in hand. I opened my laptop and pulled up my schedule for the day, trying to distract myself by reviewing the houses for which I had showings ... going over them and studying some details I thought the buyers might like.

But the moment the clock hit 8:00, my pulse quickened.

I told myself I would wait a couple more minutes— maybe 8:02 or 8:03—so I didn't seem too desperate.

Then, at 8:01, my phone rang.

I jumped, nearly spilling my coffee.

Mark.

I answered immediately. "Hey—"

"Something is going on," he cut in, his voice tight.

A cold prickle ran down my spine. I was thinking the same thing.

"With what?"

"After you left last night, instead of going home to work, I met a buddy of mine at Blue's. We sat at the bar. That Gabe guy—the one you pointed out to me before—was working." Mark hesitated. "I think he put something in my drink."

My heart lurched. "WHAT?"

"I don't remember anything. One minute I was fine, and the next, I woke up in my car at 3 am. I don't even remember how I got there."

"What did you have to drink?" I asked, trying to stay calm.

"Just my usual. Two Old Fashioneds." His voice was laced with exhaustion. "Nothing crazy. Sometimes I even have a third, and I feel fine."

I felt a shiver run through me.

"I'm driving into work now," he added. "But see what you can find out about Gabe, okay?"

"I will," I promised. Then, after a beat, I added, "Mark ... do you know if Ellie and Steven ever had a relationship? Something ... romantic?"

There was silence.

Then, finally, he said, "I don't think so. I mean, as far as I know, Gabe is the first guy she's really been involved with while we have been married. Although I wouldn't put anything past her at this point."

"Why?" He suddenly sounded more alert. "What's going on?"

I exhaled. "I'll call you back. There's something I need to look into first. But trust me—I'll fill you in soon."

A beat of silence, then—"I love you," I whispered.

"I love you too," he murmured before the call ended.

I set my phone down, staring at the folder still sitting on my desk.

I had work to do.

CHAPTER FIFTY-FIVE

I took a deep breath and dialed the phone number written in bold on the front of Steven's folder. As the line rang, I tapped my fingers against the desk, my nerves on edge.

Finally, the call went to voicemail: *You've reached Investigator Daniel Hobson. I'm unavailable at the moment, but leave a message, and I'll get back to you as soon as I can.*

I sighed, trying to steady my voice. "Hi, this is Rachel," I said. "You investigated my husband's case a couple of years ago. I need to speak with you about some possible missing documents from the file you gave me. Please call me back when you get this. Thank you."

I ended the call and leaned back in my office chair, exhaling slowly. The high back cradled my tense shoulders, but no amount of comfort could calm the tight knot forming in my stomach. It wasn't even nine in the morning, and already, the day pressed down on me like an invisible force.

My gaze drifted toward the large front window. Through the glass, Ellie's house stood quiet and still, the early morning light casting long shadows across her lawn. A strange feeling crept up my spine as I stared at her front door.

Then, my phone rang.

I jolted upright and answered it. "Hello?"

"Hi, this is Investigator Hobson. I just had a missed call from this number, and I listened to your message."

His voice was deep, gruff, but professional.

I swallowed hard, sitting up straighter. "Yes, hi. This is Rachel. I don't know if you remember me, but my husband, Steven Scheffler ... you handled his case when he died."

There was a brief pause before he responded. "Yes, I remember."

I exhaled. "You told me at the time that his case was suspicious, but there wasn't much more you could find. I was going through the file you gave me and realized that the full autopsy report isn't there. Do you happen to have a copy?"

As soon as I finished speaking, my phone beeped—an incoming call from Mark.

I ignored it.

Hobson let out a thoughtful hum. "I should be able to dig it up for you. Today's my office day, so I can try to track down the record. Give me the case number from the folder."

I quickly scanned the front of the folder and read off the series of numbers and letters.

My phone beeped again—Mark calling a second time.

I clenched my jaw. Something had to be wrong. Mark never called back to back.

"What's your email, Ms. Scheffler? I'll forward you the full autopsy report once I pull it from the system. I assume you want the complete document, including photos?"

The idea of looking at those pictures sent a shiver through me, but I needed to see everything.

"Yes," I confirmed, giving him my email address. "I appreciate it. Thank you."

"No problem. I'll send it over as soon as I find it."

We ended the call, and I slumped back into my chair, inhaling deeply. But there was no time to waste. I had to call back Mark.

I dialed his number, putting it on speaker as I sat forward.

He answered instantly.

"Something is going on, Rachel. I mean, something is *really* going on."

His voice was tight with frustration, and I could hear the sound of papers rustling in the background.

"What happened?" I asked, bracing myself.

"I got to work this morning, reached into my wallet for my keycard to get in, and—it's gone."

I froze. "Gone?"

"Yeah. And that's not all." He let out a sharp breath. "When the maintenance man finally let me inside, my desk was a mess. My personal folder—the one with all my banking information—had been shuffled. Papers were everywhere, Rachel. Someone was in my office."

A cold sensation prickled at my skin.

"Do you think anything was stolen?" I asked, already knowing the answer.

"A lot of my account documents are missing," he confirmed, his voice laced with anger. "I don't know if they got scared off by security or motion sensors, but someone was in my damn office."

I swallowed hard. "Do you have security cameras?"

"I'm checking with maintenance now. We definitely have cameras outside, but I don't think there are any inside."

"You need to check your bank accounts too," I said firmly.

"That's what I'm doing next."

There was a pause, and then, frustration bleeding into his voice, he added, "This is that Gabe guy. I *know* it is."

My stomach twisted. Something wasn't right.

"Mark, just be careful," I warned. "If someone is targeting you, this might not be over."

"Yeah, I know." He exhaled sharply. "I have to call maintenance and then check my accounts. I'll call you back."

And then he was gone. I sat in stunned silence, my heart pounding.

CHAPTER FIFTY-SIX

I tried my best to focus on work as I waited for the email from the investigator, but my mind refused to cooperate. I kept thinking of that framed picture—the scratches on Steven's arms that looked eerily similar to Mark's injuries. Then there was Mark's voice, tense and certain, claiming that Gabe had done something to his drink. And now, Steven's autopsy report was waiting for me like an unanswered question.

I let out a slow breath and took another sip of my coffee, realizing I had already finished the entire cup in just ten minutes. Stress had a way of making me consume caffeine like water.

Determined to shift my focus, I pulled up my real estate listings and started searching through houses for some clients—a retired couple. They weren't in a rush, but I had promised them a few listings today, so I forced myself to sift through options, trying to match their wish list. This took up a few hours of my morning.

Then my computer chimed with a new email. It was from Hobson.

For a second, I hesitated, fingers hovering over my mouse. Instead of reading it on the screen, I decided to print it. Holding the physical pages would make it feel more tangible, easier to process. While the printer whirred, spitting out page after page, I got up and refilled my coffee cup.

By the time I returned, the full report was waiting. I gathered the crisp sheets and settled onto the couch in my office, taking a slow sip of coffee before laying the papers out in front of me.

I hesitated.

The pictures.

I knew they were going to be hard to look at, but I had to. I had to see for myself.

Steeling myself, I flipped to the images and focused on Steven's arms first. My breath caught in my throat. His skin was covered in scratches, thin and jagged—almost identical to the ones Mark had on his body. My grip on the pages tightened. This wasn't a coincidence. The space between us had grown so wide by the end that I couldn't see past the fog of indifference—even if the evidence was right in front of me.

I flipped through the rest, scanning his legs—normal. No markings. Then his back. Something no one would be able to see in a framed picture in my dining area. Something I hadn't noticed since he started pulling away from me romantically before he died.

My stomach twisted.

His back was just like his arms—covered in deep, uneven scratches, as if someone had clawed at him. I set my coffee mug down carefully, my fingers trembling. My pulse roared in my ears. *But when? When would Ellie have had the chance to do this to him? And where? Did she lure him somewhere?*

I forced myself to move on, flipping through the pages faster, searching for the official cause of death. I skimmed over medical jargon and procedural notes until I found it.

"Cause of death: Strangulation."

I skimmed through the following sentences, and my eyes landed on the words "cord or wire."

I exhaled sharply.

I knew Steven had been found in his car near work, but beyond that, the case had always been a mystery. There had never been a single solid lead. No suspects. No explanations. Just a dead man and a case that quietly faded into the background.

Until now.

My hands felt clammy as I let the pages slip from my fingers, scattering onto the floor in slow motion.

The black duffel bag.

The wire inside it.

Ellie.

Was she planning to kill *Mark*? Or *me*? Or *someone else entirely*?

And then the bigger realization hit me like a freight train—Ellie had been having an affair with Steven.

I grabbed my phone and called Mark, my fingers gripping the device so tightly that my knuckles turned white.

He answered on the first ring.

"Hi, I found out some information," I said, my voice tight.

"Me too." He sounded anxious, on edge.

"You go first," I urged.

Mark exhaled. "Our maintenance team tracked a car parked out back last night. Someone came in through the back door and went straight to my office."

A chill ran down my spine.

"Could you see who it was?" I asked.

"No, they kept their head down, never once lifting them in front of the cameras. A hat covered their face. We saw the car. It was a black BMW."

My stomach twisted into knots.

"Did you get a plate number?"

"We only caught the first two letters on the camera: L and W."

My mind raced.

"I need you to do me a favor," Mark said, his voice firm. "Go to Blue's and see what Gabe drives. Find out if it's his car."

I nodded, even though he couldn't see me. "I will. I'll go when it's busier for lunch, so I don't stand out."

Mark sighed, his frustration seeping through the phone. "If it's him, Rachel, why the hell would he be after my information? What does he want?"

"I don't know. But I agree—he and Ellie are up to something," I said, gripping the phone tighter.

There was a long pause.

Then Mark asked, "What did you find out?"

I hesitated before speaking. "Ellie. I think she was having an affair with Steven."

The silence on the other end was deafening.

"I just ... I never thought Steven was like that," I admitted, rubbing a hand over my face. "I mean, I know I have no right to judge, but Mark ... I really think she killed him. I think she is going to do the same to you or me."

Mark let out a sharp breath. "Kill him?" His tone shifted —skeptical, almost dismissive. "That's a bit much, don't you think?"

His doubt caught me off guard.

"Mark, listen to me—"

"I mean, sure, she's capable of cheating, obviously, and of lying, but *murder*?" He let out a short, frustrated laugh. "I don't think so, Rachel."

I sat in stunned silence.

Why didn't he believe me?

Was it too much for him to process? Or ... was he embarrassed?

Something about his reaction didn't sit right with me.

And suddenly, I wasn't sure who I could trust anymore.

CHAPTER FIFTY-SEVEN

Just after half-past noon, I was ready. I picked up my phone and called in a takeout order from Blue's, keeping my tone casual—like I hadn't spent the last half hour convincing myself this was a good idea. The plan was simple: walk in, grab my food, and, in the process, confirm whether Gabe was working. If he was, I'd make my next move—checking the employee parking lot for the black BMW.

If it was there, I'd have my answer.

Pulling into the parking lot, I slowed as I approached the employee section, eyes scanning every car with meticulous precision. My pulse quickened as I searched for any sign of the BMW, but the visibility wasn't great.

I kept moving.

Instead of looping back, I parked in the front lot, angling my car so I had a partial view of the employee section. Just in case.

At one in the afternoon, I pushed open the glass doors of Blue's and stepped inside. The scent of grilled burgers lingered in the air. At the hostess stand, a young woman with bright red lipstick and a too-perfect smile greeted me.

"Takeout for Rachel," I said in an almost-bored tone, like this was any other errand.

She nodded. "Yep, that'll be at the bar."

I made my way over there, positioning myself on a seat at the far corner so I had a clear view of everyone coming and going from the bar area. Several people were sitting at the bar—two men talking quietly over sodas, a woman scrolling through her phone. No one paid me any attention.

I tapped my fingers against the counter, waiting.

And then, like clockwork, Gabe appeared.

He came from the kitchen, carrying a plate of appetizers, his movements easy, fluid, relaxed.

I forced myself to stay still as he delivered the food to a couple behind me at a table.

Then, as if sensing my presence, he turned.

For a split second, something flickered in his eyes—recognition, surprise. And then, just like that, it was gone, replaced by that same easy charm he always had.

"Oh, hey you," he said, stepping closer.

I smiled, tilting my head slightly. "Hi! I placed a takeout order."

"Yeah, I saw your name pop up a little bit ago," he said, nodding. "I'll grab it for you."

"Great, thanks."

I kept my expression neutral, pleasant. If he noticed anything off about me, he didn't show it.

The second he disappeared into the back, I exhaled, my fingers tightening around the strap of my purse. My stomach twisted. There was no way I was eating whatever was in that bag—not after what happened to Mark's drink. For all I knew, Gabe had done something to this food too.

A few minutes later, he returned, holding out the bag.

"Here you go," he said, his smile never faltering.

I took it, nodding. "Oh, great. Thank you! Can you add it to my account and throw in a five-dollar tip?" I sighed dramatically, giving him a tired smile. "I'm in such a rush. I'm helping to find a home for this retired couple in the area. Just wanted to grab something before my whole afternoon disappears."

He chuckled, tapping at the register. "Sounds like you've got a busy day ahead."

I rolled my eyes playfully. "Ugh, yeah. Non-stop." I let out an exaggerated breath, as if I were already exhausted, then grabbed my bag and walked out, keeping my pace steady, unhurried.

Once outside, I kept looking straight ahead, resisting the urge to glance back over my shoulder.

I climbed into my car, tossed the takeout bag onto the passenger seat, and let out a slow breath.

I needed to check the employee lot.

Starting the engine, I pulled out and made a careful loop around the building, turning into the side lot with a steady, deliberate speed—like I was just taking my time leaving.

Row by row, I scanned every vehicle, keeping my speed slow but not suspiciously so. The first row—nothing. The second—still nothing.

Then, as I turned into the third row, my breath caught.

There it was.

A black BMW.

Parked near the back, backed into its space, like whoever owned it wanted a quick getaway.

My hands tightened on the wheel.

I had to be sure.

I couldn't keep circling the lot without drawing attention, so I made a quick decision. I pulled into an empty space three cars down on the same side, acting as if I was checking my phone.

For a moment, I just sat there. My stomach twisted.

Do it now. Fast.

A quick glance at my mirrors showed no one nearby. No movement.

I inhaled sharply, then carefully slipped out of my car, crouching low and scanning the lot once more before creeping toward the BMW.

The closer I got, the louder my heartbeat became.

I reached the rear of the car, my breath shallow, and forced my eyes onto the license plate.

The first two letters were "LW"—the same ones Mark had seen on the security footage.

My stomach dropped. I spun back toward my car, my legs unsteady, and climbed in, shutting the door with a quiet click.

What now? What should I do?

I needed time to think. I needed—

My brain felt scrambled, everything pressing in at once.

I put the car in reverse and started to pull out of the lot.

But then—

Something caught my eye.

A car, parked across from Gabe's.

Someone was inside.

My breath hitched.

How did I miss that before?

I slowed, my pulse hammering as I tried to get a clearer look.

The person inside shifted.

Their gaze met mine.

It was Tom. The other bartender.

His expression was unreadable, but he gave me a slight nod—nothing too obvious, just a small, almost satisfied acknowledgment indicating that I was getting closer to my answers.

But something about it sent a chill down my spine.

It wasn't an *I-caught-you-doing-something-strange* nod.

It wasn't even questioning.

It was calm. Almost ... knowing.

Like he understood exactly why I was here.

And something deep in my gut told me—Tom knew more than he was letting on.

CHAPTER FIFTY-EIGHT

I eased my car onto the winding drive, leaving behind the pristine, manicured grounds of the country club. My mind was racing through the events of the last hour. I needed a moment to collect myself, to breathe, but patience wasn't my strong suit right now.

The second I turned onto the main road, I grabbed my phone and called Mark.

He picked up on the first ring. "Rachel?"

"I have some information," I said without preamble, my voice steady, though my pulse was anything but. *Stay calm. Breathe.*

"What is it?" he asked, tension already creeping into his voice.

"The car," I said, exhaling sharply. "I went to Blue's. Ordered takeout just to see if Gabe was working. I saw him inside." I swallowed. "Then I went around to the employee lot."

I could hear Mark's breathing shift—it was sharper now, expectant.

"It took me a couple of minutes, but I found the black BMW."

Silence.

"The same one?" His voice was tight, clipped. "Are you sure?"

"Yes. The first two letters of the license plate match the ones you gave me this morning."

A sharp exhale. I could practically feel his frustration through the phone.

"There's more," I continued, my stomach twisting. "When I was leaving, Tom was sitting in his car. He was parked across from me."

"Tom?" Mark snapped. "Who the hell is Tom?"

"The other bartender at Blue's," I said. "He's been there for a while—you'd probably recognize him if you saw him. He's always nice to me when I go in." I paused, pressing my lips together. "But he *saw* me, Mark. I think he even saw me go around back to look at Gabe's car." My throat tightened. "From where he was parked, there's no way he *didn't* see me."

Mark let out a slow breath. "Did he look upset?"

"No." That was the part that unsettled me the most. I drummed my fingers against the steering wheel. "That's what was strange. He didn't look surprised or even concerned. He gave me a slight smile. A nod." A shiver rolled down my spine. "It was like he *knew* something."

Mark was quiet for a beat. "So what now?"

"I have some digging to do," I admitted. "A couple of things to check into before I figure out my next move. Can I call you back in a little bit?"

"Yeah," he said, though he didn't sound happy about it.

"I need to double-check my banking records while you do that."

Gabe was up to something.

But *what?*

I pulled into my driveway, feeling relieved to be home. My thoughts were tangled, pulling me in a dozen different directions. I needed to process everything—Mark's frustration, Gabe's car, Tom's unnerving calm.

I made my way inside, tossing my keys onto the table as I grabbed the autopsy report again. Balancing it in one hand, I moved across the floor to let Jax out into the backyard. My eyes flicked over the details, but I couldn't focus. *Why am I so stuck on this?* My fingers tightened around the edges of the paper. *What about Gabe?*

I let out a frustrated breath and went to pace in front of my office window.

I felt helpless.

But I *couldn't* give up.

My mind kept circling back to one person.

Ellie.

Without thinking, I grabbed my phone and dialed her number.

She picked up on the second ring. "Hey!" Her voice was light, casual, unbothered.

Act normal.

"Hi! How are you?" I forced a smile into my voice. "Last night was fun."

I hesitated, my mind racing. *Why did I call?* I couldn't be too direct, couldn't let her suspect I knew *anything*.

"Do you want to go to Blue's tonight?" I asked, making my voice sound tired, frustrated. "I know we just had drinks last night, but I have a *ton* of new showings today, and I could really use a drink afterward." I let out a dramatic sigh.

Ellie made a sympathetic noise. "Oh wow. Sounds like a busy day."

"Yeah, tell me about it." I rolled my eyes, even though she couldn't see me. "What do you think? Just a quick drink?"

"Oh, I wish," she said, sounding genuinely regretful. "I'm actually heading over to stay with my sister for a few days—to help her with some stuff at her house. I am leaving in a few minutes. So sorry!"

We hung up after a few more pleasantries, but my mind was already somewhere else.

Ellie was *gone* for a few days. That was good. It meant she wasn't wrapped up in whatever she and Gabe were up to. At least, not *today*.

My stomach twisted.

I still needed to talk to Bennett.

I dialed his number. It rang. And rang. Then —voicemail.

I wandered back over to the door to let Jax back inside.

I left a message, though I doubted he would call back quickly.

With no other option, I called Mark again.

He picked up, his tone softer this time. "Hey, baby."

I relaxed slightly at the sound of his voice. "Hey."

"Our maintenance guys are looking into anything else they can find. And I had my financial advisor pull some records—he's supposed to call me back soon."

I nodded, even though he couldn't see me. "That's great."

"I have a couple of meetings later this afternoon," he

added, and I could hear the faint sound of typing in the background. "Can I call you back after? I just really need to focus on these right now."

I hesitated, hating the feeling of waiting—of standing still when I *knew* something was brewing.

But I didn't push.

"Yeah," I said, keeping my voice light. "Of course. We'll talk later."

"Okay. I love you."

"I love you too," I murmured, but my mind was already somewhere else.

Because no matter how much information we uncovered, one thing was certain.

We still weren't seeing the full picture.

CHAPTER FIFTY-NINE

I sank into the couch in my office, the autopsy report still clutched in my hand. My body felt heavier than it should have, the exhaustion worsened by questions I hadn't yet found the courage to ask. I leaned my head back, closed my eyes, and let the silence wrap around me like a blanket, hoping sleep would still my mind's unraveling for a few minutes.

It didn't last.

My phone buzzed, pulling me out of a shallow doze. Mark's name appeared on the screen.

"Hi," I mumbled, still halfway inside a dream.

"Hey," he said, his voice steady but worn. "I'm heading over to help Ellie."

"With what? Where?" I asked, my body tensing.

"She said her car broke down. Somewhere over by O'Brien Road. I'm heading there now."

I sat up straighter. "O'Brien Road? That's south of here. Didn't she say she was going to her sister's earlier? Her sister lives north—like twenty minutes in the opposite direction."

"Yeah, she lives north of here," Mark replied, sounding tired and unconvinced. "I don't know. I'm just going where she said her car broke down."

I frowned. "Why would she say she was going to her sister's if she's nowhere near there?"

He let out a breath. "I honestly have no idea."

I chalked it up to fatigue on his part, maybe some left-over frustration from everything that had happened lately. "Hang on—she's beeping in. I'll call you back," he said, hanging up the phone.

I exhaled slowly and let the phone rest on my lap. The autopsy papers slid to the floor beneath me. I stared blankly out the office window for a few minutes, waiting for Mark to call back. When the silence stretched too long, I stood up and drifted toward the front of the house, glancing instinctively at Ellie's place across the street.

Her garage door stood open with no cars in it, but the house was dark, silent.

I stepped outside, casually heading across the street in a performance I'd rehearsed far too often. I knocked on her front door with the practiced pretense of a concerned neighbor. "Just checking in," I mumbled to no one in particular.

No answer. Of course not.

I knocked again, for show, then called out, "Ellie? You home?" My voice was loud enough to be heard by any curious ears nearby.

Still nothing.

I circled to the backyard, careful to keep my curiosity

cloaked in innocent concern. The moment I stepped into the backyard, any illusion of Ellie's domestic perfection vanished. It was a dead zone—nothing but brittle weeds and dry, cracked soil. The front lawn had fooled us all, no doubt thanks to the landscaping crew I'd seen come by like clockwork. But back here, there was no effort, no care. Nothing had been touched in months. It was a jarring contrast to the manicured perfection of the front yard—as if I'd stepped through a portal into a dark world. But why hadn't she asked the landscaping crew to tend to the back as well? It wasn't neglect. It felt deliberate. As if she *wanted* it this way. Wild. Withered. Choked with weeds and shadows. A place where nothing grew, and nothing *wanted* to. It was unsettling—ugly in a way that felt personal. Like she found comfort in the decay.

Ellie had lied.

Suddenly, I didn't care if anyone saw me—I sprinted back across the street, adrenaline thudding in my chest. As I reached the garage and stepped back into the house, my phone rang again. Mark.

"Hi, baby," he said. "I've almost reached Ellie now. I may have to hang up in a second."

"She's still saying she's on O'Brien Road?" I asked, walking through my kitchen.

"She is. I see her car now. I just pulled off the side of the road. Wait … there's another car here too. Maybe she called someone else." Just then, I caught the faint creak and thud of his car door swinging open.

At this point, his voice cut out.

"Hello? Mark?" I pressed the phone harder to my ear. "Mark, are you still there?"

Silence.

I called him back. Straight to voicemail. Again. And again. Voicemail.

A knot tightened in my stomach like a rope being pulled too fast.

I paced. Back and forth. Over and over.

Then, without letting myself think too hard, I grabbed my purse, my keys, and the tennis shoes by the door. I didn't know exactly where I was going, only that I couldn't sit still for another second.

As I backed out of the driveway, I called him again. Voicemail.

I gripped the steering wheel until my knuckles turned white, then turned onto the main road, heading toward O'Brien. The stretch was long—at least fifteen miles—and I had no clue which part Mark was on.

Another call. Another voicemail.

As I passed Glen Springs Country Club, something in my gut screamed, *Turn around.*

CHAPTER SIXTY

Without hesitation, I swerved into a business lot, spun around, and headed back toward the country club. I didn't have a plan—just instinct.

I pulled into the circle drive, ignoring the fire hydrant in front of which I parked, grabbed my phone and keys, and headed straight inside. The hostess gave me a polite smile, but I barely acknowledged her.

I moved straight to the bar, eyes scanning.

Tom.

He was there.

I slipped between two barstools and didn't bother to sit. I looked him dead in the eyes.

"I need your help," I said firmly.

He set down a glass and raised an eyebrow. "Sure. What's going on?"

"Gabe," I said. "Tell me what he's up to. Please. I need to know."

He blinked, taken slightly aback by the urgency in my voice.

"I can't reach Mark. He was on the phone with me, on his way to help Ellie ... and then nothing. The call dropped, and now everything goes to voicemail." My voice was calm, but the panic was clawing at the edges. "You said before you thought Ellie and Gabe were up to something."

Tom shifted. "I don't know much. Just ... they've been meeting up at Gabe's car shop now and then. Pretty sure they're having an affair. That's not exactly subtle, right?"

"Gabe's car shop?" I repeated, stunned. "I didn't even know he owned one. I've seen them together here a few times, but ... she never mentioned anything about a shop."

Tom leaned in slightly, lowering his voice. "Ellie's not the type to tell you everything. You know that."

I nodded slowly, the pieces clicking together in ways I wasn't ready for. My grip on the bar tightened.

And somewhere in the distance, a new fear began to bloom.

"Have you ever been to Gabe's car shop? Where is it?" I asked, my tone sharpening with urgency.

Tom nodded slowly, squinting as he tried to recall. "Yeah ... I've been there once. Had to pick up Gabe for work one morning. It's a little ways from here. South."

"Let me guess," I said, narrowing my eyes. "Is it near O'Brien Road?"

He froze, caught off guard. "Yeah—how'd you know?"

"Where exactly? Think." I leaned across the bar, my voice low but intense. "Where is it on O'Brien?"

Tom rubbed the back of his neck, his brows furrowing as he searched his memory. "It's ... by O'Brien and Rosalie. Just north of Rosalie, I think. Yeah. It's on the east side of the road. Old rundown place, kind of forgotten. I remember there was an old lumber store sign leaning up against the building."

"That's enough. Thanks." I was already turning away.

"Rachel—let me know what happens!" he called after me as I hurried back to my car.

I slid behind the wheel, my heart in my throat, and immediately called Mark's phone. No answer. Again.

The engine roared to life, and I peeled out of the front circle drive, heading toward O'Brien Road. My thoughts tangled as I drove, every turn bringing fresh worry. I estimated it would take about ten, maybe fifteen minutes. I called Mark five more times on the way. Voicemail, each time.

At the north end of O'Brien, I turned in and started heading south, scanning every sign, every cross street.

Where is it? I thought frantically, leaning forward like it might help me see clearer. *Where's Rosalie?*

I pulled over for a moment and checked my phone's map—just one more mile to go.

Back on the road, I crept along, the street eerily empty behind me. I kept my eyes fixed to the east side, searching for anything—any break in the trees, any sign of life.

And then—a car parked ahead. It was Mark's.

My pulse surged.

I slowed almost to a crawl. No other vehicles. No people. Just his car, sitting silent. Something was wrong. Deeply wrong.

I passed it slowly, deciding to find a place to turn around. Just up ahead, the trees broke open at a wide gravel path. I turned in. It was more than a path—it was an entrance. I followed it in.

That's when I saw it.

The building Tom had described—weathered, skeletal, forgotten by time. A crumbling lumber store sign leaned against the wall.

I pulled off to the side, heart thudding. In the back, I spotted the cars. Gabe's BMW. Ellie's car. My breath caught.

I didn't have a plan. Just instinct.

I grabbed my phone and eased my door open, shutting it quietly behind me. The building looked like it had once been a gas station and had now been half-heartedly converted into a mechanic's shop. Scattered car parts littered the exterior.

I crept along the side, toward a smudged window streaked with dirt. I needed to see. *I had to know.*

I pressed close, shifting an old tire to get a better angle —and it slipped.

It hit something metal with a loud *clang*.

CHAPTER SIXTY-ONE

I froze, my breath catching in my throat. The noise echoed into the stillness like a siren.

Then—*bang*—the door flew open.

Gabe stormed out, eyes wild, and a gun in his hand.

"Inside," he barked, the weapon pointed squarely at me. "Now!"

I didn't hesitate. My feet moved before my mind could catch up.

"NOW! KEEP MOVING!" he shouted again, forcing me toward the open doorway.

Inside, the air was heavy with oil, rust, and something else—something darker. The building was a gutted shell of what it used to be. Tools scattered across a greasy workbench, extension cords tangled like snakes, two half-dismantled cars sat like wounded animals in the corners.

And then I saw him.

Mark.

He was in the center of the room, hands bound, face

bruised, but eyes locked on mine. There was no panic—just relief. *He saw me. He knew I came.*

I forced myself to stay calm, breathing shallow, my heartbeat loud in my ears.

Ellie's voice cut through the stillness. "Why are you here?" she spat, pacing a tight circle around Mark like a shark in a tank.

"I knew something wasn't right," I said, my voice steady despite the fear rising inside me.

Ellie stared at me, eyes narrowing, trying to read my face. I held her gaze, no lies, no games. Just the truth. The only thing I had left to offer.

The room was silent, waiting. And in that stillness, I realized—this wasn't just about lies anymore.

"ELLIE, SNAP OUT OF IT!" Gabe barked, his voice slicing through the stale air like a blade.

"I'll give you whatever you want," Mark pleaded, his voice ragged with desperation as he strained against the ropes binding him to the chair.

"SHUT UP!" Gabe snarled at Mark, spinning on him with wild eyes.

The shift happened in an instant—Gabe took control, his posture rigid with purpose.

"Ellie," he said, more coolly now, "get Mark's phone. We're just going to make a little transfer."

He gave me a smug smile like it was all a game to him. I glanced between the two of them—Gabe steady and brutal, Ellie wild-eyed and distant.

I understood then. The picture finally came together.

"Rachel," Gabe snapped, his voice booming through the hollow room. "Get over here. Sit. Now."

I jumped at the command, my pulse hammering in my ears. I moved quickly to the chair he pointed at with his gun.

"Give me your phone," he said, extending a hand.

I reached into my pocket and handed it over, heart pounding. He powered it off with an exaggerated flourish.

"We'll be long gone before either of you can even think about reaching your phones," he said, tossing my phone onto a high shelf.

Then he grabbed a cord from a nearby duffel bag—*that* duffel bag—and bound my wrists behind the chair. I caught a glimpse of the bag slouched against the wall. I knew what it was. Knew what it had been used for.

And I also knew this might be my only chance.

"You killed Steven, didn't you?" I shouted, my voice shaking with fury as I locked eyes with Ellie. "I know about the pen—you both had one from that same hotel. And his shirt ... the blood on it wasn't from some accident. It was from what *you* did to him.

She froze, then took a step toward me—her eyes no longer glassy, but alive with something dangerous.

"Steven was weak," she hissed. "At first, he liked it— when I clawed him, hurt him. It turned him on. But after a while ..." She shrugged. "I started to hate him."

"You ... you actually *killed* him?" Mark's voice trembled with disbelief. "Rachel tried to warn me about you two— that something was going on—but I didn't want to believe it. I couldn't."

She sauntered over to him, slow and taunting.

"You never fought back, did you, Mark?" she said sweetly. Then, without warning, she spat in his face.

"There's just something *so* satisfying about clawing into a man," she added with a wicked grin, her voice dripping with venom.

"Ellie!" Gabe shouted. "Focus. We need to move. Do the transfer."

With a frustrated huff, she reached into Mark's pocket and pulled out his phone, her fingers tapping quickly across the screen.

"There," she said after a moment, triumphant. "All done. The transfer is done."

Gabe snatched the phone from her, double-checked, then powered it off and hurled it onto the same shelf as mine.

"Let's go," he said. "We've got a plane to catch."

He kissed her hard—right in front of Mark.

They were gone within seconds. The door slammed shut behind them.

Silence.

I twisted in my chair, fighting against the cords. "What do we do?" I asked Mark, panic rising. "My hands—he tied them so tight."

"Damn it!" Mark groaned, yanking against his own restraints.

Then—minutes later the door creaked open.

"Tom!" I cried, seeing him rush in.

He didn't hesitate. "They were here, weren't they?" he asked, untying Mark first.

"Yes," Mark said breathlessly, then moved with Tom to free me next.

"We've got to move—now. She killed Steven. They're heading to the airport," I said, bolting for the door.

"Our phones," Mark reminded me, reaching up to the shelf. We powered them on as we rushed outside.

I dug into my pocket for my keys, already planning the fastest route. But as we reached my car, I froze.

All four tires had been slashed.

CHAPTER SIXTY-TWO

"Get in," Tom said, unlocking his own car. Mark jumped in front, and I slid into the back.

As Tom sped off, I scrolled through my contacts and dialed a number.

First call—no answer. Second—nothing. Third—

"Detective Hobson," he answered cautiously.

"It's me—Rachel Scheffler. You just sent me the report on my husband's death," I said, breathless.

"I remember. Is everything all right?"

"I know who did it. It was her—Ellie Duncan. She *admitted it*. Right in front of me and others."

"Ma'am, slow down. Take a breath."

"She's leaving the country—with Gabe. They're heading to LaGuardia. There's still time. Can you stop them?"

"Rachel Scheffler, from Glen Springs?" he confirmed, then repeated my age and address.

"Yes, yes—please stop her," I said.

"I'm dispatching officers now," he said. "And I'm heading there myself."

The call ended.

"Mark, what's wrong?" I asked, noticing him staring at his phone, scrolling rapidly.

He let out a soft laugh.

"Nothing," he said, a strange calm in his voice. "Everything's worked out ... perfectly."

I didn't have time to ask what he meant. We pulled into the airport minutes later.

"Just park up front," I told Tom. "If we get ticketed, or towed, whatever—I'll pay it."

As we neared the terminal entrance, flashing blue and red lights filled the circle drive.

Police cars. At least four of them.

Tom threw the car in park. We leapt out.

But Mark ... stopped staring at the departure screen.

And for a split second, I saw something in his eyes that didn't match relief.

It was something else.

"I know the airline," Mark gasped, breath catching as clarity hit him. "They're flying to Paris."

We sprinted toward the overhead screen glowing with departure times, our eyes scanning it frantically.

"Gate C7," Tom called out. "Flight to Paris, boarding now—leaves in twenty minutes!"

"Come on!" Mark shouted, charging forward, weaving through the crowd like a man possessed.

We tore through the terminal, dodging suitcases, bumping into shoulders, and brushing past startled travelers. The polished floors echoed with our pounding footsteps. Gate C7 loomed in sight, the final call already flashing in bold red letters.

We reached the gate just as the boarding door sealed. The plane was fully loaded.

I rushed to the wall of tall windows beside the gate, pressing my hands to the glass as I scanned the plane parked on the tarmac. There it was—just feet away, cabin lights glowing like a cruel tease.

"There they are!" I shouted, breathless, pointing toward the side of the aircraft.

I looked left, then right—Mark and Tom weren't beside me. I pressed my finger harder against the window. "They're right there!"

Across from me, in the third row of windows, Ellie sat poised in the window seat. Even from here, I could make out her smug expression. Gabe sat beside her, half-turned. She locked eyes with me through the glass and laughed —*laughed*. Then she nudged Gabe and pointed toward me.

He leaned closer to the window and gave me a slow, mocking wave. Another laugh. Their silhouettes were wickedly calm, as though they had already won.

But then Mark reappeared beside me, holding up his phone. His expression was unreadable. Focused. He tilted the screen ever so slightly, enough to catch Ellie's eye.

She looked down at her own phone.

Her smirk vanished.

Her head snapped upright.

"No!" I could read it on her lips, even through the thick glass. "NOOO!"

She started thrashing—legs kicking, fists pounding into the armrests like a tantrum. Her rage was unmistakable, raw, and furious. The flight attendants leaned in quickly, trying to calm her. Gabe's arm flailed—he grabbed something and hurled it across the cabin.

"What just happened?" I whispered, stunned, eyes still glued to the chaotic scene inside.

Mark didn't look away from the glass. His voice was low, steady. "She thought she had wired $7.2 million into a joint account for her and Gabe. What she didn't realize ..." he turned slightly to me, "was that she had sent it to an old account we opened together—back when we were thinking about buying a house in the islands."

I blinked, stunned.

"We never used it. I already moved the money into my investment account."

He turned to face me fully now, a calm in his eyes that hadn't been there in weeks.

"I let her walk into her own trap," he said. "And she never saw it coming."

Behind the glass, Ellie continued to spiral. Gabe was shouting at someone now, a flight attendant holding up a phone and waving toward the front of the plane. Red and blue lights began flashing outside the terminal, making sure the plane didn't leave.

"I love you," Mark whispered, his voice full of quiet relief as he reached for my hand. "We don't have to hide anymore."

Fingers entwined, we stood side by side, watching it all unfold.

Just ahead, several uniformed officers surrounded the gate agent, showing badges and giving hushed, urgent instructions. The woman nodded and unlocked the secured door, and within seconds, two of the officers stepped onto the jet bridge.

Through the tall glass, we saw it all happen.

One officer reached down and gripped Ellie's arm, pulling her firmly from her seat. Another yanked Gabe to his feet. The smugness they wore just moments ago had been replaced by panic.

They were marched off the plane like fallen royalty—no longer in control, no longer laughing.

Mark and I drifted closer to the gate. The storm had passed. The reckoning had arrived.

"It's just us now," he said with a soft smile, turning to kiss me gently.

That's when Ellie saw us.

Handcuffed and wild-eyed, she was being dragged forward, screaming and twisting like a feral animal. Her eyes locked on us—and her rage ignited.

"No—no, let me go!" she shrieked. Her shoes skidded against the tile floor.

She halted just a foot from us, eyes narrowing, venom in her voice.

"I told you Steven was weak," she spat. "I should've taken care of *you* too, Mark. Or maybe both of you."

Then she lunged.

But the officers yanked her back before she could get near. Ellie snarled, still laughing as they dragged her down the corridor, her laughter echoing through the terminal like a bitter ghost.

I exhaled.

Then, from the corner of my eye, I spotted him—Detective Hobson, approaching from the security checkpoint. He looked composed, observant as ever.

"Detective," I said as he neared, "I don't think you'll have any trouble getting her to admit it now."

He gave a small nod, adjusting his coat. "I'll be in touch soon."

With that, he turned and followed the officers into the crowd.

We slipped out of the thick crowd—uniformed officers and curious onlookers buzzing like flies around chaos. The air outside the terminal was cooler, calmer, a strange contrast to the storm we'd just come through.

As we approached the front of the airport, my eyes locked with someone waiting just inside the door. It was Bennett. I gave Mark a subtle nudge to follow, though he looked puzzled, unaware of who we were walking toward.

"I got your text, young lady," Bennett said, his voice steady, but laced with concern.

"Yes," I replied, glancing at Mark, silently telling him I'd messaged Bennett from the car.

"You were right," I added. "She *was* up to something. But it's over now. The police have her."

"Good," Bennett said with a nod. Then he extended his hand toward Mark in greeting.

"You must be Mark?"

"I am," Mark said, shaking his hand firmly. "Thank you for watching out for Rachel," he added, sliding his arm protectively around my waist.

"My pleasure," Bennett replied with a slight tilt of his head.

"I'll call you tomorrow, fill you in on the details," I said. "Right now ... we're just ready to breathe."

"I understand. Take care," Bennett said gently, giving

my arm a reassuring pat before turning to disappear into the night.

Mark looked at me, his thumb brushing across my knuckles.

"Let's go home, baby," he said.

ABOUT THE AUTHOR

Penelope Rose Palmer is a modern-day American author of fictional suspense thrillers. She loves letting her mind unravel to set the pathway for a story that will leave you guessing.

Her books often deliver intrigue, emotional ups and downs, and hidden points that tie everything into place for the ending.

When she is not writing, she can be found spending time with her family, walking, and exploring beaches.

Find her on Instagram @penelope_rose_palmer.

84240704R00198